RISE OF
KNIGHT AND SWORD

D0851850

RISE of KNIGHT and SWORD

MIRIAM WADE

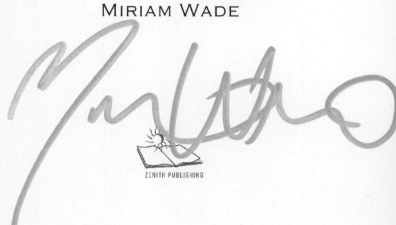

ZENITH PUBLISHING

Copyright © MIRIAM WADE 2020

Supervising Editor: Caitlin Chrismon
Associate Editor: Gabriella Grace
Internal Formatting: Jack Oliver, Alexandria Boykin
Cover Designer: L. Austen Johnson
Map Designer: Amanda Wade

All rights reserved. No part of this publication may be reproduced,
distributed, or transmitted in any form or by any means without the prior
written permission of the publisher, except in the case of brief quotations
and other noncommercial uses permitted by copyright law. For permission
requests, write to publisher at Info@genzpublishing.org.

GenZPublishing.org
Aberdeen, NJ

ISBN: 978-1-952919-03-9

To Ryan –

For encouraging me from the start, for being my most honest critic and biggest cheerleader, and for never letting me doubt myself.

A MAP OF THE
AVALON
REALM

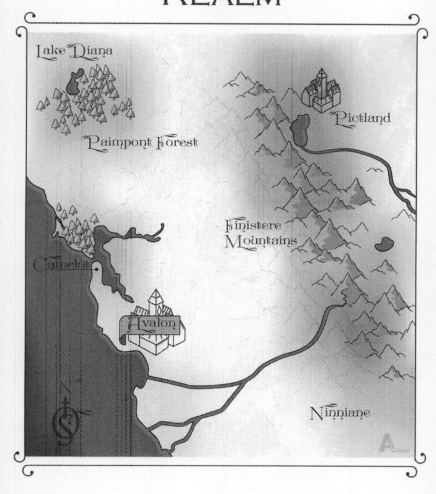

Lake Diana

Pictland

Paimpont Forest

Finistere
Mountains

Camelot

Avalon

Ninniane

Chapter One

The moon hung over the Avalon sky, its beautiful shine reflecting off the lofty towers near Camelot. A few lonely airships were moored at the tallest buildings and let out wispy puffs of smoke from their idling boilers. Ocean waves lapped gently at the city's western bank, and the skies were empty as far as the horizon. Even the pterodactyls, which in Avalon were ubiquitous like seagulls, were missing. Sometime in the next hour, they would begin their daily commute toward the sea, catching their fill of fish and posing for wealthy tourists. But for now, the port city was quiet.

Guinevere lived in a small apartment across the eastern bay from Avalon. The walls were paper thin, and her neighbors liked to stay up partying. By the time she could finally sleep, her alarm would let out an ear shattering shriek. This morning was no different. Guinevere reached out carelessly for the clock, lost her balance, and tumbled onto the floor. She laid there, eyes closed, longing for a few more moments of rest. When they didn't come, she let out a frustrated groan and pushed herself off the floor.

Wandering the short distance to the kitchen, Guinevere looked for something to eat. She opened the icebox and sifted through. Inside were several beers, a half-molded block of cheese, a head of cabbage, a couple apples, and a glass jug filled with curdled

1

milk—just as she had left it. Grabbing one of the apples for breakfast, she let out a long sigh and promised to stop by the market on the way back from work.

Back in her room, Guinevere finished getting ready for the day. She selected a simple long-sleeved white blouse, paired it with black balloon corseted shorts, and finished the look with knee-high calf brown leather boots. Hearing a cry outside, she looked out the window and caught a glimpse of a lone pterodactyl flying past. It was time to go. With added quickness, Guinevere threw the half-finished apple into her satchel, slipped the bag over her shoulders, and hurried out of the apartment door.

Thundering down two flights of steps, she stumbled into the empty street. She set off towards her transit station, walking past several blocks of apartments and into a park. The oasis of green trees offered her an escape from the industrial landscape of the city. Here, Guinevere was tempted to remove her shoes. She wanted to walk alongside the creek, feeling the overgrown grass poking up between her toes, the damp soil squishing beneath her feet. Instead, she breathed deeply, letting the crisp, cool autumn air fill her lungs, and headed to the station. More pterodactyls soared overhead as they eagerly ventured to the ocean. Stars still speckled the sky, as the first rays of the sun began to peak over the horizon. Soon, they would disintegrate into a backdrop of blue, leaving the sun and moon alone in the Avalon sky.

***

The transit line rose up from the ground, supported by pillars of black steal. It stood tall over the main throughfare, waiting to be

2

filled with pedestrians and motorcars. The elevated station was pressed up against one of the brick buildings lining the street. A faded mural adorned its surface, with soot and ash smudging its features. One could just barely mark the outline of a man with the fabled sword Excalibur in his hand.

I'm late, Guinevere thought as she hurried through the turnstile and ascended the cold, metal staircase. Her footsteps resonated with each step. Reaching the platform, Guinevere looked up at the large analog clock that hung above a gathering of benches. *Half past five.* There were still five long minutes until the train's arrival.

Guinevere made her way to an abandoned bench, taking care to avoid eye contact with the other early morning commuters. They all looked as tired as she felt. Most were slightly disheveled in mismatched clothes. Suddenly self-conscious, Guinevere adjusted her socks beneath her boots. She fidgeted with them for a time before leaning back against the bench, her bag padding her shoulders. Trying unsuccessfully to relax, Guinevere got up from the bench and quietly purchased the daily from the paperboy. She mindlessly flipped through the pages and began reading a travel advertisement.

"The fabled streets of Avalon offer many exciting sightseeing opportunities. So numerous, in fact, that the *way* you tour is more important than what you see. Try our amazing packages, from the electric nightlife to world-class culinary adventures. Here are a few of our most memorable offerings.

"The City Icon: Camelot looms large over downtown Avalon and is a must for first-time visitors. This guided castle tour will check-off your favorite royal sites without leaving you to figure out the logistics.

"The Adventurer: Want to explore hidden stairways, picnic in a magical urban forest or climb to the summit for breathtaking views? Want to view the variety of dinosaurs that calls this city home? From the high-flying pterodactyl to the water-dwelling ichthyosaurs, everyone will find something unique. Avalon's ample greenspace and natural beauty make our urban adventures one-of-a-kind.

"Find out more by visiting the Avalon Ministry of Tourism on 5th and Arrowhead."

What a sham! Guinevere thought, setting the publication down on the bench. She adjusted the straps on her satchel and brushed her long brown hair over her shoulders. *I can barely pay rent or buy my next meal. While the ministry is touting our city as a traveler's paradise, the rest of us are doing all we can to just get by. And the gall to advertise "dinosaurs" after shuttering the conservatory last year. Seems the government only cares if they can be used for sugar-coated propaganda.*

* * *

A low steam whistle cried out as the locomotive barreled into the station. The engine kicked up a cloud of smoke as it passed by, and Guinevere coughed from the soot. As the air cleared, she boarded the already busy commuter train and stood in the aisle. One hand grasped an overhead strap and the other clung to her satchel for fear of it sliding off. With two high notes, the car began to move.

4

The unrelenting motion of the train threw her back and forth as it accelerated. After a while, her legs grew tired from standing and her wrist ached where the strap twisted around.

Peering through the rest of the crowded car, she looked out the window. Old-growth redwoods passed by her vision, blurry with the speed of the train. Their branches glowed in the early morning light. In rapid succession, the trees gave way to rolling hills, the hills to row houses, and the houses to taller buildings. Bicyclists, pedestrians, and motor carriages filled the streets in every direction. The train slowed as it neared South Metro station. Passengers hurried in and out during a brief stop, and Guinevere snagged a vacated window seat.

Seconds later the train pulled forward. The rhythmic motion of its pistons reverberated through the floor with ever increasing frequency. Soon they were speeding onto a long bridge that connected the two sides of the bay. Guinevere peered down into the water below, hoping to catch a glimpse of an ichthyosaur swimming beneath the water's surface. Instead, she spotted a lone sea lion basking in the early morning sun on one of the bridge's many pylons.

As the train passed back onto land, it entered the Port District of Avalon. Trails from smokestacks billowed fumes into the sky and the sprawling shipyards were a frenzy of movement. People and goods scurried around to find their correct ship to board. Some were headed towards freighters docked at the water's edge, while others hurried towards the neighboring airfields where lighter-than-air ships waited to take off in flight. Just past the docks, a large crane was in motion. Row upon row of stacked wooden boxes stretched out in the yard. The crates came in a variety of shapes and sizes, making it possible to guess at their contents. Some were clearly designed to transport animals, and a few were purpose built for the illicit dinosaur trade. Guinevere was not naïve about the goings on in her city, but this was one of its more shameful pastimes.

The scenery quickly changed from industrial to residential, with rows of crates replaced by neatly lined houses. As the train neared the urban core, the rows of dollhouse-like structures were pushed further into their respective neighbors. The yards similarly narrowed until there was barely a patch of grass between the front door and the street. People were hurrying out of their homes: some to motorcars, others on foot, but most to catch an electric streetcar. The row houses continued along the train route for a distance—a corner store here, an apartment block there. Soon the number of businesses outnumbered the residential ones, and the buildings grew into the sky. Guinevere's station was next.

When the train came to a halt, torrents of people pushed in and out of the passenger doors. Guinevere gripped the straps of her satchel and pushed her way through. Once on the platform, commuters dispersed in a multitude of directions, their paths crisscrossing and narrowly avoiding collisions. Conversation and footsteps reached a dull roar. They were augmented by the mechanical vibrations of nearby locomotives, which hissed and clanked with cooling jets of steam. The Central District Station was one of the largest interchanges in Avalon. From here, one could venture to the furthest realms of the kingdom. Arched windows above the walls let in streams of early morning light. Banners hung beneath them, bearing the proud portraits of King Uther and General Gorlois. Towering openings at either end of the hall offered views of the surrounding city. Just barely, through the numerous buildings that had risen over time, she could make out the library. *Almost there,* she thought.

After walking a mile and turning down a few side streets, Guinevere reached the Avalon Central Library. The structure once served as an engineering marvel, towering over the streets with its three stories. Now, although still prominent—with its ornate stonework, massive ascending granite steps, and large wooden double doors—it was dwarfed by the new and more modern sky towers. Sadly, it was not protected in the same way as the castle, which stood on a tall hill at the northern tip of the peninsula.

It was quieter here in the library district than in the rest of the Avalon metropolis. The stillness was punctuated by the occasional electric trolley that unleashed a swarm of tourists into the streets. Guinevere quickly ascended the granite steps of the library and fumbled with a lock. An audible click rumbled outward, followed by the gratifying mechanical sequence of gears and levers unlocking. The large wooden double doors swung open and Guinevere stepped inside. Sun beamed in behind her, illuminating specks of dust as they hovered in the air. The hanging lanterns in the large space were off; the three-story vaulted room was quiet without patrons to mill about. Time had frozen here overnight, unmoved by Guinevere's small presence.

A large wooden welcome desk rested nearby. It sat empty, waiting to be staffed in the moments before the library opened.

Guinevere walked behind the desk and reached inside its mahogany hood. With the flip of a small insignificant switch, the torches ignited successively toward the back of the library. Guinevere smiled. *That never gets old*, she thought to herself. The lanterns were simple in their silhouettes, with intricate cutout details, pressed patterned glass panels, and a gold finish.

Behind the welcome desk, down the center of the library's great hall, sat several large wooden tables. At each one, chairs encircled it: the cushions were red velvet, the chairs' soft top layer had been rubbed away, their edges were worn smooth, and the wooden legs were decorated with carvings. Rows and rows of shelves lined the walls on either side of the hall. Numerous books were softly coated with layers of dust, their leather bindings bearing a mild, earthy smell with sweet overtones from vegetable tanning and natural dyes. The yellowing pages of the books collected remnants of the smells of readers past: tobacco, coffee, and cheap perfumes. As Guinevere passed the shelves of books, she dragged her finger along their edges, feeling their spines. Dust floated off them and into the air. It lingered there for a moment before falling to the ground.

The surface beneath Guinevere's feet showed signs of age, with commonly traveled paths worn into the floor. The large patterned ceramic tiles gave off a coolness that was much welcomed in the hot summer months, but in this autumn season, the coolness served to chill the bones even further. The tiles had begun to fade from their original black and white to the current, more vintage, cream and gray. In areas where the tile succumbed to the sheer amount of traffic, haphazard repairs had been made to the chips and cracks in the floor. Grout and new tiles had been placed gradually over the years, but without a full restoration, the newly introduced patches stood out as awkward strangers, creating an accidentally eclectic pattern of vibrant against aged—old against fresh.

Her feet struck the floor in a staccato rhythm, making the only noise in the wide and airy room. The silence was eerie, but Guinevere had become used to it. She wasn't a fan of arriving so early but admittedly enjoyed the time to herself. Guinevere walked across the open room as if she owned the place: no staff to chat with, no managers to contend with, and no patrons to ask her questions. Interaction with the immediate public didn't so much bother her, but it wasn't exactly part of her job as an archivist either. Her purview was to study old manuscripts: to preserve them, to translate them, or to duplicate them if they were past saving.

As she reached the back half of the great hall, the ventilation system came to life and broke the silence. Here, the library split into three separate stories; each opened toward the front of the library and was guarded off by ornate marble railings. From her station, the stacks of books could be seen on each floor. The large spiral staircases housing the collection—wide and made of sturdy granite—sat on each side of the room, making their presence known. Guinevere headed to the one on the right and made her way to the third story. As she climbed, she looked down to the floors beneath her. The books grew smaller and the colors of their bindings became the only distinguishable feature. Soon, she was far enough away that they were mere smudges: reds, browns, blues, tan, and black mixed into a sea of muted colors.

When she arrived on the third floor, Guinevere walked further toward the back of the building. Here, there were more shelves of books, more wooden tables, and more velvet chairs. Past all of that were several offices, one of which Guinevere shared with several fellow archivists. Together, they worked on projects and shared resources. The light in her office had been left on, leaving a soft glow beneath the door. It guided Guinevere like a moth to light. Before entering the room, she slipped her satchel off her shoulders and felt around for her work badge. She pinned it to her blouse and reached for the door. Finding it unlocked she turned the handle to see who was inside.

"Hey," sing-songed one of her coworkers. Blanche was hovering over a stack of crates, busy with work.

"What are you doing?" Guinevere asked.

"The last shipment arrived this morning."

"It's here already? Those weren't supposed to arrive until next month!"

"Yep. Our friends on the Caerleon Expedition are really pulling their weight."

"I wish I could have gone with them. It would have been amazing to collect these documents from the ruins."

"Yes, but I know you. As much as you daydream, your favorite part is spent with your nose in the artifacts, not chatting with the locals or digging through rubble. Plus, the Rangers were in charge and we all know how irritating Agravain is to work with."

"You make a good point," Guinevere replied. Agravain was General Gorlois' right hand man. Everyone knew not to cross them as they had the ear of the current ruler, King Uther. Guinevere wanted nothing to do with the politics of Avalon, but this was yet another example of it intersecting with her work. "Are there any more crates in the loading bay?"

"Raynell's getting the last of them and should be back any minute. We waited for you to open them up."

"Thanks, Blanche! You know me too well."

The freight elevator dinged, and Raynell entered the room, pushing a dolly stacked with crates. "Let's get started," she said.

With that, the three coworkers began what an external observer would have called a 'choreographed ballet.' Together, they emptied each crate, pulling out documents, maps, books, paintings, and drawings, and arranging them on rows of tables. Blanche managed the packing list and checked off items as they were sorted. Raynell disposed of the hay that packed the crates by unceremoniously throwing it out the back window. Guinevere took shorthand notes on the condition of each document. Many of the items were rare or the only known copy. It was without doubt that the Caerleon Archaeologists had ensured their authenticity before sending them. Even so, Guinevere knew it was best to double check before moving forward with any kind of study or restoration.

After unloading all that the first crate contained, the three of them stood back and gazed at the tables filled with numerous ancient books, old maps, a couple pieces of art, and other manuscripts. They hardly knew where to start. Overwhelmed by the quantity and value of the collection, the archivists buzzed with sheer excitement and a bit of adrenaline.

"Why don't we all take a break?" Blanche said, speaking to all of them. "Then we can come back and figure out where to begin."

They nodded in agreement. Guinevere followed them out of the office into the main part of the library. She walked toward the front, stopping at the railing to look down on the floors below. The library had become a bustle of activity. People were mingling about looking for books, reading, and socializing. Even with all the patrons, the library had barely more than a hum of noise. The overhead lanterns were purposefully dim in favor of desk lamps to read beside. This was done to preserve Avalon Central's vast collection for years to come. Guinevere also preferred the general sense of calm that the low light and orange glow brought to the space.

Being nearly high noon, the library was filled with a diverse cross-section of the district: men and women came during their lunch breaks; parents with children; nearby school kids studied. They all had an indescribable harmony and sense of community. The people wore a mixture of clothing. Many of their choices looked impressively utilitarian: linen, cottons, and comfortable walking boots. Others were more artistic: metal accents, ruffles, and leather. The women in the library were mostly wearing corsets composed of brocade or leather with steel-boning. This corset was met with bell skirts, trumpet skirts, and bustle skirts. But each wearer gave them a unique twist.

Guinevere caught Raynell heading back to the office and turned to follow.

"Want to head to the archery range after work?" she asked.

"I'd love to!" Raynell responded. "I've been practicing over the weekend, but I'm not sure it's helped much."

"Let's see what we can do about that," Guinevere said as they reached the office.

Blanche was waiting for them and the three archivists gathered at the far end of the room.

"Let's start by categorizing the artifacts," Blanche said. "I expect you already took good notes so this should be straight forward."

As Guinevere and Blanche started working, Raynell returned to the crates. Something about their construction had been bugging her. She began to disassemble them with a crowbar and stack their boards along the office walls. When she removed the side wall of the last crate it revealed a hidden compartment.

"Hey!" she called. "I found something." She reached inside the cavity and pulled out an envelope with the Ranger's seal. Raynell handed the envelope to Guinevere. "Here, why don't you open it?"

Guinevere took the envelope in her leather gloved hands and gingerly broke the seal. Inside was a lightly folded parchment. She gently un-creased the edges and set it on the last vacant patch of table. The three of them huddled over it.

"What is it?" Raynell asked.

"Looks like it's some kind of map," Guinevere responded, picking it up and turning it around to see if there was any more information. She leaned over to get a closer look. The parchment was filled with pictograms and illustrations depicting ancient cities. Only Camelot, distinguishable by the royal crest of Constantine, seemed to be in its rightful location. Unintelligible runes were scattered over its surface, written in an unknown code.

The door opened, and Agravain walked in. His eyes widened as he saw the broken crates.

"What are you doing?" He barked.

"Our jobs," Blanche grumbled as she slipped the document off the table and hid it behind her back.

Agravain didn't reply, which was typical. He often strutted around the world as if it were beneath him. Having an in with the shadow king had its perks. He walked briskly toward the crates and reached into the opening Raynell had created.

"Where is the envelope?" Agravain asked again. He stood there for several seconds, studying the group. The three archivists awkwardly milled around the room, ignoring his question.

He muttered under his breath before hurrying out of the door. The archivists stood motionless in his wake.

After a few moments, Raynell spoke up, her voice cracking, "I think we just found a map to Excalibur."

"What?" Blanche responded. "That's impossible."

"I recognize a few of the runic symbols, and this edition of Constantine's crest places the document in the same era as the sword's disappearance."

"But Excalibur is just a myth."

"I wouldn't be so sure," Guinevere interjected before getting lost in thought. The Caerleon Expedition was excavating one of Constantine's lost Archives. The Rangers involvement made it likely that Gorlois was up to something. Uther was weak, but his legitimacy kept Gorlois from acting outright. If the sword fell into his hands, it could give him a rightful claim to the throne, to Avalon, and to the surrounding realms.

Guinevere bit her bottom lip. *What would become of Avalon?* Her mind started enumerating through all the worst possible outcomes. There was no space to think positively. Avalon was about to change—and not in a good way.

Outside she could hear Agravain in a heated exchange with the library director. Guinevere locked eyes with each of her coworkers and communicated wordlessly. The trio moved into action, hiding the map in Guinevere's satchel, and placing a decoy in the original envelope. Holding it over the flame, they resealed the wax and completed the subterfuge with seconds to spare.

Agravain entered the room with the library director in tow. Blanche held out the envelope.

"I believe this is what you are looking for," she said.

He snatched it out of her hand and smirked, looking her once over. Guinevere held her breath as Agravain focused his attention on the envelope and ran his finger over the seal. He gave a quick smile to the library director who looked as white as a sheet. She could only speculate what Agravain had said to him. Agravain left the room as quickly as he had arrived, and the director followed at his heals. When the archivists were finally alone, they let out a sigh of relief. Raynell grabbed Guinevere's bag from under the table and helped it over her shoulders.

"You need to go," Blanche said.

"Rain check on my archery lesson?" Raynell asked.

Guinevere smiled. Raynell always found a way to distract her. "Yes, we can go as soon as I get back."

With that, her friends returned to processing documents. Guinevere walked to the doorway, looked back one last time, and left.

Chapter Two

"Scotch—neat." Mordred said in a gruff voice as he sat down on a stool at the end of the bar. The pub was a small establishment, split lengthwise by a half-flight of stairs and an open railing. The bar counter was on the upper floor, covering the entire right wall. Behind it were brightly illuminated shelves lined with a collection of numerous drinks and mixers. Except for this display, the lighting in the pub was poor and a smokey haze hung over the establishment. Several patrons were scattered throughout the dingy room at high top tables. Most were sipping drinks; some were playing cards. No one was eating.

Mordred's scotch came, and he slammed it back. "Hit me again," he said before the bartender even had a chance to move. Startled by his forceful persona, the bartender nervously bumped into his coworker in a way that made him seem new to the job. Glass shattered when they collided, but no one turned to look.

A gust of cool autumn air blew through the open backdoor of the pub. Beyond it, a second-story deck sat sadly, occupied only by leaves for the season. The breeze could not penetrate the smoke of the room, smelling like a mixture of fresh rain and tobacco.

The bartender returned with the drink and quickly retreated. Mordred took a swig and turned his gaze across the bar. A lone man

17

sat at the other end, looking as if he hadn't slept in weeks. His hair was unkempt, and his outfit was disheveled. The shirt rumpled, misbuttoned, and untucked. His face matched the rest of him: bloodshot eyes and dry lips. Mordred got up, his drink in his hand, and walked over to him.

"Edern Nudd," Mordred said, running his metallic left hand through his once black, now mostly gray, hair. The internal metal workings of his bionic arm were exposed, the gears turning as he completed the motion.

Startled to hear his name, Edern turned to look at who had spoken. Mordred stared back at the man, eyes piercing his soul.

"What do you want?" Edern asked suspiciously.

"Heard you are a wanted man," Mordred replied.

"You've got the wrong guy," Edern spoke rapidly. "I'm innocent."

"This says differently." Mordred pulled a small metal disk out of his pocket, placing it on the bar. He pressed the top, and the device expanded in a telescopic motion. The side opened up momentarily, revealing intricate machinery. A glass lens flipped out of the opening and snapped to the top of the device. An orange light ignited in the bottom, building in luminance, and letting out a high-pitched electric whine. Moments later an amber beam of light burst forth, and Edern's wanted poster flickered in the air like the mesmerizing sparks of a campfire.

"I don't care what you may or may not have done," Mordred continued. "I only care about the bounty offered for your head."

Mordred reached for his drink and knocked it down, taking several long gulps. Seeing an opportunity, Edern leapt up but tripped backward over his stool. Catching himself with his hands on the ground, he prepared to run. Instead of bolting forward with speed, he crumpled headfirst into the arms of a young man who had appeared before him. Edern straightened himself out and brushed off his clothes, disoriented. It was only after several long seconds that he noticed the man standing in front of him.

His features were strong and defined, as if molded from granite. He had dark eyebrows that sloped downwards in a dour expression. Simple black slacks covered his legs and a brown jacket hung perfectly over his upper body. His coat was pulled back at the sleeve, exposing a black dragon tattoo on the inside of his left forearm. Leather holster straps held two pistols across his chest. Cargo boots, caked with mud and dirt, were on his feet. A bandana was tied around his neck, ready to be pulled up for cover if needed. The young man grabbed hold of Edern and spun him around to face the bar.

"You can let him go, Arthur," Mordred said. He squeezed the side of the mechanical projector, and it returned to its original form on the counter. Scooping it up, he turned to Edern and growled. "Come. Sit and finish your drink before we leave."

Edern hesitantly obliged, sitting down.

"We can do this one of two ways: either come with us willingly and we will do you no harm, or all bets are off. Personally, I enjoy the second option," Mordred said, moving his jacket back slightly to reveal the guns strapped to his waist. "What will it be?" he asked.

Edern sat stiffly, staring at his drink. He hadn't touched it, unable to relax. Throwing a cautious glance over his shoulder, he noted Arthur was standing guard. Edern eyed him over for a moment contemplating his next moved. He slunk back in his chair and picked up his drink, sloshing the liquid around. Without warning, he leaped backward out of the chair and threw the glass at Arthur's head. It was easily dodged and the glass crashed over the balcony into an unlucky patron. Arthur responded with a sharp kick to Edern's left knee. He stepped back at the sudden pain, spewing out a flood of curses. Enraged and dizzied by the pain, he threw several wild punches which Arthur deftly blocked. But, in a moment of pure luck, Edern managed to connect with Arthur's right eye. Edern flashed a dumb grin, but his victory was short lived. Arthur countered with a series of sudden blows and knocked him backward onto the floor. Edern lay there, gasping for breath.

Mordred stood up from his seat and walked over to join. He towered over Edern, his weapons brandished. Arthur pulled his pistols out of their holsters and motioned for Edern to get to his feet.

"You could have just shot him," Mordred mocked Arthur, while staring straight ahead at Edern.

"I have to stay in shape somehow." Arthur smirked, casually twirling one of his guns around his index finger before stopping it to aim at their captive. Edern stood in before the two men with his hands up, watching them carefully and waiting for their next move.

"Give it a rest. Let's go." Mordred rolled his eyes and motioned toward Edern to move. He began to lead him out of the building, passing fellow patrons. A few people were still preoccupied with an ongoing game of poker, but the majority had noticed the struggle and were raring for action. Some likely wanted to claim the bounty for themselves.

Arthur took a moment before joining his companion, walking up to the bar and unloading several loose coins onto the counter. The bartender nodded at him, acknowledging the payment.

As Arthur turned back around to follow Mordred, a fight broke out on the barroom floor. Quickly, he scanned the room for his partner.

"And I thought the drinks were good here…" he heard someone muttering next to him. Turning his head slightly to the left, he noticed that this someone was actually a young lady, standing with a drink in hand and smiling up at him. She had layers of flowing golden curls cascading over her shoulders, flawless ivory skin, and stunning blue eyes brighter than the sky itself. Her eyes could have pierced even the soberest of patrons.

"I couldn't say," Arthur replied. "I'm just stopping through…" He spotted Mordred trying to shuffle Edern toward the front door of the pub without getting mixed up in the fight. His guns were drawn, prepared to shoot anyone who tried to take away his prize. This tactic kept most of the crowd at bay. Glasses shattered and liquor sprayed the floor as the mob threw alcohol-fueled punches at one another.

"Care to join me?" the lady asked, looping her arm through his. She danced her fingers on his dragon tattoo and gazed openly at his sharp jaw, chin, and cheekbones. Arthur turned back to look at her, flashing two iridescent eyes: sharp, warm, and blue like the ocean on a summer day, with flecks of silvery light swimming across their surface. His dark eyebrows were fierce but graceful and his tousled brown hair was thick and lustrous.

Arthur stared blankly at the mysterious figure, enamored with her charm. She reached up and caressed his cheek with her soft hands. He grabbed her wrist pulling her hand away from his face.

"Would you like to?" she asked him.

Before Arthur could respond, someone broke a chair across his shoulders, and he staggered to the floor. He grabbed the edge of a table, pushing himself on to his feet. Arthur's heart pounded and a flash of anger rippled across his complexion.

"I'm a little busy right now," he said to no one in particular. He furtively looked around the room trying to spot his assailant. Instead he spotted Edern, who had somehow escaped and was trying to sneak out the bar by way of the back patio.

Arthur started forward, but someone grabbed his wrist from behind. He whipped around indignantly, only to find the woman staring back at him. She pressed a note into his palm.

"Find me some time."

Arthur nodded, closing his palm into a fist. She released him and he charged off to pursue his quarry.

Arthur reached the patio door and shouted Edern's name. He was out on the far end of the covered patio, contemplating a jump to the ground below. Edern quickly turned around with fear evident in his eyes. Arthur took a step toward Edern as Mordred joined them on the patio.

Edern's eyes darted rapidly between the two men. With only a moment of hesitation, he carelessly leapt off the edge of the patio. Luckily for him, an ample pile of leaves and foliage broke his fall, but the wind was knocked out of his lungs. By the time Edern had collected himself, Mordred had detached the wrist of his metal arm and repelled down the railing on a thin coil of wire. When he had reached the ground, his hand released its grip, and the coil spooled back into its housing. He stood over Edern, waiting for him to get back on his feet.

"Don't try to run again," Mordred said as he twisted his metal wrist and locked it in place. He flexed his arm, making sure all the metal workings were back in place. Satisfied, he grabbed his gun out of his waistband and gruffly lifted Edern by the collar.

Taking much more time than the other two, Arthur vaulted the railing, landing much more gracefully than Edern.

"I think a lady was inviting me back to her place," Arthur said as he turned to face Mordred, completely ignoring Edern.

"Well, what are you doing out here?" Mordred asked him, as if they hadn't just chased their bounty off a building.

"I couldn't let this idiot escape," Arthur explained very reasonably.

"I had it covered. You always have an excuse and back out. Eventually, you'll have to take someone up on their offer," Mordred dragged Edern by the collar around to the front of the pub. "At least for the company, if not for more."

Arthur shrugged.

"Let's go," Mordred barked, shoving the barrel of the gun in between Edern's shoulder blades. He stumbled forward with his hands held up in the air.

Arthur passed them and the group walked the short distance to their airship. It was an old-style Stallion class vessel with the name 'Hengroen' painted crudely on the side near the door. Most vessels of this type were used by smugglers to transport their goods; Mordred and Arthur were no different.

The gondola of the airship was angular in shape, cutting off near the back of the craft into a straight edge from which a large rudder protruded. Two fans were mounted on either side of the frame with short stubby wings. The trio entered the vessel just aft of the helm. From there, two hallways ran the length of the ship, encircling a central mechanical room that housed the boiler. Surrounding it were four cabins. The first—and most immediate— had been converted into a makeshift holding cell. Another housed the galley and lounge. The last were a pair of crew quarters for Arthur and Mordred. An expansive cargo hold completed the ship tucked in the aftmost quarter in front of the rudder.

The ship was well worn and had seen better days. The varnish on the wooden floor was scratched and worn, caked in layers of dirt tracked in by the crew. The walls, previously covered in new textured paneling, had now begun separating at the seams. Unidentifiable stains patterned the surface. In some places, the paneling had completely disintegrated, exposing the bare metal and rivets of the ships frame. The ceiling was open, and piping ran in a myriad of directions. They clanked and hissed with pressure from the still active boiler. In the not-so-distant past, the airship had been top of the line. Now it was a few bumps away from being sold for scrap. Even so, it was still Arthur' home. The place gave him a warm feeling every time they returned from a job.

Mordred guided Edern to the holding cell and stopped at its threshold. Edern hesitantly stepped forwards taking in the space. The surfaces were an amalgamation of earthen tones: tan walls, off-colored ceiling, brown floor, and almost-but-not-quite-beige furniture. There was a small bed sitting against the back wall, accompanied by a rickety chair, both of which looked very uncomfortable. In the corner of the room was a closed-off stall, which was probably the closest thing to a bathroom Edern would have access to.

Dissatisfied with his slow progress, Mordred shoved him into the space with the barrel of his gun. Edern stumbled in unwillingly. He spun around to plead with his captors.

"I didn't do what they said I did," he said.

Mordred stepped towards him, stone-faced. Edern flinched, cowering with his arms in front of his face. With a blunt shove, Mordred lifted Edern up against the wall and pressed his metal arm into his throat. Mordred gradually pushed harder, making it difficult for Edern to breathe.

"Be happy that the reward is for you to be delivered *alive*." He hissed into his ear. Edern tried to speak, but his voice only came out as a small squeak. Mordred released his grasp, and Edern slumped to the floor.

Mordred walked out of the room and shut the cell door. It closed with a resounding thud. The two men then walked the short distance to the bridge.

The helm was surrounded by a glass dome, offering a nearly 180-degree view for the pilot in all directions. Only the nose of the dirigible prevented them from seeing up into the sky. A large captain's chair dominated the space, whose gray fabric upholstery was tattered and coming undone at the seams. The dash in front of it was covered in a variety of steam gages and mechanical switches.

"Chart a course to Avalon," Mordred said as he left the helm.

Arthur hung his coat on the headrest and took a seat in the captain's chair. His hands moved quickly across the dash flipping several switches until the outboard fans roared to life. He pulled back on the throttle, and Hengroen lifted into the air. Once they had reached a decent altitude, the fans pivoted forward, and the vessel picked up speed. He brought the airship around and set its bearing by the metal compass built into the dash.

Arthur spotted a group of pterodactyls and altered course. They were fierce creatures, and he did not want to get entangled in an arial scuffle. He watched as their triangular formation retreated out of view. Once he had traveled some distance further, he allowed himself to relax and look around. Beneath his feat, the heads of brachiosaurs poked out over the canopy. They watched as his airship passed them by, turning their necks in a long sweeping arch.

The forest continued on for some time before abruptly ending. The trees were replaced with water and a bay stretched out to the eastern shores of Avalon. Arthur could just make out Camelot in the distance. It stood on the tallest hill in the northwestern most corner of the peninsula. Camelot towered over the fledgling sky towers of downtown Avalon. Those structures, having only been constructed at the turn of the century, were mere blips when compared to castle's storied history.

Camelot had been built many kings ago: before Uther, before Constantine, before the city had grown out beneath. Its pristine stone walls looked as if they were untouched by time. Throughout the years the Realms of Avalon had been challenged by foreign armies and rival kings. The castle's survival was due in no small part to its naturally defended position. Just north and west of its foundations were sheer cliffs that steeply descend into the ocean. To the east, was a steep ascent that was impassible by mounted forces. This made the only easy approach from the south—from downtown—which was protected by a series of gates leading up the Castle Hill.

I wonder what it's like inside those castle walls. The few times Arthur and Mordred had delivered bounties to the crown, he had waited behind to watch Hengroen. He rarely left the shipyard during their time in Avalon and let Mordred do most of the talking.

The airship crossed over the peninsula approaching the airfields. Arthur slowed the craft until it hovered over the landing site. As the craft descended from the sky, Arthur looked out over the ocean on the opposite side of the peninsula. Its blue surface sparkled in the sunlight. The view was quickly muddled with other airships descending and rising.

When Hengroen neared the ground, Arthur let loose several mooring lines for the grounds crew of the airfield. They pulled the craft in until the vessel made contact with the ground. The ropes were tied off as Arthur shut down the fans. Soon after, Mordred appeared on the bridge.

"You should put some ice on that." Mordred said. "Don't want to get a black eye."

"I've had worse," Arthur replied.

"You were beat up by someone wanted for tax evasion. That's got to be a first."

"I didn't get beat up. He landed one punch."

Mordred smirked.

"Actually, why are you badgering me. You're the one who let Edern get away."

Mordred shrugged, "What can I say, the chase helps my reputation. And unlike you, I don't have a black eye."

Arthur rolled his eyes.

"I suppose I did recruit you for your piloting skills, not your fighting expertise," Mordred relented.

"Recruited? More like you begged me to join. As I recall you spent several hours pumping me full of whiskey before I gave in."

Mordred laughed. "That is definitely not how it happened. I'm going to collect our bounty. Stay and watch the ship," he commanded.

"As always."

Arthur readjusted his position in the captain's chair, lounging back and putting his feet up on the dash. Looking out over the airfield, he could see several airships refueling, loading, and unloading cargo. The whole place bustled with activity. He spotted a large group of Rangers patrolling the shipyard with their weapons at the ready. *That's odd,* he noted before drifting off to sleep in the comfy chair.

Chapter Three

The door to the archival room closed with an audible click. Guinevere froze, looking around the hallway to see if anyone had noticed. *No one's there,* she thought, remembering to breathe for the first time since leaving her friends. The staff hallway of the library was silent save for the recurring tick from the wall clock. Self-conscious, she took a moment to readjust her satchel and make the straps more comfortable. She could feel the map burning a hole through the canvas. Even though only Blanche and Raynell knew she had it, her theft felt obvious.

Moving down the hall, she approached the fire escape window. She opened the sash and slid it upward, the old frame groaning at her command. Guinevere looked over her shoulder sharply, her gaze darting around to check just one more time if anyone was watching. Her heart was in her throat, pounding with the rush of adrenaline. Shaking, she focused again on the window before her and forced herself through the opening. Her boot lace caught on the sill. In her haste, she tripped forward, twisting midair toward the metal platform. Swinging her hands around to catch herself, the satchel slipped from her arm and hurtled over the edge to the alley below. There was nothing she could do to stop it, so she concentrated on the predicament at hand. Steadying herself on the platform with one hand, she managed to free her boot. The loss of her anchor, however, caused her to lose her balance. She fell on her back with the full force of her weight, knocking the wind out of her lungs. She lay motionless on the platform. For a few long moments, she stared at the sky, unable to breathe. *You're okay*, she told herself unconvincingly.

Regaining her composure, Guinevere stood up and dusted herself off. She closed the window and cautiously made her way down the stairs. The fire escape had been haphazardly bolted onto the side of the library. Most days, she despised its ugly appearance, but today she was thankful for the makeshift escape. Reaching the ground, Guinevere walked across the empty alley to her bag and checked its contents. Everything was there, but she rummaged through it several times for good measure. Pulling the drawstring shut, she slung the satchel over her shoulder and gripped its strap. Guinevere stood up and made her way toward the main thoroughfare. Her grip continued to tighten with every eager step forward. She rounded the corner and walked down the street, heading toward the Central District Station. On her way out of downtown, she could devise a plan before someone realized that the map was missing; before someone realized that *she* was missing.

Guinevere tried to hide the sense of urgency in her transit, but all she could hear was the sound of her boots hitting cement and echoing off the walls of the city. The early afternoon sun beat down on her, its rays penetrating through her clothes. Beads of sweat began to collect on her back, but she pulled the bag closer to her anxious body. She felt the straps of her satchel slipping in her sweaty hand. Her heart skipped a beat. It pounded loudly filling her head.

Upon arrival at the station, the clock struck its latest update: five minutes until the next arrival. Guinevere sighed and readjusted her satchel. *Okay,* she thought, *I'll just wait a little bit longer.* Sitting was the last thing she wanted to do, but instinct took over as she took advantage of the rare open seat. Feeling nervous, she started to fidget. She smacked her heels to the floor in an alternating motion and began bouncing her hands on her thighs. As her body was becoming a symphony of ticks, she willed herself to stop. Returning her hand to the straps of the satchel, she gripped them like a child on the first day of school. When another person joined her on the bench, she forced a smile to her new neighbor. The lady seated next to her didn't return Guinevere's gaze. She was more interested in the Daily Camelot Gazette's crossword than any type of human interaction. For this Guinevere was thankful.

Thoughts of Blanche and Raynell entered her mind. She wasn't sure what would happen to her co-workers, her friends, since they had helped her runaway. *I can't worry about them*, she thought. *I need to focus on getting myself away from here. They are resourceful and more than capable of handling a sticky situation.*

Although it felt like hours to Guinevere, the train arrived a couple minutes later. She boarded a nearly empty car toward the back and sat down on one of the bench seats. She slipped the satchel off her shoulder and onto her lap. She clutched it close to her chest and her thoughts drifted to the map. Thinking back to the few moments she had to examine it, Guinevere realized that the map must be in code. She wouldn't be able to decipher it without spending significant time to sit down and study. For that, she would need a safe space. Her home would likely be the first place the Agravain and the Rangers looked, so she'd have to disappear to somewhere new. *The shipyard. I'll stop there and look for a hideout.*

Ten dreadful minutes later, the train finally arrived at her intended destination. Guinevere got off the train and slipped her satchel on, desiring for once to get lost in the crowd of people returning from their lunch breaks. Pushing her now haphazard hair out of her face, she scanned around the new environment. She had never been to the docks before; she only ever looked out at them from the window. *Should she hide in one of the storage containers?* She didn't want to get shipped away or boxed in—an irrational, albeit very real, concern. Maybe she would join the crew of a sailing vessel, but they might ask too many questions. Whatever she chose, she needed to do it quickly.

Further into the shipyard, Guinevere watched as a large cataphract-class airship was repaired. The vessel must have returned to port from battle, as there were scorch marks emblazoned on its hull. The crew hustled around it, fixing the landing struts and patching sections of its torn balloon. She looked out toward the end of the yard and out to the bay. Yachts, military vessels, cargo, and passenger ships were bobbing up and down in the water.

She headed away from the maintenance district and toward the skyport. Here, airships were loading and unloading cargo and passengers alike. Suddenly, Guinevere stopped. Up ahead, several Rangers were talking with Agravain. *Was I followed?* she thought as blood rushed into her face. Her mind was filled with an impending sense of panic. Guinevere hid among some travelers waiting for their luggage.

The Rangers turned to walk away, and Guinevere took the opportunity to run. "Hey!" she heard someone shout. Her mind went silent. All she could think to do was place one foot in front of the other in an all-out sprint.

She did not stop until reaching a remote part of the airfield. There were few people there and even fewer places to hide. Up ahead she spotted a grouping of airships. One of the smaller vessels had its door open, so she ducked inside.

Staring up at the ceiling, she began to count. Her breaths were sharp, and her heart pounded loudly as she recovered from her sprint. Each beat shook her body and seemed to resonate into the world around her. She didn't dare poke her head back out the door to see if they were gone. She couldn't risk them finding her. Instead, Guinevere gathered herself together and walked further into the vessel. *I'll just hide around the corner until the coast is clear.*

Looking around, she recognized the craft from her studies. It was an old model, formerly used by members of the royal guard. The ship was reminiscent of another time in Avalon's history and Guinevere could not help but feel the old airship tug at her heartstrings. She reveled in the feelings of nostalgia before an unpleasant thought crossed her mind. The small nimble crafts had been mostly discarded by previous kings, and they were excellent at transporting goods undetected. Bounty hunters and smugglers had taken to them. She felt the blood drain from her face and suddenly felt sick to her stomach. She wanted to get out of the ship but knew the Rangers were likely waiting outside.

Guinevere paced along the back corridor of the ship. Each tread was carefully and slowly placed in an attempt to keep her footfalls quiet. She breathed in and out deeply, attempting to control the rapid flux of her mind. She paced to keep herself occupied. Was she noticed? *No one saw me*, she told herself. *No one saw me*, she repeated. *No one saw me.* If she reiterated it enough times maybe she would start to believe it.

What am I going to do now? You can't rush this. I just need to be patient. I need to take this one step at a time. After the coast is clear, I'll find another place to hide out. This is not where I thought I would be this morning when I left for work. I never imagined I might meet bounty hunters. Don't panic. She tried to calm any negative thoughts that wandered into her brain. Once she felt ready, she turned around and headed back toward the door.

A thud and a rumble, undoubtedly coming from the airship's turbines, reverberated around the ship. Guinevere peered around the corner just in time to see the exterior door swing shut. Slumping against the wall—head hung in her hands—she thought, *I can't do this. I've got to get out! I need to get away while I still can.*

Peering around the corner, the hallway was empty. She got up on her feet and ran to the door. She pulled the handle and the door swung open, revealing that the craft was already in the sky. Before she could move or close the door, the craft leapt forward and knocked her off of her feet.

Too late now, she thought. *I either need to confront the crew or find a place to hide until this aircraft reaches port.* Unsure of what would happen if she got caught, Guinevere started to panic. *What kind of people would they be? Are they reasonable or would they throw her out of the moving airship? Ruthless or merciful? Lawless or trustworthy?*

Hurrying into an adjoining room, she opted to find a place to hide. The room appeared to be a cargo hold but was poorly lit. She walked forward slowly in the dark, trying to stay quiet and keep balance in the moving airship. She was surrounded by towers of wooden crates.

Guinevere bumped into one and grabbed hold of the rim to steady herself. The lid was slightly ajar and fairly light. She reached inside to see if it was empty but found a few apples rolling around in the bottom. This was probably someone's stash and wouldn't make a great hiding spot. She animatedly replaced the cover and tiptoed away from the crate for good measure. *Don't want to tick someone off by eating their food.*

With her last step, the floor rang hollow. She turned back to the spot and knelt to the ground. Running her hands along the floorboards, she felt for an opening. After a few attempts to find one, she succeeded in lifting the hidden panel from the floor. Guinevere peered down into a small cavity. Cobwebs hung in the corners and it looked unused.

Perfect. She smiled, releasing her satchel into the void. The bag landed with a soft thud and kicked up a cloud of dust. Guinevere stifled a sneeze. She crawled into the space and lay down on the floor. It was a bit cramped, but the panel fit when she lay on the ground. It thudded noisily into place, and she held her breath.

Pulling her legs up to her chest she wiped the dust off her knees. *I guess that's one good thing about a smuggler's ship. There are lots of places to hide.* Guinevere breathed a short sigh of relief as she waited for the ship to land. She clutched her bag tightly and rested her head on it. Her heart echoed in her ear, and she felt it resonating through her satchel. It beat in sync with the ship's rotors. Guinevere smiled to herself in a moment of calm. She had found a place to stay. But like before, the moment passed, and her smile faded. She pressed her lips together tightly as her anxiety returned. *I hope they don't check this compartment,* filled with an all too familiar panic.

What seemed like hours passed as Guinevere lay alone with her thoughts. Time crawled. Every second felt like a minute, and every minute felt like an hour. The fear of discovery kept her awake and alert. She couldn't risk being turned into the Rangers. Her mind tried to form a plan, but coherency evaded her. The only thing left was a bleary-eyed focus on her growing tiredness. She stayed in this pattern of faux vigilance until exhaustion took over, and she finally passed out.

Chapter Four

"Hello, sleepyhead," Mordred said, giving a whack to the back of the captain's chair. Arthur flinched, nearly falling out of the seat.

"Don't do that," he said. "You know I hate it."

"Were you inviting over guests?" Mordred asked, a wry smile forming across his face.

"What? No. Why do you ask?" Arthur furrowed his brow.

"You left the hatch open," Mordred walked up behind the captain's chair and placed his hands on Arthur's shoulders, massaging them gruffly.

"I seem to recall you being the one who left the ship," Arthur replied. "That would make you responsible for the door." He winced as Mordred dug his fingers in a little too hard for comfort.

"I mean, if you want to invite strangers onto our ship, that's your prerogative."

Arthur rolled his eyes.

"Where to?" he asked.

"Your pick." Mordred turned his head toward Arthur. "We just need to find a place for the night." With that, Mordred left.

Arthur flipped a few switches, and the beast came to life. He felt the familiar vibrations of the pistons course through his bones like the rhythmic heartbeat of a healthy stallion. Instinct took over as he held the throttle; a surge of energy flooded his veins. With gentle goading, he led Hengroen forward. The ground fell away, and the wind rushed past. Soon they were galloping into the sky, surrounded by nothing but blue. Here, in the stirrups of a proud airship, Arthur felt alive. He reveled in the moment, awash with delight.

Arthur piloted the Hengroen away from the capital city, leaving Camelot far behind. They flew for several hours over the neighboring mountain range to the east, finding a valley between the tree studded slopes. The ship touched down on a smooth patch of grass just as night was beginning to fall.

Looking out the cockpit window, Arthur watched the sunset. One moment, light entered the cabin in scattered, gleaming rays. The next, the sky was filled with a hazy orange glow. The stars came out, shyly at first, obscured by the red afterburn of the distant sun. Before long, the last rays had faded, and the stars dominated the night's skyline.

Arthur leaned back in his chair. He was fairly certain Mordred had retired for the night. With time on his hands, he considered leaving the ship. *It might be nice to enjoy a nighttime stroll.* He walked to the door of the Hengroen and peered outside. The wind rustled the waist high grassland. In the distance her heard a low growl. Outside, he was just one dinosaur away from being on the dinner menu. With that thought in mind, Arthur pulled the door firmly shut, checked that it was firmly latched, and retired for the night.

***

A rthur lazily yawned and flipped over onto his side. He could hear the faint mechanical ringing of an alarm clock. Arthur pulled the covers around his body tightly and smushed his pillow over his ears, hoping to fall back to sleep. Instead, the ringing grew noticeably louder, refusing to be ignored. *It can't be the morning already,* Arthur thought, letting out a loud yawn. He opened his eyes and stared up at the ceiling. *Alright, it's time to get up.* He flopped out of bed and silenced the clock. He did not pause to look at the time, knowing by the light that it was midmorning. Instead, he turned back around and grabbed his clothes, brushing out the wrinkles in his shirt. His stomach growled as he headed to the lounge.

"Look what the cat dragged in," Mordred said as Arthur walked into the room. Mordred was sitting in a booth, lounging back, and sipping a steaming cup of tea. It was likely spiked, as indicated by the adjacent bottle of whiskey on the table. He smirked at Arthur who shrugged.

"We aren't in a hurry to get anywhere." He walked over to a cupboard and looked inside. It was mostly empty, save for a few bottles of hard liquor.

Mordred chuckled. "Drink?" he asked.

"No," Arthur replied as he turned to leave. "I'm looking for something with a little more sustenance."

"Really? You don't say," Mordred said. "Fetch me something while you're at it."

Arthur didn't bother to reply and walked the short distance to the ship's hold. Inside, he headed for the crate of apples and grabbed out his favorite snack. He held it out and brushed it off with his shirt before taking a bite. *We really need to get more*, he thought before turning to leave the room. As he walked across the floor, something sounded off. Retracing his steps, he found the noise again. *This compartment should be empty*. He rocked the loose panel back and forth with his heal.

He reached down and unhooked the cover. He half expected to find one of Mordred's various side hustles. *Maybe it would be edible*. With his foot, he slid the hatch aside revealing a sleeping figure. She was curled up in the small compartment with her knees drawn up to her chin. Her long brown hair was draped over her legs.

This is new, Arthur thought. Stowaways were uncommon. Rather, they were nonexistent on Hengroen—Mordred's temper had a bit of a reputation. But beyond that, the young lady did not look like she belonged: she was too put together, too proper, and too clean to be a drifter. *Better to get her off the ship before Mordred finds out*, he thought. His choice was less out of pity and more to avoid Mordred's unnecessary badgering. He crouched down and rested on his heels.

"Hey there." Arthur called out, soft but firm.

Her eyes fluttered open, and she reached up to rub them. She pushed herself upright, head popping up over the edge of the floor. Her gaze was unfocused and confused. Arthur studied the figure's expression. Her eyes were milky brown, her pale skin was dusty but smooth, and her bowlike lips were slightly chapped. She moved suddenly and snapped to attention, glancing furtively around the room.

"Like the ship?" Arthur asked, staring curiously at the stranger. Her head spun around to face him, and a loose strand of hair fell in front of her eyes. She brushed it aside hastily, her eyes flush with momentary anger. He tried to anticipate what she would say, but the figure did not speak. She looked him over instead: his head, his boots, his tattoo, his holstered weapon. Her eyes widened.

"Oh," he said, removing the gun from his belt. She reeled backwards.

"It's all right," he said, realizing his mistake. He quickly set the weapon on the floor beside him. "See?" He held up his hands to show that they were empty. She didn't relax.

"Is there something I can get you?" Arthur asked.

"I didn't mean to…" she answered him. Her voice sounded dry and raspy. She wrapped her arms around herself and hunkered into the corner of the space. Arthur waited a few moments, but she did not continue.

"Don't worry," he stated, "I'm not going to hurt you."

She shook her head, noticeably overwhelmed.

"I'm Arthur," he started again, "Who are you?"

"I'm not… I didn't mean to…" The words fumbled out of her mouth.

"Where's my snack?" Mordred hollered as he lumbered into the room. Arthur closed his eyes letting out a long sigh. He stood up to intercept, placing himself between Mordred and the uninvited guest.

"Here, have this," Arthur said, hoping to distract the other man. He tossed the half-eaten apple to Mordred, who grabbed it out of the air with his metal arm. But his eyes had already locked onto the stowaway, and a mischievous smile formed at the corner of his cheek.

"Arthur, did you sneak a lady aboard our ship?" he teased.

Arthur shrugged in response, glancing backwards to see how she was doing. The stowaway had hoisted herself out of the compartment and was presently crouched at the edge of the void. Arthur kicked the covering back into place, and the young lady to flinch.

"Is that so?" Mordred glowered. Instinctively, the young lady pushed herself back toward a wall of crates. Her hand bumped into Arthur's gun.

Everyone in the room froze, as if holding their breath. In a burst of motion, Mordred shoved Arthur out of the way and reached for his holstered weapon. But she was faster at the draw and took aim at Mordred's head.

She stood up and breathed deeply, steadying her form. Her composure had changed: gone was the terrified stowaway; in its place was a collected presence.

Mordred slowed his approach and cheekily raised his arms.

"Alright, you've got me," Mordred cooed at her.

The girl remained silent.

"Do you know what we do to uninvited guests?" He asked while producing Arthur's half eaten apple. Mordred crushed it with his metal arm, sending a spray of fluid all over the room. He rolled the pulverized remnants of its carcass through his fingers.

"We drop them in the forest and let the dinosaurs take care of them. Or we leave them in the desert and let the elements kill them. Which would you like?" He grinned at her.

"Option three," she replied. "I kill you and take your ship."

"Hah!" Mordred exclaimed. "I like this one." The woman cautiously lowered her weapon and pointed it afield. Mordred crossed the distance to Arthur and rested his hand on his shoulder.

"She's got spunk," Mordred whispered and glanced at their guest. Mordred walked to an adjacent wall and leaned up against it, crossing his arms. Arthur stared at the woman with curiosity.

"Who are you?" He muttered to himself a bit louder than he intended.

"Guinevere," she replied softly. Her arms were now down at her sides.

"Why are you here?" Mordred barked from across the room.

"I was being stalked," she said. "I passed through your ship to hide, but the door closed before I could leave."

"We don't give out free rides." Mordred said. "You appear to have no money or valuables to pay for this trip."

She didn't reply. After a moment's pause, she crossed the room to Arthur and held out the hilt of the pistol.

"Let me join your crew." Guinevere said, offering the gun as an olive branch.

"I think we could work out a deal," he told her. "What skills do you have? As you can probably tell, I'm the smart one, and he's the hired gun."

Mordred rolled his eyes.

"Well, I'm an archivist at the Avalon Central library…"

Mordred let out a hearty laugh. "What kinds of skills is a librarian going to provide us?"

"Archivist," Guinevere countered. "I can verify the authenticity of artifacts, manuscripts—you name it. That could prove useful to a couple of…smugglers?" She paused. "I'm also a skilled archer."

"I'm sure you are," Mordred said dismissively.

Arthur spoke up. "I can think of a couple jobs where we could use her as a grifter or a third pair of eyes in the sky."

"Humph." Mordred looked between the two of them.

Arthur studied Guinevere. Behind the bravado, he could sense her icy resolve cracking. *She must be terrified of Mordred,* he thought. Her eyes were fixated, unblinking, on the elder man, watching and waiting for his next move. She noticed Arthur's gaze and gave him a half-smile.

"Alright. You can have the guest quarters," Mordred turned to leave. "I don't want any more surprises today."

Arthur motioned for Guinevere to follow and they traveled a short distance towards the front of the ship. "Here we are," Arthur chimed, pointing to the door on the left. "I'm afraid it isn't much. We don't typically have guests."

He pulled the handle to the wooden door and walked in. He watched as she hesitantly stepped forward.

"I'll go fetch you some water," Arthur said, disappearing out of the room. Arthur heard Guinevere slump onto the bed.

He left the door open behind him. There was nowhere she could run while they were in the air, and she was unarmed. Reaching the galley, he unlatched a cupboard and pulled out a glass from the shelf. He filled it with water and walked back. *Can I trust her?* He barely knew anything about their mysterious guest. She'd been light on the details of who was chasing her. Something about it seemed fishy. Arthur had several questions that he wanted to ask, but simply handed her the glass of water when he reached the room. He watched as she guzzled most of it down.

"Let me know if you need anything," Arthur said. "I'll be just across the hall."

She didn't reply, appearing lost in thought so Arthur turned to leave the room.

"Thank you," she said, filling the silence.

He paused, not quite sure what to say, and waved awkwardly in response. He shut the door on his way out and locked it out of habit.

***

"What do you make of our stowaway?" Arthur asked Mordred. They had rejoined each other on the bridge of the ship.

"She's hiding something," Mordred said, turning to face Arthur.

"Yeah. Something seemed off, but I do think she could help us," Arthur replied.

"I don't trust her, and neither should you," Mordred warned. "She's clearly a city girl, and we are not cut out of fine cloth. Having said that, I do believe this is our chance to do the job in Pictland. It has been on my list for a while now, and I think her skills as a librarian will help her blend into the Pictland crowd and get close to Hueil. You and I both know he'd just look at us like rocks."

"So, let me get this straight. You don't trust her, but you're willing to gamble the Pictland job?" Arthur said. "I know how important that job is to you, what with your lady friend and all."

Mordred shrugged. "Might as well go for a major score since we have the means."

"I don't know. That job is risky."

"If she's going to be on our ship, she'll need to earn her keep."

Arthur eyed him suspiciously. "For now, let's just head out to the next outpost. We need to refuel."

"Make sure it has a tailor. We're not going to fool anyone with our typical attire," Mordred said, walking out of the bridge.

Chapter Five

Arthur tinkered with the ship's boiler as he waited for Mordred's return. They had landed several hours before, and he took the time to perform much needed maintenance on Hengroen. He laid back on a wheeled dolly, working within the heart of the machine. The rachets and clanks of his tools formed a strange mechanical symphony that echoed off the metal space. Arthur was covered with sweat and oil, occasionally dabbing his face with a towel. The work kept him busy and helped pass the time, but his mind still wandered. He was intrigued by their hitchhiker and was surprised when she hadn't appeared looking for a meal or asking to leave the ship. But her door was closed when he had checked earlier, and he thought it best to give her space.

With a final twist of his wrench, Arthur pushed himself out from under the machine and admired his work. He placed his tools aside and pulled a large lever in the wall. Flames burst forth within the metal contraption, casting shadows that danced around the room. Arthur checked his work one final time and replaced the metal cover of the firebox. It would take some time for the pressure to rise, so he left the room to clean up. He wiped down his arms in his cabin and changed into clean clothes.

Arthur's stomach growled. *Must be dinner time.* He headed to galley and prepared a meal on the stove. *Might as well make enough for three.* He whipped up some food and found himself standing in front of the holding cell with a plate of food in hand. The door was locked.

Shit! No wonder she hasn't come out. Arthur reached forward and unlocked the cell. The hinges creaked as the large metal door swung inward. He looked into the room. Guinevere sat on the bed, looking dejected. Her eyes were puffy, and her tears had formed paths through the dust on her cheek.

"Hey. Sorry for locking the door earlier. That was my bad." Arthur fidgeted with his hair and looked at an inconspicuous point on the ceiling. When Guinevere didn't respond, he turned to face her. She averted her eyes and stared at the floor.

"I brought you something to eat," Arthur said, setting the plate of food beside her.

Guinevere scooted against the wall and pulled her feet up on the mattress to sit crossed-legged. She moved the plate into her lap before taking a bite out of the freshly cut fruit. Arthur watched as she ate several more pieces, trying to get a read on her expression.

"Where are we?" she asked between mouthfuls of bread. "I could feel us land, but I can't see out the window."

"We are at an outpost—to refuel and gather supplies. Mordred is gathering some intel on our next job."

"Can you show me?" she asked.

"Sure, but there's not too much out there…"

"That's alright, I'd just like to look around."

Arthur stepped sideways and motioned out of the room. Guinevere passed him, likely knowing the way from her short time on the ship. They rounded the corner, but Guinevere stopped in front of the exterior door. She stood there motionless.

"Is something wrong?" Arthur asked.

"No," she said stepping aside from the door. "After you."

Arthur nodded and walked up to it turning the handle and stepping through. The brightness of the outside world blinded him for a time as he walked down the ship's ramp. He reached the bottom before realizing that Guinevere had not followed. Looking back up at the entrance, he could not see her.

"What's up with that?" Arthur furrowed his brow. He looked around the tarmac spotting several figures: a mechanic, a street peddler, a few Rangers, and uniformed security. Seeing nothing out of the ordinary, he shrugged and walked back up the plank towards the ship.

Before he could cross the threshold, Arthur felt Guinevere's hands grab his torso and pull him into the ship. She held him tightly against her. He braced his palms on the wall for balance, his arms on either side of her frame. He glanced down at Guinevere curiously, but she looked away and let him go. Arthur didn't move, confused as to what just happened. Realizing how little space was left between them, Arthur took a step back and closed the door to the ship.

"Are you okay?" he asked, kicking a nonexistent piece of dirt.

"No." She slumped, sinking to the floor. Guinevere held her knees to her chest and looked down the hall.

"Mordred should be back shortly," he said. "We can leave as soon as he arrives."

Guinevere didn't move, and the seconds ticked by.

"Sorry," she muttered, hanging her head, "I just thought…" Her voice trailed off. She rested her chin on her knees.

"It's alright." Arthur sat down against the other side of the hallway.

She looked over at him, her eyes betraying her careworn temper.

"So, you were running away from someone?"

"Yes," Guinevere nodded. "I had to get out of Avalon."

He searched her expression, trying to glean any insight as to what had happened. After a pause, he continued his questioning. "What was your plan? To hitch a ride with us and then…?" He raised his shoulders questioningly.

"I don't really know. Tag along with you, I suppose?"

"Is there a reason you didn't just book passage on a civilian ship?"

"I couldn't," she said with a hint of indignation.

"Don't get me wrong. It just looks like you could have afforded something a little more luxurious than this"

"They were following me. They would have known."

It was clear that Guinevere wouldn't simply volunteer the mysterious entity who was stalking her. Why she wouldn't say was beyond Arthur's comprehension.

"What's it like in Avalon?" Arthur asked.

"Huh?"

"What's it like living in the capital city?"

"I live in the next town over," Guinevere replied, "and, honestly, it is not much different than here."

Arthur didn't quite know what to make of her response, so he stood up and offered her a hand.

"Here," he said. "Why don't I show you around the ship?"

She looked at him tentatively before taking his hand. She stood up but lost balance. Arthur caught her by the waist before she hit the ground. Guinevere looked up at him, relieved.

"This way." He guided her around the small ship, showing off its handful of rooms. They passed the boiler room, the lounge and galley, a few closets, Mordred's quarters, the lavatory, and Arthur's room. When they had completed the loop, Arthur showed her to the bridge. Stepping inside, he held out the captain's chair. Guinevere settled in, obviously worn out.

"We are halfway to Pictland." Arthur motioned to the navigation charts sprawled out across the dash. He traced his finger on the path they had taken. "Out there," he pointed beyond the glass, "is the Red Rock Pass of the Finistere Mountains. This post serves as a shelter during inclement crossings for both wanderers and airships alike."

Arthur watched as Guinevere stared out the window. The valley before them stretched on for miles, and numerous buildings dotted the landscape. The craggy mountains beyond were both ominous and inviting; the peaks were already capped with snow.

"It's beautiful." Guinevere admired the view. "The mountains make me feel a bit cold, though."

"Hold on," Arthur said. "I'll be back in a moment." He returned with a blanket which he draped over her shoulders. Guinevere pulled it tightly around her.

"You can stay here if you'd like. The chair's a bit comfier than the bed in that room."

Guinevere nodded, and he turned to leave the room.

"Arthur?" She called, and her voice cracked. "Don't go."

He hesitated for a moment, before pulling down one of the jump seats from the back wall.

"I'm here," he said a bit clumsily.

"Thank you," Guinevere said sleepily as she settled into the captain's chair.

Arthur kept a watchful eye over her.

She's something else, he thought. Outside, the sun set over the Red Rock Pass and the mountains gleamed in the last light.

"Arthur," Mordred barked sometime later.

He got up from the jump seat and pushed the older man from the room. He shut the door quietly behind them. Mordred looked at Arthur, judgement written on his face.

"I don't trust her," Mordred said sternly. "Maybe after the job in Pictland, but not now."

Arthur nodded solemnly.

"Chart a course to Pictland and meet me in the lounge first thing tomorrow. Bring your girlfriend."

"She's not…" Arthur started, but Mordred had already walked away.

***

53

"Thank you for joining me," Mordred said with a wry smile as Guinevere and Arthur entered the lounge. He was sitting on the booth side of a small round table. From his perch, he commanded the entire room.

"Take a seat." He motioned and Guinevere pulled out one of the chairs. She did not drop her gaze as she sat down and eyed him warily. Arthur crossed the table and took a seat next to Mordred on the booth.

"Drink?" Mordred asked, lifting up a bottle of whiskey.

"It's not even lunch," Guinevere answered shortly.

Mordred eagerly topped off his glass and passed the bottle off to Arthur. The younger man poured one for himself, but before he could take a drink, Guinevere had stolen it. She took a large swig and slammed it on the table.

"I didn't say no." she said.

"I think I'll have tea," Arthur passed the nearly empty bottle back to Mordred.

"Oh, Arthur," Mordred muttered. "You're something else." He turned to face Guinevere. "I don't trust you, you don't trust me, and bonehead can't think straight. I think that pretty much sums up where we all stand."

Mordred turned to Arthur, who had gotten up to tend a whistling kettle. He drummed the table impatiently with his metal arm. Arthur mixed several varieties of dried leaves before returning to the table with several cups of hot liquid.

"Back to the matter at hand," Mordred said shortly. "I want to discuss our next job—give you an opportunity you can't refuse."

He ticked off on his fingers. "Dinosaurs, desert, and maybe a skydive."

Arthur rolled his eyes.

"In any case, I have 'approved' your request to join this crew—provisionally, of course. For your first task, you will help us with a small job in Pictland. Consider it a trial run."

"What's the job?" Guinevere asked, clearly unphased by his vague threats.

Mordred set a small silver disk on the table between them. He pressed its top and an amber figure was projected over the table. The man, probably in his mid-30s, was of average height and build. He was clothed in an expensive suit and covered with jeweled rings.

"This is Hueil," Mordred explained. "He is the kingpin of the dinosaur trade. Poaching, breeding, fighting, you name it and he's the man. We need you to steal a time piece from him."

"What's so special about it?" she asked, adjusting her posture to better view the image.

"That—" Mordred clenched his jaw and grated his teeth as he paused to regain his composure "—is not relevant." After a moment, he smiled and continued talking. "Due to its importance, Hueil always keeps the pocket watch on his person. According to my sources, he is hosting an art auction in the gallery below his penthouse. This will be our best chance to get in and have you pickpocket him."

"And you can't do this because…?"

"He's not interested in men," Mordred answered matter-of-factly.

"What does that have to do with pickpocketing?"

"Hueil only appears when something interesting is on the floor. Surely you understand."

Guinevere mulled over this new information.

"Be careful," Arthur warned. "Hueil has a reputation with women. Just give us a signal and we'll bail you out"

"Great pep talk," Mordred chastened.

Guinevere faced Mordred. "Can I count on you to back me up?"

"If you do disappear, don't expect much from me. I'll be waiting on the ship." Mordred stared at Arthur. "And if the two of you fail to return, I will not hesitate to ditch you both in Pictland."

"And if I decline this job of yours?"

"By the simple fact that you're still on this ship, I'd wager you don't have another option," Mordred said.

"Fine," Guinevere said, relenting. She slowly looked from Arthur to Mordred and smiled. Despite all his bluster, Mordred had made her a part of the crew, however dysfunctional. "Let's go steal a pocket watch."

Chapter Six

The coat check in the lobby smelled of moth balls. Their musty odor trickled in with the patrons, riding in on the cool breeze that lay beyond the gaudy double doors. In the main hall, the scent of expensive perfumes rose into the air. Their overwhelming fragrances all mixed with the smoke of cigars wielded by the wealthy men wandering from painting to painting. They carelessly allowed the ashes from their cigars to fall near priceless works of art. The open bar bustled with activity. Workers filled and refilled glasses of champagne. The smell of the bartender's sweat became a medley with that of the alcohol. An elevator was in the back of the gallery for the lucky few who were wealthy enough to either spend the night in the hotel or—even more exclusively—own one of the condos.

Guinevere felt nauseous. She saw no sign of the target yet. She walked slowly around the gallery, glancing toward the drink table where Arthur—along with several other young men—stood refilling guests' glasses. She caught his eyes for a moment before quickly looking away. A shadow of a smile flickered across his face.

Guinevere felt self-conscious in the outfit Mordred had selected for her. She wanted to tug at the single sleeve that covered her left arm. The fine gold and jewels that draped over her other shoulder lightly touched her skin and rustled with her every movement. Each contact with her shoulder, enticed Guinevere to swat at them.

She recalled the two men's expressions when she joined them on the bridge of the airship, moments after changing into her new outfit. Her long hair was pulled up into a single braided ponytail, exposing her face beyond the usual curtain of brunette locks. She felt utterly foolish in the dress on the bridge, but the two men seemed impressed.

"Good," Mordred said. "Glad to see that you are ready. It's just about time to go."

"You look stunning," Arthur said, admiring.

"Do I really have to wear this?" Guinevere asked.

"Yes," Mordred blurted out instantly with no further explanation. Guinevere did not argue further, ready to get the next few—what she assumed to be hours—over with.

Even now, she knew that her outfit made her appear at home amongst the rest of the crowd, but she still felt like she stood out. Guinevere stole a quick glance back at the bar, hoping to meet Arthur's eyes once more, but he was busy attending to his duties. Feeling slightly disappointed, she turned back to viewing the art. She had been to art galleries in Avalon before, but they were nothing quite like this. Here, priceless and lost works of art were being displayed, all available for purchase.

"What's a pretty young thing like you doing here alone?" Guinevere heard behind her.

She turned around to see a man not much older than her. Guinevere looked him over. He was of average build, wearing a long black overcoat. Several gold metals were pinned across the left breast. He wore sleek black boots; they were in pristine condition without a single blemish or speck of dirt on them. There was nothing special about his outfit, but, nevertheless, his appearance emanated wealth. In his ring-encrusted hands were two champagne flutes.

"Drink?" he asked.

"Thank you," Guinevere said as she gently took the glass from him. She took a sip. "And I'm not here alone." She nodded toward Mordred, who was standing near the wall, watching her.

"Your date?" the man asked.

"My security," she answered and took another sip of champagne. This was their target.

"Hueil," the man introduced himself, taking Guinevere's free hand in his jeweled one and delicately planting a kiss.

"Guinevere," she responded.

"I've never seen you around before."

"Well," she lingered on the word, drawing it out, "I've made quite the journey to be here tonight."

"Are you enjoying yourself?" he asked and then took a sip. He looked at Guinevere over the brim of his glass, his rings reflecting multicolored light onto her.

"I do enjoy browsing, and sometimes a purchase if I see the right piece," she replied as she walked past him. She stopped to look at the next piece of art. "This one here—" she motioned with her champagne flute toward a large oil painting "—is too boring. I want something with a little more excitement in my life." She took another swig of her drink. "What about you?"

"I'm always in the market for art. Particularly something new—something I've never seen before." He put his hand on her upper back. She flinched slightly with his touch. She tried to hide her distress at feeling cold fingers invasively caress her bare skin. The metal of his rings sent small chills down her spine. Hueil guided her to the next painting.

"Have you found that here?" she asked him, already knowing his answer.

"I think I may have," he told her. She downed the rest of her champagne.

Hueil motioned to the bar. Guinevere watched as Arthur moved to come to the pair, but another bartender had already intercepted them and refilled their glasses. Disappointed, Arthur returned to the bar, and Guinevere moved her attention back to Hueil.

"What would you recommend?" Hueil asked as she continued sipping on her champagne. She tried avoiding making eye contact.

"Not sure." She walked slowly away down the row of paintings. Guinevere turned to face him. "I'm not sure if I've found the right piece yet."

The two of them walked around the auction some more. Hueil kept looking over his shoulder at Mordred, but Guinevere didn't seem to notice. She finished her second glass.

"Want to go somewhere with better champagne than here?" Hueil asked.

"What do you have in mind?" Guinevere asked, motioning to a bartender to take her glass.

"I have a rare bottle up in the penthouse."

"But I will miss the end of the auction."

"Pick any piece and I'll make sure that it's yours." Hueil motioned over the officiate of the event, whispering something inaudible to him. The man nodded in response and then walked away. "What do you say?"

"Show me the way."

Guinevere followed him out of the gallery hall to the elevator at the end of the room. An attendant opened the golden gate for them. Mordred followed, hurriedly moving to catch up with the pair before they made it into the elevator. Hueil turned and noticed him.

"Don't worry about him. He's harmless," Guinevere said, placing her hand on Hueil's arm reassuringly. She motioned for Mordred to follow. He walked closer to her, nodding his head slightly in submission. Before he could fall in line beside Guinevere, Hueil put up a hand to stop him.

"Sir?" Mordred questioned.

"We don't need any tag-along, rent-a-Ranger security. She'll be back before you even realize she's gone." Hueil smiled at Mordred as he palmed Guinevere's fingers that rested on his arm. His hold was tight, griping her hand such that she was unable to slip it away.

"Ma'am, I can't let you go alone."

Guinevere met his gaze, trying to mask the fear behind her eyes. After a noticeable pause, she opened her mouth to speak.

"How much is she paying you?" Hueil asked before Guinevere had a chance to speak. He released his grasp on Guinevere's hand, which she quickly slipped off his arm.

"I am not sure I understand the question, sir." Mordred tilted his head, slightly focusing back on Hueil while keeping Guinevere at the edge of his vision.

"How much is she paying you to act as her security tonight? Fifty credits? A hundred?"

Mordred did not reply.

"Two hundred? *Five hundred* credits?" Hueil let out a laugh at the proposition. Mordred remained stone-faced. Shaking his head, Hueil pulled out a coin purse from inside his jacket. "It doesn't matter. Here." He reached out, handing Mordred the entire coin purse. "There should easily be a couple thousand credits worth of coins in there. Go get yourself a drink and relax a bit."

Mordred took the weighty coin purse in his hand.

"Don't worry. I won't hurt her," Hueil added. "Besides, I have real security if something were to happen. They'll look after her too."

Guinevere sincerely doubted Hueil would look after her. It was likely that she was walking into a trap. She was afraid to go with Hueil alone but didn't see an alternative way forward. At this point Mordred couldn't follow her without arousing Hueil's suspicion. Mordred and Guinevere stared at each other, both in an impossible situation.

"What do you say?" Hueil asked.

It took a moment for Guinevere to realize that he was addressing her. Hesitantly, she turned to look at him. The way he was smiling made her want to squirm, but she pushed her feelings aside and turned to Mordred.

"I left my cloak at the coat check," she said. Her voice shook slightly.

"Ma'am?"

"My coat," she snapped.

Mordred nodded and turned around.

Guinevere got into the elevator with Hueil. She took a final glance out into the gallery as Mordred walked away. Farther into the room, Arthur stared back at her. The attendant stepped out of the elevator and closed the metal gate to the elevator.

Hueil pressed one of his signet rings into an opening in the control console. The elevator started moving upward, without stopping at any other floors. The two of them rode in silence. When they arrived at the penthouse, moments later, Guinevere let out a small gasp.

The main hallway of Hueil's apartment was nearly two stories high. Above their heads hung a crystal chandelier. The light from the city bounced off its many reflective surfaces, casting tiny rainbows on the blank white walls. No paintings or ornamentation ordained their surfaces. Guinevere found it slightly odd that someone at an art auction would have such bare walls. What was the point except to show them off?

The farthest wall from them at the end of the hallway was full of glass. It looked out over the glistening lights of the city. Other sky towers' windows glowed with an eerie yellow light. Airships buzzed over their tops; their running lights visible in the late evening sky. Few stars were visible beneath the light of the futuristic cityscape.

A bar filled the space on the east side of the hall. Simple but elegant drink instruments sat on its surface. Three lonely barstools leaned against the mahogany countertop. In the middle of the west wall stood a large brick fireplace. It sat empty, cold air blowing down the flume and mixing with the warm air of space. The fireplace's sooty existence was a blunt juxtaposition from the rest of the over-glamorized penthouse. A set of double doors were next to the fireplace, leading—presumably—to the master suite.

In the center of the room sat a large, circular leather couch, its surface without blemish or speck of dirt. A bearskin rug covered the floor, hiding the dark wooden surface.

"Wow," Guinevere whispered, walking into the room. She headed straight for the window to get a better view of the city. As she walked past the couch, she dragged her hand across its edge.

"Genuine tyrannosaurus rex," Hueil told her. "Please make yourself comfortable."

He went to the bar, removed his jacket, and opened a bottle of champagne. Guinevere took a seat on the sofa so that she could keep looking out the window.

"It's an incredible view," she told him as he brought a glass of champagne. He sat the bottle in an ice bucket on the coffee table in front of them. It was a large circular slab of quartz marble seated on top of three large carnivore's teeth. Hueil took a seat next to her as she took a sip of her drink. He pulled a cigar out of his pocket and lit it, taking a long drag so smoke billowed around the two of them. "And what delightful champagne," Guinevere added.

He smiled at her.

"Do you ever get worried about your safety with all of these windows?" Guinevere asked as he draped his arm around her. She flinched slightly as his greedy fingers once again touched her skin. She glanced at him quickly, but he didn't seem to notice. He continued to smoke.

Hueil chuckled. "I've got plenty of security. They just know how to stay hidden."

"Are they here with us now?" she whispered.

He laughed. "Here? No, but they are close. Plus, I have men stationed on other buildings in case someone tries to get in through the windows. Although, I'd like to see someone try. This building can withstand an attack from the largest pteranodon." He motioned his cigar to the pane, its trail of smoke seemingly floating in the night sky.

Guinevere was genuinely impressed. He continued pointing out and bragging about the features and furnishing of the penthouse. She had no need to act, having never been somewhere so nice with so many high-end trappings. She guessed that the bottle of champagne she sampled was more than a month, no, a year, of her apartment's rent. She was way outside her. What had Mordred and Arthur gotten her into? She knew she needed to keep her cool as she took a sip of her drink.

"What do you do to afford such a lavish place?" she asked him.

Hueil paused for a moment, taking a long drag of his cigar, before answering: "Let's just say I transport dinosaurs."

Guinevere finished her glass of champagne. Hueil removed his arm from around her, reaching forward to grab the bottle off the coffee table, and refilled her glass. She took a sip as he returned the bottle to the table.

I've got to stay focused, Guinevere reminded herself. *I need to find the pocket watch*. She started to ignore what Hueil was telling her and attempted to scan his person for it. His outfit contained many pockets, most of which were concealed within his jacket. Guinevere took another sip of her champagne, looking back at Hueil. She smiled politely and feigned interest. She glanced down at his lap and noticed a small gold chain leading out of his pants pocket. *The time piece!*

She set down her champagne flute onto the table and looked at Hueil. He placed his right hand on Guinevere's bare leg, the lit end of the cigar dancing dangerously close to her skin. She wanted to brush it away, but she didn't. If he was distracted, she might be able to steal the pocket watch. He started to slowly move his hand up her thigh, ash dropping off the tip of his cigar onto her exposed skin. His fingers glided then stopped when they reached the hem of her dress. Hueil squeezed her upper arm. His nails and rings dug in and pressed the metalwork of her dress against her skin.

Hueil leaned in, boxing her against the back of the sofa. Pulling her closer, he started to lift the hem of her dress. Guinevere pushed down her disgust and reached for the pocket watch. Hueil delicately reached his hand under the fabric of her dress. Guinevere stole herself, removing the watch, as his hands moved further up her dress and touched her inner thigh. She hid the watch in her palm and brushed his hand aside. She stood, picking up her drink and walking toward the window. Trembling, Guinevere tucked the watch into the front of her dress and downed the rest of the champagne.

"Do you do this a lot?" she asked, turning back around to face him. Hueil was leaned forward, fixing his jet-black hair. He was transfixed by her, smiling that unsettling grimace of his. The cigar balanced between his fingers, ash dropping onto the rug. It seemed like it would never extinguish. "Do you bring girls up to your penthouse, show them this incredible view, buy them expensive art, and get them drunk on pricey champagne?"

"Would you be offended if I said yes?" He rose from his seat and joined her by the window. He stood close to her; she looked up at him. She could smell the tobacco on his breath. He was looking at her, a hunger in his eyes.

She pursed her lips and replied, "No, but everyone wants to feel special."

She took a small step away from him. He walked closer to her, and she stepped back again. Hueil approached her once more, removing the remaining space between them as Guinevere's back collided with the window. Her shoulders rested against the glass, absorbing the cold from its surface. She was trapped.

"What would make you feel that way?" he asked, but it didn't feel like a question; it was a demand. His words were menacing, but his expression was even more so.

She turned her head to look out the window, to gaze out over the city lights, and to look away from Hueil. She raised her arm to take another sip of her empty glass, but he caught her wrist. His grip was so tight and so surprising that she dropped the flute. It fell to the ground and shattered, spraying her legs with tiny particles. He backed her up against the window and leaned down to her ear.

In a low, suave voice, he repeated, "What would make you feel special?"

It wasn't a request. A shiver went down Guinevere's spine. With his free hand, Hueil brushed a loose hair behind her ear, delicately running his hand across her cheek. He reached behind her head, pulling it toward his own, continuing to pin her arm to the window behind her.

Hueil tilted closer; his face was so close to Guinevere's that she could smell the sweet fragrance of the champagne and the musty scent of the cigar still lingering on his lips. He pushed into her until their lips met. Hueil kissed her. Guinevere could taste his breath. It made her want to gag. Hueil pressed harder. Guinevere could feel the hot ashes falling on her arm, but it was his grasp of her wrist that hurt more. She tried to pull away, but she couldn't.

Chapter Seven

Arthur watched as the elevator gates closed in front of Guinevere. He locked eyes with her for a moment before she rose out of view. *This is not the plan.* Part of Arthur wanted to drop the tray of champagne and run after Guinevere, but it was already too late. There was no way to follow her. He felt himself get angry with Mordred who had simply turned and walked away.

"You, boy," Arthur heard someone behind him. He turned around to find a disgruntled couple. Arthur's eyes were immediately drawn to the man's large gold clasp which was ordained with several vibrant jewels. It held together a bright red cape that flowed down his back and draped partially in front of his chest. The woman on his arm had a sour expression. She clasped a cigarette and took a long drag, releasing a cloud of smoke.

"Are you going to get us more drinks?" The man said as he tapped his foot on the ground.

"Yes, sorry, sir," Arthur muttered, turning his gaze down. He took their empty glasses and lowered the champagne tray. They snatched two flutes from the platter and strutted away.

As he turned back to the bar to return the empty glasses, his eyes caught those of an attractive young woman. She motioned at Arthur with her champagne glass. She was dressed in a delicate flowing gown; its creamy ivory color was covered with embroidered flowers that cascaded down the dress in a spiral of red roses and green leaves. Her long golden hair was pulled up and styled. In one hand she held a small clutch purse that coordinated with her attire. Arthur nodded at her and altered course.

Arthur handed her a fresh flute and she smiled sweetly at him. She reached into her purse, pulled out a metal hotel key, and slipped it into Arthur's jacket pocket before he could object.

"I'm staying across the street," she informed him. She took a long sip of her drink. "Room 312."

"Thanks, but I, uh—" He moved to pull the key back out, but she stopped him. She rested her hand on his, holding it tight, until he let go. He continued speaking, "I appreciate it, but I can't."

"Do you know who I am?" She scoffed, clearly offended that Arthur had rejected her offer.

"No, miss." Arthur shook his head.

"If you did, you wouldn't be so quick to say no." She snatched the key back out of his pocket. She dismissed him with the wave of her hand, glaring slightly at him. Arthur rolled his eyes and turned around to return to the bar.

"Did you really just turn down Elaine of Garlot?" Mordred asked, approaching Arthur from behind.

"Is that who she was?" Arthur sounded unimpressed. He set his tray down on the bar and returned the bottle to its ice. Turning to Mordred, he whispered forcefully, "Weren't you going with Guinevere?"

"I was," Mordred replied at a normal volume, "but Hueil wouldn't allow it."

"You should have gone with her," Arthur insisted. "You should still go after her."

"She'll be fine," Mordred said. Arthur read between the lines and noted Mordred's unease. He wasn't one to relinquish control and be comfortable. "Besides, I have an errand to run. You're free to come with."

"Right..." Arthur said. *This can't be good.* Mordred running an "errand" meant things had gone way off script, and he needed a pick me up. That usually meant someone was going to get beaten up. Arthur glanced around the room to make sure that they weren't being watched. Satisfied, he turned back to Mordred who motioned for him to follow.

They slipped through a door behind the bar and entered the kitchen. The space was occupied by a small handful of dishwashers and bus boys. They walked past the workers, past the large stoves, past the empty shelves that littered the walls, and past the vacant countertops whose stainless-steel surfaces glistened in the bright light. They exited the kitchen and entered a large, dimly lit corridor.

"This way," Mordred said as he turned left and hurried down the hall. Arthur followed close behind. They briskly walked for a short while before stopping. Before Arthur could ask where they were headed, Mordred turned into the next room on their right. Arthur didn't follow but peered around the corner.

Two security guards blocked the entrance of a storage room.

Mordred stumbled into one of them. "Sorry," he muttered between feigned drunken laughs. The guard pushed him away. "Can you show me where the bathroom is?" Mordred slapped his hand on the man's chest, leaving it there to balance himself. "My friend over there—I think he's drunk," Mordred whispered to the guard, but his voice came out as a shout.

The guard shoved Mordred off again but was unenthused. "I guess not," Mordred mumbled. He turned and shouted to Arthur, "He doesn't know."

In one swift movement, Mordred charged the guards. Without even a struggle, he knocked them unconscious.

"You could have at least tried to help," Mordred told Arthur as he cracked his neck.

"At least you didn't get us killed. But hey, that performance of yours was quite entertaining."

Mordred shook his head, and they both laughed.

The two of them walked over the guards' bodies and entered the storage room.

Inside, the room was filled with the art that had already been purchased. They were packaged up neatly in wooden boxes, ready and waiting to go home with their buyers. Many flat rectangular ones leaned against each other along the walls. On the back, shelves were littered with smaller boxes. Arthur surveyed the room as he took in the expansive collection. A smile crept across his face as he realized their good fortune: a neglected room filled with numerous items ready to be snatched up.

"We only have a couple minutes before more security loops back around," Mordred barked, "so we need to work quickly."

Arthur nodded, walking up to a small crate in the back of the room. Mordred rushed over to a picture box and pried it open. Out of it, he pulled a large, framed portrait.

"A little creepy for my tastes." He showed the painting to Arthur, mimicking the gaunt face of its subject. Arthur laughed in agreement. Mordred turned back to the portrait. He pulled his knife out, cut the painting out of its frame, rolled it up, and stuffed it inside his jacket. He slid the frame back inside the crate and secured the lid.

Meanwhile, Arthur opened his crate. He tossed the lid aside and peered inside, pulling out the hay that filled its empty space. Once enough was gone, he reached inside and pulled out a large golden goblet. Arthur held it up. The chalice, although large and imposing, was simple in design with no ornamentations or carvings. It was made of hammered gold. Arthur sat it aside and went back to the crate, checking to make sure nothing else was inside.

He was interrupted by a noise coming from the hallway. The pair looked at each other and then at the door. *Security is back early*, Arthur thought. "I'll distract them," he said, hurrying past Mordred. "Meet you back on the ship."

In the hall, he nearly collided with the armed security.

"Sorry," Arthur muttered, trying to avoid making eye contact. Still holding onto the goblet, he moved it behind his back to hide it. The security guards were barely distinguishable from the other guests, as they wore dark suits, but unlike the patrons, the guards had tactical belts strapped around their waists, complete with guns and additional ammunition.

Arthur turned to leave but was stopped. One of the security guards reached out, grasped his shoulder, and spun him back around. The guards quickly looked him over.

"Aren't you one of the bartenders?" he asked after noticing his uniform.

"Yes," Arthur answered.

"What are you doing out here?" the other guard asked. They eyed him with suspicion.

"I, uh—" Arthur quickly tried to think of an explanation. "I was sneaking off to make out with one of the guests." He gave them a half-smile.

"Really?" The first guard replied, peering around Arthur's shoulder and noticing the goblet.

"Ugh. Just my luck." Before they had a chance to pull out their weapons, he pushed his way between the guards and took off running down the hall. Without a moment of hesitation, the guards turned and pursued him.

"Stop! Thief!" They shouted after him.

Arthur continued his sprint, glancing over his shoulder to track the guards' movement. They were still on his tail. Up ahead, the hallway curved around a section of the gallery. He used the reduced visibility to slip into one of the adjoining rooms and press himself against the wall. A few tense seconds passed as the guards' footsteps echoed down the hallway. Arthur held his breath until they were gone and exhaled deeply.

74

Stepping back out into the hallway, he adjusted his uniform and straightened his apron.

"Freeze!" Arthur stopped moving and cautiously turned around. One of the guards had doubled back and brandished his gun. Arthur raised his hands as the guard took several steps towards him. With a concealed motion, Arthur whipped the goblet through the air. It collided with the guard's face and knocked him unconscious.

Arthur ran down the maze-like passages of the service corridors until he found an open room. Sighing, he slumped against the wall.

"Hiding from the party?"

Arthur looked around looking for the source of the voice. A young lady was leaning up against the wall opposite Arthur. She wore a long black dress that flowed down in several layers. The straps sat at the ends of her shoulders plunging down into a deep V-neck, and a burgundy leather corset cinched her waist. She wore a long, delicate gold chain around her neck; at the end of it hung a raw uncut rose quartz crystal. A variety of gold bangles adorned her wrists. Part of her short black hair had been pulled away from her face with two braids that were pinned back. The rest hung down delicately grazing her bare shoulders. She shuffled a deck of cards in the open air between her hands.

"Something like that," Arthur replied as he glanced back out into the hall. The lady laughed sweetly. It was light and airy. "How about you?"

"Avoiding potential suitors," she replied, "especially those who are just after the family money."

"If it's so bad, why even come in the first place?" Arthur asked.

"My father... And you?"

"It's a job. Speaking of which, I should get back to it."

"Don't go yet. Your aura—it's fascinating. Let me at least tell your fortune." She held out the deck of cards and stopped shuffling them. She walked into the middle of the room and crossed her legs on the floor. She flopped her long gown over them as she placed the deck in front of her. Arthur hadn't moved from the wall, so she motioned for Arthur to sit down.

Hesitantly, he obliged.

"Merlin," she said, extending a hand to Arthur. Gently, he lifted her hand and lightly planted a kiss on it in a regal gesture.

"Arthur," he said.

"Well then, Arthur," she smiled, "have you ever had your fortune told before?"

He shook his head, looking uncertainly at the deck of cards on the floor.

"You seem skeptical."

"Not sure I believe fortune tellers. They just seem to be swindlers after a quick paycheck. No offense," he added.

"Did I ask to be paid?"

"No..."

"Alright then." She handed him the deck; her bracelets jangled with every movement of her wrist. "Shuffle the cards."

Arthur followed her instructions and mixed the deck several times before handing it back. Merlin set them down on the floor and flipped over the first card: the three of pentacles, reversed. Three people stood together upside down from Arthur's point of view. Above their heads were a trio of stars. Merlin tapped her fingernail on the card. Her nails were long and painted with a soft, glittering polish.

"There is missing camaraderie and a lack of collaboration. Where you should be working together, self-interest is getting in the way."

"Sounds accurate," Arthur reflected on the cards meaning and leaned back. *There are some growing pains in this new partnership, but it should work itself out. Everyone must have some conflict in their lives. Doesn't mean that she can actually tell the future.* Despite his dismissal, Arthur decided to play along. "We have a new teammate," he volunteered, "and there isn't a high degree of trust."

"Hmmm." Merlin nodded in understanding. She flipped over the second card and sucked in her breath: the ten of swords.

"Is it bad?" Arthur asked.

"It isn't good. Disaster will strike when you least expect. It will be swift and unavoidable. There is something here beyond your control and it will leave you with a feeling that you are a victim of circumstance. Betrayal, back-stabbing, and defeat are all present in this card."

"Switch it out for a better one." Arthur was not pleased with this development. Even if he had little faith in the value of fortune telling, this future sounded unpleasant.

Merlin let out a laugh that floated around the empty room. "Remember, I am just revealing your cards. They depict what the future *can* be. It's ultimately up to you to control your fate."

"Alright, just show me the rest."

Merlin flipped over the third and final card: the ace of swords. In its center, a single sword was depicted. A crown rested at its tip and a snake wrapped around the blade. Although he meant to look away, Arthur's eyes were drawn back to the card. It seemed to be staring back at him. He shook off the feeling.

"Victory, raw strength, and a sharp mind. The potential for immense power and success is evident, but the sword is double-edged—depending on who wields it, the power can be used to shelter and protect or to mercilessly strike down for cold and ruthless self-gain."

"So, my present is filled with team conflict, and my future is full of betrayal," Arthur rose and shook his head. "This is why I haven't had my fortune read." He turned to leave the room, but Merlin reached out and grabbed his arm. Her hold was gentle but commanding.

"We don't read the cards, Arthur. The cards read us."

"Is that my future? Defeat?"

"No. It's a warning. My advice: your team—the one that has the current conflict—should face it head on. And be careful of who ultimately wields the power of the sword."

"What sword?" Arthur asked.

"Excalibur."

"Excalibur?" Arthur scoffed. "That sword is a myth."

Merlin smiled at him. "No more mythical than dragons. They live and breathe and give life to this world."

"Well… Thank you, but I need to be going."

"Back to your heist?"

"I—uh, what—?"

Merlin laughed. "Yeah, you aren't fooling anyone. It's pretty obvious that you don't belong here. Art thief, I presume?"

"And what if I am? What would you do?"

She shrugged. "Nothing really. I wasn't honest with you either. I'm not here because of my father."

"Wait, what?" Arthur felt foolish for believing her so easily.

"I have my own nefarious plans. Actually, I could use an extra set of hands, if you'd like to help."

"I need to hurry back to that dysfunctional team of mine. We are supposed to meet up."

"Alright, I'm sure we'll meet again."

Arthur nodded and hurried out of the room.

***

"Welcome back," Mordred said, "Any sign of Guinevere?"

"No, I had a rough time with the guards. Between that and this fortune teller, I only had time to make it back here."

"Your distraction scored us a good haul."

"I suppose, but that's not why we are here. While we sit around Guinevere is who knows where with Hueil. You were supposed to stay with her."

"I'm sure she is just taking her time. That, or she decided not to come back."

"Taking her time? With Hueil?" Arthur scoffed. "Do you hear yourself?"

"You think she's coming back for you, don't you?" Mordred teased.

"Hell no. That's way off base. I thought this job was important to you. She is the key to getting that timepiece. Or have you given up on seeing Morgan?"

"No." Mordred rose from his seat and gritted his teeth. "I'm going to the lounge for a drink…or ten."

"Fine. But I'll be out looking for Guinevere."

"Suit yourself."

A chirping noise interrupted their bickering. All eyes turned to the dash. The projector disk had unfolded, and an amber light was building.

"Looks like we've got a new bounty opportunity," Mordred said.

An image burst forth from the top of the device reading: "Wanted: Crimes against the Crown." Above it was a face Arthur easily recognized: Guinevere Cornwall.

Chapter Eight

Guinevere wanted to disappear as Hueil pressed his lips against her. She fought to hold back tears and her legs trembled. With each passing moment, her mind detached further from her body, becoming a spectator to the scene. Hueil eventually withdrew, but a growing hunger was evident in his eyes. Somehow, she had managed to swipe the pocket watch, but now she had no exit strategy. She was at the whim of his desire.

"What would make you feel special?" He whispered, sending a cold shiver down Guinevere's spine. *Say something.* Guinevere shouted at her careworn body. *He's giving you an out!* Hueil leaned in to kiss her once more but was stopped by a finger on his lip.

"Dinosaurs," she said, her voice fawning and sweet. Hueil's face listed to the side in curiosity. He released Guinevere's arm and took a long drag of his cigar, blowing a puff of smoke in her direction. She turned away from him and looked out at the lights of the city. Her ghostly figure reflected off the glass and screamed at her to run.

"What makes you say that?" Hueil asked. Guinevere took time to fix her hair, making him wait for a response. She took a deep breath and turned around to face him.

"Don't play dumb with me," Guinevere said. "I know you trade dinosaurs. I mean, look at this couch: T-Rex leather isn't legal on the open market. Honestly, I wouldn't be surprised if you had an underground fighting ring too." She forced herself to look him in the eyes. He was considering her request. "A man like you keeps tabs on his work, so it is never far away. There's no way you would have a place like this," she waved her arms around the room, "away from your animals."

Hueil smiled.

"Clever girl. You've got more than just looks. I'll take you to see them and then we can finish our soirée."

Hueil stepped into the center of the room and shoved the butt of his cigar into an ash tray on the table. The red coals smoldered in the glass container.

"Dinosaurs you want to see, dinosaurs I will show you." He reached out his hand and she reluctantly took it. Naively, Guinevere allowed herself to relax as they walked into the elevator. But as Hueil closed the gate, he wrapped his arm around her waist and whispered in her ear. "I wouldn't mind showing off some more."

***

When the elevator gates opened, four, maybe five, security guards received them. There was little light in the substructure of the tower, and no one else was around. The guards parted to allow Hueil through, but one approached holding out a white fur jacket. Hueil removed it from the hanger and draped the coat over Guinevere's shoulders.

"It's a bit of a stroll," Hueil explained before motioning to the guards to get going. The procession moved down a narrow walkway below the galley. Faint music filtered through the floor and reminded Guinevere of the erstwhile party. Somewhere, up there, she had left Arthur and Mordred behind. Now more than ever, she regretted that fateful decision.

When they reached the end of the hall, two guards opened a set of double doors letting in a crisp gust of Pictland air. Guinevere clasped the front of her jacket as she adjusted to the temperature. The cold stung her eyes, and she blinked several times before the scene came into focus. A concrete patch stretched out from the door to the lakefront. Overhead, the night sky was thick and hazy. All the celestial bodies were drowned out by the electric lights of the city. Several large warehouses lined the water's edge with large piers extending out into the water. The structures' lights reflected in the glassy surface, the water still and quiet in the night.

Guinevere took in a deep breath of the fresh air, happy to smell something other than Hueil's cologne. She eyed the buildings as they approached, realizing they were much taller than anticipated. The vast compound stretched around the lake, and she found herself wondering which one they would enter. Guinevere tried to remain cool and collected, but a part of her was giddy at the prospect of seeing dinosaurs up close. The Avalon Conservatory was one of her favorite spots and the frequent subject of her childhood memories.

The long night was testing her resolve, and she found herself haunted by the encounter with Hueil, replaying it over and over in her mind's eye. He was clearly very powerful and more dangerous than his charming looks let on. She needed to plan her escape.

The procession stopped in front of a nondescript warehouse. Hueil walked up to the door and pressed his ring into a lock. He stepped back, as a mechanical rumbling emanated from the door and it cracked open. One of the guards stepped forward and held it for the pair.

"After you," Hueil said.

Guinevere stepped into the warehouse and out of the brisk, dry air. She wiped her dripping nose on the back of her sleeve and felt the warm, humid air hit her lungs. The smell of animal droppings and the sweet fragrance of cedarwood drifted through the hallway. Several doorways lined the corridor, some with windows, others completely obscured from view. One appeared to contain an array of specimens and samplings that men in lab coats vigorously studied. One technician extracted venom from a pair of dilophosauruses, another tested it on mice.

At the end of the hallway was another set of double doors. The room beyond was expansive and looked to occupy the full width of the warehouse. Embedded into the walls of the structure were iron barred stalls. Each housed a different creature more exotic than the last.

"Amazing," Guinevere whispered, as she walked up to the cage of a lumbering stegosaurus. Fins jutted out of its armored backbone and spikes protruded from its tail

"Watch this." Hueil snapped his fingers at the beast which looked terrified by the comparatively smaller man. It lowered its head to the ground in obedience and pressed it gingerly against the walls of the cage. Hueil reached out and stroked the snout of the dinosaur.

"Now you," he said. For a moment Guinevere was totally enraptured by the creature. She allowed Hueil to place her hand on the dinosaur's snout. It snorted, sending a puff of hot air in her face and Hueil let out a jolly laugh. Then the dinosaur licked her hand, and she allowed herself to smile.

Her hands nuzzled the head of the dinosaur to say goodbye before walking to the next enclosure. It housed a group of small bird-like creatures covered in iridescent feathers of blues and greens. The small animals were huddled together in the back corner of the stall. They moved as a collective, with the smallest protected in the middle of the grouping.

"What are these?" Guinevere asked

"Gallimimus hatchlings."

"They are incredible," she said, mesmerized by the light refracting off their features.

"Come here," Hueil said. "I want to show you one of my favorites." He grabbed her hand and pulled her away from the docile creatures.

Guinevere's smile faded as they passed by a triceratops with a large gash above its eye. It looked like it had fought in battle with a larger carnivore. The next stall had a torvosaurus with blood dripping from its teeth. The half-eaten carcass of a goat dangled in the corner of the cell.

Finally, they stopped. Hueil grabbed Guinevere by the shoulders and started to trace his hands down her arms. He let the fur of the jacket run through his fingers before stopping at her waist. It was yet another reminder that this was not the conservatory, not a happy childhood memory. She furtively glanced around the stable, looking for a way out. The security guards were standing in the shadows and casually ignored their boss's actions.

"Look," Hueil said, pointing into the stall of a juvenile stygimoloch.

"Isn't she a beauty?" He let go to pull out a cigar and held it to his mouth. One of the guards rushed to his side and lit it for him. Hueil took a long drag and rested his hand back on her shoulders. The ashes fell between the fur tuffs of the jacket. She could feel the heat from the smoldering end of the cigar, too close to her face for comfort.

"She's gorgeous," Guinevere said, squirming out of Hueil's grasp and taking a couple steps forward. "Can I touch her?"

Before Hueil had a chance to answer, the stygimoloch ran full speed and rammed its head into the stall door. Guinevere twisted in shock, tripping and falling into Hueil's arms.

He looked down at her feeble body, and she looked up with wide, terrified eyes. He smiled and offered his hands to help her up.

"Careful, wouldn't want mud to get on that nice fur jacket."

Guinevere blushed as Hueil lifted her up and she clasped the back of his hand. *The signet ring.*

"I think someone might have given me too much champagne." She rolled out of his grasp and slipped the ring off of his finger.

"Whoa," he said, grabbing her arm, "let's not get too hasty."

Fear flooded Guinevere. *Did he notice?* She panicked, but Hueil didn't seem to care. He twisted her arm and pressed her up against the cell. He leaned in to kiss her. She tried to move again, but Hueil twisted her wrist behind her back.

A loud explosion rang out from across the stables.

"What's going on?" Hueil shouted at his guards.

"Sir, the dinosaurs! Someone has—" The guard screamed as an arrow plunged through his chest.

"Stop them!" Hueil growled as a volley of arrows rained down upon them. The shots barely missed Hueil and the handful of nearby guards.

"You two, get her out of her." Hueil's eyes threatened them, and they nodded with understanding. They rushed Guinevere out the side door to the stables and away from the commotion. Outside, it had begun pouring rain. The water soaked through her jacket and turned the ground into mud. The trio trudged between two neighboring warehouses. Several more explosions rocked the compound and the guards ducked for cover from the falling debris. Guinevere took the opportunity to bolt, sprinting away from the compound and towards the ongoing auction.

Guinevere could hear the guards shouting behind her, calling out for her to stop. *Why would I listen to you?* She thought, before hearing distant gunfire. Guinevere ran for her life, attempting to weave across the field and dodge a spray of bullets. Her shoes sunk into the muddy ground hindering her flight, and she was certain one of the guards would hit her.

A creature roared in the distance. When Guinevere turned to look, she could see the torvosaurus chasing the guards. They were firing wildly at the creature, not her. The dinosaur caught up to one of the guards and ate him whole, letting out a guttural cry. It paused momentarily to swallow its lunch before charging forwards.

Up ahead, Guinevere could see the back doors to the gallery. She was almost there; she was so close. Without warning, she tripped and fell to the ground. Her shoe stuck in the mud behind her. Looking up from the ground, she could see the remaining guard and the torvosaurus closing in on her. She couldn't waste another moment. Full of mud, Guinevere reached out and grabbed her lost shoe. She slipped it back on her foot, stood up, and charged for the door.

Guinevere pushed it open and stumbled into the gallery. All eyes turned to her, and silence fell over the room. She was suddenly self-conscious of the mud smeared across her face; she reached up and wiped it off with the sleeve of her jacket but made it worse. Shrugging her shoulders, Guinevere strolled further into the gallery. There was nothing she could do about the judgmental looks of the crowd.

The patrons quickly forgot about Guinevere as the last guard burst through the double doors. Seconds later the torvosaurus entered the gallery and let out a roar. The patrons ran screaming in conflicting directions as the scene was thrown into chaos. Guinevere used the distraction to slip down the main corridor undetected and out the front doors of the hall.

Chapter Nine

Guinevere bolted into the Hengroen as Arthur and Mordred were having a heated conversation. Arthur leapt into action, facing the helm, and slamming the throttle open. The outboard turbines and their mechanical linkages groaned in protest under the full force of the steam boiler. They held, nevertheless, and shuttled the Hengroen into the sky with uncharacteristic speed.

"What do you think you were doing?" Mordred snapped.

"Following through with the heist." She walked up to the helm, purposely stepping between the two men. "One pocked watch, as promised, and Hueil's signet ring," she said, slamming them onto the dash.

"You should never have gone alone with Hueil."

"You think I don't know that?" She held out her wrists where bruises were forming. "Where were you anyway? Drinking booze while I did all the real work?" Guinevere was fuming and her body trembled. She matched Mordred's fervor.

"You could have jeopardized everything."

"Really? *I* could have jeopardized everything? There was no heist without me. *You* needed me." At this point Guinevere broke down and the tears rolled down her cheek. "You were, and I quote, 'pretty much rocks'."

Guinevere spun around to face Arthur. "And where were you? Mordred, I get, but I expected better from you."

"I—" Arthur stammered. But before he could defend himself, before Guinevere could lay into him further, Mordred shoved Guinevere backwards into the wall and got into her space.

"Do not," Mordred said, "talk to Arthur like that again."

"Seriously?" she snapped, shoving him, not caring how he would respond. "You are going to rail on me for how I react?"

Mordred stepped forward to charge her again. She stared at him, eyes squinted and burning with fury.

"Mordred. That's enough," Arthur said, restraining his partner. Mordred threw off Arthur's grasp and fumed.

"I'm thinking about leaving you at the next outpost," he said coolly. "Then you can see how long you last with bandits and bounty hunters."

"What?" Guinevere said, looking at the man aghast.

Mordred reached up over the dash and slammed his fist on the top of the projector disk. An amber wanted poster flickered above the console.

"Dead or alive," Mordred whispered in Guinevere's ear as he placed a hand threateningly on her back.

Guinevere stared at the projected image. Her photo was plastered in the center, her smile a contrast from the rest of the poster. As if this shitty day couldn't get any worse.

Guinevere's thoughts were a blur. *What am I going to do now? The map must be real. Will I be thrown off the ship or will Mordred come around?*

"When was this released?"

"Just a few minutes ago," Mordred barked. "You should have told us you were a wanted criminal."

"As if you aren't!"

"We don't have bounties on our heads. We hunt those people and turn them in. We hunt people like you."

Guinevere paused for a moment before responding and glanced over at Arthur. He looked visibly distraught.

"I didn't know there was a bounty." Her voice had softened. "Honest. I would have mentioned it if I did."

"Why should we believe you?" She could feel his hot breath on her face saturated with the smell of alcohol.

"Mordred." Arthur placed a hand on his arm. "If she knew about the bounty, why would she come back? She could have taken the pocket watch for herself, but she didn't. Guinevere brought back what you could not acquire on your own. What more will it take for you to trust her?"

"So, what will it be?" Guinevere said, holding her wrists together for them to see. "Are you going to turn me in or not?"

Mordred looked at Guinevere, then back at Arthur who reached out and punched the man in the shoulder.

"We'll see," Mordred said reluctantly. His voice had leveled out. It could not be described as calm but was no longer fuming. "First we have a pocket watch to take care of. Maybe you can stay out of trouble there."

"Where are we heading?" she asked, happy to change to subject.

"To Ninniane to visit Morgan Le Fay at her outpost," Arthur told her. Guinevere had only heard rumors about Ninniane. It was a lawless place in the middle of a desert. If the heat didn't kill you, a carnivorous dinosaur would. And if you were lucky enough to survive, any number of bandits would finish you off.

"You will be coming with us when we talk to Morgan," Mordred told her. "I want to keep my eyes on you. And I suppose that if all else fails, we can get ourselves a million credits from one of the Rangers that stop by sometimes to collect from bounty hunters." He started walking off the bridge of the ship. "Arthur, take her back to her room. We should be arriving in a few hours," he said as he walked away.

"A million credits?" she asked Arthur once the two of them were alone. "But the poster simply said 'reward.'"

"Crimes against the Crown offer a minimum of a million credits. The reward only goes up from there, depending on the state of the body upon delivery," he explained.

"How many rewards like that are available right now?"

"Just you," he answered. He spun a dial on the side of the projector disk and several dozen wanted posters phased in and out. She stared at them.

"Some of these people are wanted for assassination or multiple murders or extortion." She listed the crimes as the posters blipped by, holding fast to the dash to maintain her balance. "Or treason. None of those are worth a million credits?"

"Crimes against the crown are the highest offense. It goes without saying in our world," Arthur told her. She looked at him fearfully. *Should I tell him?* Guinevere wondered. *Is this a man I can trust?* Arthur smiled at her and place his hand on her shoulder.

"What?" Guinevere asked.

"I'm not going to let Mordred ditch you at the next outpost. And believe it or not, Mordred doesn't get that mad unless he cares. So somehow, you've gotten into the big man's heart," Arthur gently repositioned her coat before lowering his arm, pulling the edge up to cover her shoulder. Guinevere flinched at the gesture.

"Sorry, I—uh—" Arthur looked away.

"No," Guinevere interrupted him. "It's alright." She reached out and rested her hand on his. He looked up at her and she gave him a slight smile.

Arthur awkwardly dropped his arms to his side. A few seconds passed until one of them spoke.

"So, what did you do?" Arthur said.

"What do you mean?"

"What crimes against the crown did you commit?" He turned back to face her.

"I may have stolen an important document." She looked sheepishly at the wall. "It's in my bag in the compartment where you found me."

"What kind of document would warrant such an extreme reward? Are you a spy of some kind?"

Guinevere shook her head. The proposition of her being an actual sanctioned spy made her laugh slightly. Her heart pounded and excitement built up as she thought about her quest.

"It's a map to Excalibur, but it's written in code. A few of my friends and I accidently stumbled upon it at work."

"Excalibur? But that's a myth," Arthur said.

"Maybe. Maybe not. After seeing the wanted poster, it sure doesn't seem like a myth."

"Why didn't you mention this before?"

"Would you have believed me when I first arrived? I didn't say anything about the map because if it is true, I could not let it get into the hands of smugglers—no offense," she quickly added. "The sword holds too much power. It will overturn the current royal family and appoint the next heir to the throne."

"Why are you telling me all this?"

"I'm not quite sure. I guess at the end of the day, you have treated me fairly."

"Why should we trust you anymore?" Mordred interjected. Arthur and Guinevere turned to see him standing in the doorway, arms crossed, and staring at the duo.

"How long have you been there?" Arthur said.

"Since she mentioned Excalibur," Mordred turned to look at Guinevere. "Is it true?" he asked her. His tone was no longer spiteful, but serious. He was uncharacteristically calm and collected.

Guinevere looked directly at him.

"Yes, it's true," Guinevere insisted. "I wouldn't make it up."

"It seems pretty convenient that you are telling us all this now, considering there is a bounty on your head."

"I know. I know. But I'm not making this up. The library was ordered to turn the map over to Agravain, General Gorlois's aid.

King Uther is nothing more than a puppet and Gorlois is running the government behind the scenes. I believe that Gorlois seeks the sword in order to claim the throne for himself and overthrow Uther. I can't let that happen. So, I stole the map for my country. If I don't stand up for Avalon who will?" Guinevere took in a deep breath after her impassioned speech. She felt more confident than before about her goal.

"You have to believe me," Guinevere pleaded with Arthur.

"It's not me you need to convince." Arthur said. "I have my own reasons to take you at your word."

"I believe her," Mordred said and broke through the tension.

"You do?" Arthur and Guinevere said in unison. They glanced at each other and then turned back to Mordred.

"Yes," he said. Mordred stopped leaning against the wall and walked up to the dash. "Sit." He motioned to the chair across from him. Guinevere obeyed; both men remained standing in front of her.

Mordred reached into his pocket and pulled out a parchment. He unfolded it, laying it out on the dash for Guinevere to see. Her eyes widen as she recognized the symbols scrawled across the weathered paper. It was the map.

"Turns out the librarian had more to offer," Mordred spoke to Guinevere directly.

"Where—how—?"

"A strange woman hides on my ship in the smugglers hold. Did you really think that I wouldn't check it?" Mordred smirked.

Guinevere shrugged. *One could hope.*

"By the way, thanks for the extra hundred credits," he added.

For a moment she looked at him confused before he dangled out her coin purse.

"You can have this back," Mordred reached out, tossing her the library badge. She snatched it out of his hand.

Guinevere looked down at the metal emblem of the Avalon Library Crest. All she could think about was the friends she left behind.

"If the bounty hadn't presented itself, were you ever going to tell us about the map?" Mordred asked, drawing Guinevere's attention back to him.

"That depends. Right now, I don't trust you and you don't treat me like a member of the crew. Were you actually going to let me in?" she retorted.

"How were you planning to search for the map if you were masquerading as part of this crew? It's not like there's much privacy around here"

Guinevere shrugged. "I was still figuring that out. Probably just ask—or lie. If that failed, kissing Arthur probably would have worked."

Arthur widened his eyes, unaware both Mordred and Guinevere could see him in their peripherals.

Mordred scoffed.

"Oh, did you want me to kiss you instead?" she asked. Arthur stifled a laugh.

"I'm serious," Mordred snapped. He slammed his fist down on the dash. The sound of metal colliding with wood startled Guinevere. She jumped to her feet.

"Sorry," she muttered with a quiver in her voice.

"Do you want to work together or not?" Mordred asked.

"You—you want to work together?"

Mordred simply nodded.

"Yes!" Guinevere's eyes sparkled with excitement.

"As long as everything goes smoothly at our next stop, we will make sure the Rangers don't find you while you figure out where to find Excalibur."

She nodded.

"And after that," Mordred went on, "you will continue to help us, perhaps as a permanent member of the team, for your ongoing protection. You were quite successful in dealing with Hueil after all."

Guinevere nodded again. "Why are you doing this. What's in it for you?"

"I figure that if you find the sword, and take the throne of Avalon, I can expect a handsome reward for my services."

"And what's to stop you from taking the throne yourself."

"It's not my style. Politics is too much work. What do you think?" Mordred turned to Arthur.

"Let's go find a sword."

* * *

Guinevere figured several hours must have passed when she was awoken by the airship landing. It took her a minute to put together where she was. The room was still as small and as bland as she remembered it. Mordred may have called it the "guest" room but, in reality, it was nothing more than a cell. She didn't want to be unthankful, but she could hardly call it hospitality. She looked around the room before getting up out of bed, her eyes dancing along the empty walls.

She sat up in the bed and rubbed the sleep out of her eyes. Realizing that Arthur's jacket was covering her instead of a blanket, she pulled it off. *I must have been really tired,* she thought, *to have not noticed him coming into this room last night.* Guinevere rummaged through the pockets, not sure of what she would find. To her disappointment, they were empty. She gently tossed the coat aside.

Guinevere swung her feet over the side of the bed, nearly kicking over a glass of water. She picked it up and downed it in one swallow. Even after drinking the fluid, she still felt parched. Guinevere stood up and saw that Arthur had also left her a change of clothes. She took the fur coat off, dropping it on the floor, wanting to forget the night before. She stripped out of her gallery clothes and changed into the outfit that had been left for her. She put on a long white cotton dress that ruffled slightly at the bottom. Her arms, including her bruised wrist, were covered by its long flowing sleeves. She slowly worked to lace up a brown leather corset.

A faint knock came from the other side of her door. This time, when Arthur had left, he had made sure to leave it cracked just in case Guinevere wanted to leave her room. She appreciated being treated like another team member and not one of their bounties. After last night, she hadn't been sure if things would continue that way.

"Come in," she called out.

It swung open and Arthur walked in.

"You back for your jacket?" Guinevere asked. She was sitting on the bed to put her boots on but twisted around to grab his coat.

"How are you feeling?" he asked as he slipped it on. Arthur had two guns strapped to his hips and a belt loaded with bullets. He adjusted his coat and weapons, so they hung comfortably on his body.

She ignored Arthur's question. "Do I get a weapon?" she asked, likely knowing the answer.

"Follow orders and you won't need one," Mordred said, stepping into the room. "Here." He handed Guinevere a brown leather cowl bandana and a coordinating full-brimmed hat. "You should probably hide your face."

"Thanks," she muttered and put them on. She felt exposed compared to what Mordred and Arthur were wearing. Both men had various arms strapped to their bodies. Their arms were protected by leather jackets, whereas hers were covered by a single layer of cotton fabric.

"When we leave this ship, don't talk to anyone and don't look at anybody. Don't even think of looking at anything," Mordred repeated himself with intensity. She nodded in agreement.

They filed out of the room. When they had walked far enough that they could see outside, Guinevere glanced out the window. Her view was clouded by the dust that was kicked up by the ship.

"Welcome to Ninniane," Mordred said.

Chapter Ten

Guinevere followed Mordred across the desert and Arthur walked behind her. She sensed that his hand was resting on his holster. She wasn't sure if that was about her or the animals in their surroundings. As they walked, she saw silhouettes of apatosaurus in the distance. Pterodactyls swooped overhead, only landing to feed. Their shrieking calls made it difficult for her to resist the impulse to cover her ears. Other travelers, bandits, smugglers walked or drove by them, kicking up a wake of dust and sand in their passing. Guinevere avoided making eye contact with any of them. She kept the hat pulled down and the bandana cowl pulled up, both to hide her face and to protect herself from the air.

In the distance, Guinevere could see the silhouettes of buildings, their forms hazy in the dusty air. The town was small; it was no Avalon. It consisted of only the necessities, being nothing more than a stopping point for travelers. Only a few buildings had been constructed. Ninniane was a town with few permanent inhabitants. Most of the passersby were travelers and outlaws. Some stopped by to refresh themselves—others, to pick up or drop off cargo. That was what the three of them were doing after all.

The town had its own code outside the control of Avalon. Rangers held no station here and were not allowed to patrol within

Ninniane's borders. Over time, the outlaws and travelers had developed a culture of their own, a blend of survival and chivalry. Being on the edge of civilization had driven people toward self-dependence and individualism, where your word was more valuable than any bounty you could collect. Extrajudicial justice, such as vigilantism and gunfighting, was not uncommon. Many duels had been employed to solve disagreements.

Guinevere looked to her left, to the north. Through the sand and dust, she could see smoke billowing. Living in Avalon, she was used to seeing the occasional wildfire. Smoke from northeast of the city would be blown down by the wind, blanketing the sky. It looked like fog but dirtier. This fire, however, seemed much closer than anything she had experienced in Avalon. She looked at Mordred and Arthur, and then around toward other travelers who were walking nearby them. No one seemed alarmed. No one seemed worried that the fire might travel toward them. What was there to burn, after all, except sand?

The sun beat down on Guinevere's skin. She could feel the rays penetrating through her dress sleeves. The warmth felt nice compared to the chilly weather she had just experienced in Pictland, but the warmth had grown to hot quickly and was no longer refreshing or comfortable. She looked up toward the sky, the sun hitting her right in the face. She squinted her eyes and tilted her head back down, her cheek feeling hot. A pterodactyl screeched overhead, swooping down like vultures in front of their path. Guinevere jumped, startled by the size of the dinosaur. She froze for a moment before she felt Arthur's hand on her back. She started walking again, the dinosaur taking off into flight shortly thereafter.

Guinevere looked toward where they were headed. They were close now. The buildings were becoming clearer, their signs now visible through the dust. Just south of a hotel, Guinevere saw Morgan Le Fay's Outpost. The wooden sign hung slightly ajar in front of the door. They were almost there. It felt like they had been walking all day, but it had been just over an hour. Resting in front of the outpost were several motorcycles and a hadrosaur tied to the front post. The building had seen better days. The pillars that held up the front porch were starting to sag. The red paint that once covered the wooden parts of the structure had chipped and faded. The rest of the building was made up of cinder blocks, which had retained their color. On the south side of the building, a mural had been drawn, proclaiming the shop as Morgan Le Fay's in case the sign on the front wasn't clear enough.

Guinevere, Mordred, and Arthur sat down at the bar. The west end of the building emitted the smell of alcohol. The mixtures of different spirits filled the air: the yeast-filled smell of beer; the sweet, fruity scent of wine; the piercing smell of hard liquor; and the creamy, sugary smell of malt liquors. Their odors mixed in with the dusty air brought in by the patrons, making for an odd combination. The wooden surface of the bar nearly ran the entire length of the room, leaving a space on the southside for the spiral staircase leading up to Morgan's suite. In the main area of the outpost, several tables of differing heights filled the space between the bar and the entrance, which was situated on the northeast corner of the building.

The smell of sweat, dirt, and smoke filled the area, ashes and the corpses of used cigarettes littering the ground. The floor, and nearly all surfaces, were sticky with once-spilled, not fully cleaned up alcoholic drinks. The buzz of flies created a white noise beneath the sounds of chatting and music. South of the door was an upright piano where a man was sitting, downing beers and pounding out music. Its tingly off-key sound filled the room, slightly drowned out by the dull hum of conversations. The light in the saloon was dim. The room was only faintly illuminated by overhead lights, which many of them were either missing or contained burnt-out lightbulbs.

There was an air of exhaustion and anticipation in the room. As they had walked past several people on their way from the door to the bar, Guinevere had noticed that everyone had been armed. There wasn't a single person in the room who wasn't enjoying a drink and carrying a weapon or two. Many people were simply stopping on their own journeys. Others were there feeding habits or addictions. She felt their eyes follow her as they walked up to the bar. She pulled her hat down further, fearing that she would be noticed. Barmaids bustled around the saloon, clearing tables, refilling drinks, and making sure everyone was being taken care of.

Guinevere sat between Arthur and Mordred. The building was poorly lit, and she could barely hear her thoughts over the din. Mordred was already on his second glass of whiskey, even though they had just sat down. Arthur was nursing his drink and Guinevere was staring at the drink in front of her, feeling slightly hungover from the previous night's quantity of champagne. She turned to look around the outpost. She got a quick glance at the pianist before

Mordred grabbed her head—forcing her to face the bar again with one hand—while he drank his liquor with the other.

"Stay focused," he told her. They were waiting for Morgan Le Fay to be ready for them. She was meeting clients in the office space above the bar. 'Walk-ins only,' a sign read. "Drink," he commanded, sliding the beverage closer to her.

Guinevere pulled the cowl down, shooed away a stray fly, and threw back the drink until the glass was empty. She slammed the container down on the bar top and glared at Mordred.

The barmaid came over and asked her, "Would you like another, honey?" She was wearing a ruffled black top that plunged her chest and matching short skirt, which was mostly covered by an apron. She had a towel in her hand, which she used to wipe off the bar top after picking up Guinevere's empty glass.

"Make it a double," Mordred told her.

"Here you are," the barmaid said and filled it for Guinevere.

Guinevere picked up the drink and swirled around the liquid, staring at it. She sat it down again on the counter and leaned back in her chair, trying to relax. She rubbed her hands together in her lap nervously. She did not feel comfortable in the outpost. Something about the atmosphere was off-putting and awkward to her. Everyone seemed to be holding a secret of their own, hiding it from everyone else in the room. Guinevere felt naked by comparison, as if everyone could see through her disguise with ease. They would be able to look beneath her hat, behind her cowl, and see her face, revealing to them what she had done. That was somehow worse than the secrets and mischief of these strangers.

For a while, the three of them were silent. Mordred finished his drinks and instantly ordered more. His glass was continuously refilled. Arthur fidgeted in his seat, one hand resting on his weapon and the other holding his never changing drink. He glanced around the outpost, eyes gazing but not focusing. He ran his hand through his hair after once again picking up and setting his drink on the counter, without taking a sip. Guinevere sat between them, looking mindlessly ahead at her drink, not touching the glass. Her own thoughts ran wild, taking up all her headspace.

She longed for a glass of water or something to eat. Or something to help kickback the hangover she was developing. Her stomach growled with the thought of food. She had been too nervous to eat when she had been with Hueil, even though he had offered her an array of exquisite hor d'oeuveres. Now, although she was anxious, her hunger had become strong enough that it couldn't be denied. She sat forward in her seat, leaning her elbows on the bar top. She turned to look at Mordred, who was leaning over his drink.

"Can I get something to eat?" she asked him.

"Something to eat?" he replied with a hint of anger in his words. "What do you think this is?"

Puzzled, Guinevere went to answer him, but before she could, she was interrupted.

"Morgan is ready to see you now," a man said behind Mordred. He had descended the spiral staircase.

"Thank you," Mordred said impatiently, turning away from Guinevere to look forward. He finished his drink, set the glass down firmly on the bar top, and got up from the stool. Guinevere followed suit and got up from her seat. Arthur did likewise.

The messenger put his hand up to stop Guinevere.

"Just Mordred," he said.

"Okay, sorry," she said, walking backward with her hands up slightly, until she retook her seat.

"Watch her," Mordred told Arthur, nodding toward Guinevere. Mordred headed up the spiral staircase, following the man.

Arthur sat back down next to Guinevere, both staring blankly at their now room temperature drinks. She spun her glass and watched the golden liquid swirl in it, pieces of ice dissipating with every turn. They continued to sit there without talking to each other, or even looking toward the other. Eventually, Arthur ordered himself another drink, but Guinevere had barely touched hers. She pushed it away from her and leaned over the bar, draping her arms out in front of her so that her fingers lightly touched her glass. She laid her head down on the counter, despite it being slightly sticky from drinks of past patrons.

"You okay?" Arthur asked.

"I'm fine," Guinevere muttered, her voice slightly muffled from resting against the bar.

"Alright," Arthur replied. "Stay here and I will be back shortly."

"Where are you going?" Guinevere asked, but Arthur didn't say anything else; he had already gotten up from his seat and headed out of the room.

Guinevere watched as Arthur walked out of the outpost. As she turned around to face the back of the bar, her eyes caught a table of men sitting near the exit. She was drawn specifically to one. He was sitting in the middle of the group, leaning backward in his chair, its front legs casually lifting off the ground. He held a drink in his hand and was engaged in a lively conversation with the rest of his table.

He was dressed in a dirty white shirt and dark jeans, holsters strapped across his chest. His face was rugged, but a smile was plastered across it as he laughed at what had been said. There was an air of familiarity to him. His two guns were visible. The fingers on his right hand were lightly resting on the hilt of one of them. Guinevere squinted to get a better look and accidently caught his eyes.

Agravain, Guinevere realized quickly, turning back around. A shiver of fear went down her spin. How could she forget the Ranger who tried to take the map to Excalibur from her at Avalon Central Library? *What is he doing out here? Does he recognize who I am?*

She heard footsteps approaching. *He's coming this way.* She panicked, but it was too late to do anything about it.

"Can I buy you a drink?" Agravain asked as he sat down on the empty stool next to Guinevere.

She picked up her beverage, gesturing it toward him as if to say *'thanks, I got one. Now leave me alone.'* Instead, she decided to keep it semi-polite. "Thanks for the offer, but I'm still finishing this one."

"Let me buy you the next one then." He motioned for the barmaid. "Another drink for the lady and one for myself," he said.

Another glass was set down in front of Guinevere. "What brings you here?" Agravain asked her as he picked up his drink and took a sip.

"Just passing through," Guinevere replied.

"You been here before?"

She shook her head no, trying to avoid eye contact as she took a sip.

"I swear I've seen you before," he said, placing his arm on the bar to turn to look at her squarely.

"Is that so?" she asked. Her palms were sweaty as she held the glass, her body tensing up.

"Must not have," he said, "because I don't think I would forget a face as stunning as yours."

Guinevere wasn't sure how to respond. *Is Agravain really trying to flirt with me?* She almost let out a laugh. The thought was comical. She picked up first drink, finished it, then reached for the new one. She held it in her hands but didn't move it to her lips. Guinevere turned to face him.

"How about yourself?" she asked him, motioning slightly with her glass. "What brings you here?"

Agravain started talking, but Guinevere didn't hear a thing. All she could think of was how Agravain must recognize her. Her mind wandered, thinking about the worst possible outcomes.

"Hold on," he said as if he had just made a realization. "I know where I recognize you from." He set a projector disk on the counter and pressed the button on it. Guinevere's wanted poster emerged from the medallion with a faint glow. "I swear this looks just like you."

She squinted at it. "Can't say it does," she told him nonchalantly. She looked away from the projection and back to the bar. She pressed the glass to her lips and finished the contents. Before she could do anything else, Agravain grabbed her hat and pulled it off her head. Startled, Guinevere jumped off her seat.

"Looks like we've got ourselves a wanted outlaw." He threw his drink back and slammed down the glass with so much force that it shattered. Guinevere flinched. Terrified, she scanned the bar to see if Arthur had returned. He was nowhere to be seen.

Where did he go? Guinevere thought. *Why isn't he back by now?*

Guinevere looked back at Agravain, who was still standing across from her. She wasn't sure what she could do. She didn't think she would be able to fight her way out of the situation, and she wasn't sure that talking would work. Before she had a chance to try either, Agravain grabbed her arm.

"I'm taking you back to Avalon—to Camelot," Agravain told her. She didn't object, knowing that he was armed. Reluctantly, Guinevere allowed herself to be led toward the exit of the outpost.

As they were halfway across the room, the door crashed open and in rushed Arthur. He was holding a new bow and quiver of arrows. Seeing Agravain trying to leave with Guinevere, he strapped the weapons to his back and headed straight toward the two of them.

"Where do you think you are going?" Arthur shouted, running across the bar toward the duo. He pulled his gun out of its holster. "Let go of her," Arthur commanded, pointing his pistol at Agravain's head.

Instead of listening to Arthur, Agravain pulled Guinevere in front of himself, using her body as a shield. He pressed his forearm into her throat, causing her breathing to be cut short. She struggled helplessly to free herself from his grip. She was so close to him that she could smell his tobacco-scented breath, its fragrance only strengthened by the other odors of sweat and musty leather that made up much of his clothing. She felt her body growing weaker and her vision started to blur. With his free hand, Agravain pointed his gun at Arthur.

The other people at the outpost watched. The piano player had stopped the music. Others were pulling out their weapons. They looked around, trying to figure out who they should be fighting if the exchange took a turn.

"Let her go," Arthur repeated with more force, taking a step closer to them. Agravain did not respond.

I've got to do something before it's too late for either of us. Guinevere thought of the gun pointed at Arthur. With a flurry of adrenaline, Guinevere elbowed Agravain in the stomach. With as much force as she could muster, she dug the elbow into his gut.

He loosened his grip from around her neck just enough that she could slip out from his grasp. He slouched over slightly from the sudden influx of pain. Guinevere dropped to the floor and rolled away. She caught her breath and quickly got back onto her feet.

"Get behind me." Arthur hissed. She obeyed and scurried around him.

111

"Look at you, tough guy." Agravain sneered.

"She's mine to collect the bounty on," Arthur said, sensing what was going on. With his free arm, he reached behind himself to grab Guinevere's wrist and hold her squarely behind his body.

"Deputy Ranger Agravain," the man said as he pulled his identification papers out of his back pocket. Arthur squinted at it to verify that it was genuine. "Hand her over."

"Not until I receive the bounty that was promised."

"You will receive it once she is handed over to the king."

Arthur released his grip on Guinevere's arm.

"Run," he told her in a forceful whisper.

She turned to go but froze when another Ranger appeared behind them. "Arthur?!" The panic was clear in her voice.

He spun around as the Ranger pulled a gun out of his holster. Before they had a chance to shoot, Arthur pulled the trigger.

"We've got to go." He pulled Guinevere's arm and charged through the crowd of patrons.

Before they were able to make it out the door, she was separated from Arthur. She twisted her arm around, throwing the man who had grabbed her to the ground and freeing herself. Another gunshot ran out. The bullet nearly grazed her arm. "Get down!" Arthur shouted.

Guinevere dropped to the floor. Arthur returned fire. Another Ranger approached Guinevere, pulling her up from the ground and Arthur ran to her side just as quickly. He punched the Ranger in the face. Stunned, the Ranger stumbled back, away from the two of them. Arthur put a hand on Guinevere's back and led her out the door before any more Rangers could stop them.

Guinevere looked back. She saw that Morgan Le Fay had walked down the spiral stairs and was standing on the bottom step. Her long blonde hair faded into blue at the ends. She was wearing a simple white ruffled dress with a colorful open robe. A coordinating multicolored wrap held her hair back from her face. Mordred came down behind her. His shirt was partly unbuttoned and untucked. He was belting his pants and holding his coat. He slipped it back on.

"Who let the Rangers into my outpost?" Morgan said.

Arthur pulled Guinevere out of the building before anyone could answer. They rounded the corner and nearly ran into the hadrosaur. Arthur stopped for a moment unstrapping a bow and quiver from his back.

"Here," Arthur said.

Guinevere took the weapon, surprised by the gift. Arthur did not wait for her response and moved quickly to a modified motorcycle with a second seat. The metal body was all black with gold lines outlining its shape. He fidgeted with the vehicles controls and worked to turn over the four-cylinder engine.

"What is this?" Guinevere asked.

"It was going to be a surprise for you later, but I think we need it now." The engine roared to life, and he motioned for her to get on. "You said you were good at archery? Now would be a good time to prove it. Hold tight," Arthur said while revving the engine.

Guinevere gripped tightly around Arthur's waist as they sped away from the outpost and kicked up a cloud of dust. Agravain and several other Rangers had started a chase. Several patrons ran after on foot, firing bullets angrily into the air over their stolen bikes. The noise upset several pterodactyls perched nearby. They screeched and took off into flight, knocking over several of the patrons. Mordred appeared, grabbing the last remaining motorcycle, and speeding off after the Rangers. They closed in on Guinevere and Arthur, whose bike was slowed by the weight of the second rider.

"Use the bow," Arthur shouted over the howling wind and the roar of the engine.

"What?" Guinevere called back.

"The bow!"

Guinevere gripped tightly into the bike with her legs and released Arthur's. She grabbed the bow off her back and examined the weapon. It was the nicest recurve bow she had ever held. Its riser and grip were covered in elegant etchings, inlaid with a gold leaf paint. The carvings ran the length of its hickory limbs, where the tightly wound hemp strings met their knocks. She was hesitant to use it.

Now is the time to prove myself, she thought. *No pressure.* She took a deep breath as she pulled an arrow out of the quiver and nocked it into the bowstring.

"Hold steady," Guinevere said. She shot out the tire of the nearest motorcycle. Its rider lost control as the front shaft of the motorcycle blew sideways and caught in the ground. The

114

momentum of the craft threw him over the handlebars as the motorcycle tumbled end over end.

"Nice shot," Arthur said.

Guinevere took a deep breath and sighted the next vehicle. The rider tried to dodge but turned too sharply. He fell sideways off of the bike, rolling across the terrain in a cloud of dust. The riderless bike veered rightward, colliding with another Ranger, and exploding in a fireball. The shockwaves nearly threw Guinevere from her seat.

As Arthur closed in on the parked Hengroen, Mordred pulled up between two riders. He let go of the handles and pulled out two handguns, his long black trench coat flapping in the breeze. Time slowed as he pulled both triggers, and the riders slumped forward in their seats. Mordred casually threw his weapons aside before accelerating after the final grouping of rangers.

Arthur banked his motorcycle sideways, skidding toward Hengroen's gantry. They jumped off before it had stopped and sprinted for the doorway. A spray of bullets pelted the ground at their heels.

"Get inside!" Arthur said. "I'll hold them back until Mordred gets here."

Arthur knelt low to the ground and unholstered his twin pistols. He released a volley, forcing the motorcycles to swerve and stop firing. When Arthur stopped to reload the pistols, they circled around to make another pass. Mordred rocketed past them and ran up the gantry.

"Go go go!" He shouted, running past Arthur and into Hengroen. Arthur fired off several more shots to cover his retreat before sprinting to the bridge. Mordred and Guinevere were already there, strapped in and ready to take off. Arthur took the captain's chair. He pulled several levers, flipped several switches. The outboard fans spun up, and they rocketed into the sky as a volley of bullets chased after them.

The trio let out a collective sigh.

"Is everyone unharmed?" Mordred asked. Arthur and Guinevere nodded.

"What were you thinking? I told you to keep your head down and not talk to anyone!" Mordred barked at Guinevere. Before she could answer, Arthur spoke up.

"She didn't do anything. It was my fault." He stepped in front of Mordred, who had moved toward Guinevere. She held the bow lazily in her hand. She looked around Arthur to find Mordred fuming.

"Don't defend her." He shoved Arthur out of the way.

"I was the one who engaged, and I was the one who started the fight. I was the one who left the outpost and left her alone," Arthur pleaded with him.

Mordred took a step back.

"Alright," he said. "Go clean yourself up." He dismissed Guinevere with a wave of his hand. "I'll deal with you later." He turned back to Arthur.

Guinevere hurried off the bridge and around the corner. She stopped there instead of heading back to her room as Mordred had instructed. She clutched the bow, Arthur's gift, close to her chest and pressed her ear to the wall to hear.

"Why would you leave her alone?" Mordred said.

"I had things I wanted to do in Ninniane. She should have been fine. Rangers should never have been in the outpost in the first place." Guinevere could hear the anger growing in Arthur's voice as he continued talking, "Without her, you would have had no excuse to visit Morgan."

"You helped her evade the Rangers. They are going to be coming after us now," Mordred shouted back.

"That's nothing new. They have always had a reason to come after us if they wanted. They just haven't."

"Why are you standing up for her?"

"Because you won't treat her like a member of our team," Arthur accused him.

"That's because she isn't!"

"Well, she should be."

"She might jeopardize everything. I should never have listened to you in the first place and handed her over for the bounty while we had a chance."

"She saved me. Don't pretend like you didn't see that."

"After she got us into this mess in the first place. And after you had to defend her at the outpost. I don't trust her."

"I don't care if you don't trust her. I trust her. You needed her to get the pocket watch from Hueil. You knew that neither one of us would be able to get close enough," Arthur said.

There was a long pause.

"We are supposed to be partners," he said with an even voice.

"We are partners, but if she messes up again, I'm going to hold you responsible. And," Mordred added, "I won't hesitate to hand her in and receive the bounty on her head." His anger had simmered down slightly.

Mordred stormed off the bridge. Guinevere didn't have time to react; he turned and faced her. He rushed over to her and got up in her face. She stood, back against the wall, nowhere to go. She clutched her bow tightly.

"I thought I told you to go clean yourself up," he said. She nodded slightly. "How much did you hear?"

"More than enough," she muttered under her breath. Mordred let out an angry huff and stepped away from her.

Arthur, hearing the commotion, left the bridge and came to Mordred's side.

"Where did you get that bow?" Mordred asked Guinevere, snatching it out of her grasp before she could object.

"I got it for her," Arthur explained, stopping Mordred in his tracks.

"Now why would you do that?" He snapped at Arthur who shrugged as a response. "Was buying this bow—" he wagged it in front of Arthur "—the thing you wanted to do that left her alone at the outpost?"

"So, what if it was?"

"How could you be so reckless? I'm tempted to get rid of it just to teach you a lesson."

"You better not. It cost me my share of our bounty from finding Edern Nudd."

118

"Are you serious?" Mordred snapped, incredulously.

"Yes, I am. Now give it back," Arthur retorted, snatching the bow out of Mordred's hands. He turned to Guinevere. "I was going to surprise you with this bow after we got back from Morgan's…to welcome you officially as a part of this team, but someone—" he jabbed Mordred in the ribs "—seems to be having second thoughts."

"She's a liability," Mordred responded, not looking at Guinevere.

Arthur walked forward, ignoring Mordred, and handed Guinevere back her bow. Graciously, she took it.

"You didn't need to do this," she said quietly to him.

"I wanted to," Arthur assured her. He walked back over by Mordred.

The three of them quietly stood there in the hallway, none of them quite sure what to say.

"Look," Guinevere said, "I know you don't want to trust me. I don't blame you. I wouldn't trust me either. But you clearly need my help and you've risked a lot to protect me." Tears were welling up in her eyes from exhaustion. She blinked to hold them back. "I don't have anywhere else to go. Without Arthur's help in Ninniane the Rangers would have turned me over to the king with barely more than a struggle on my part. You know we're on each other's team." Her voice quivered slightly. "I'm scared," she admitted in a barely audible whisper.

Mordred stood there speechless, clearly uncomfortable by the display of emotion, but somewhat softened by the speech. Arthur looked from Guinevere to him and back to Guinevere. A tear escaped from her eye as she squeezed them shut to control her emotions.

"We'll keep you safe," Arthur said. "Won't we, Mordred?"

Mordred simply nodded.

A small smile snuck its way across Guinevere's face. She looked to Mordred. "Can I go shower then we three can talk and figure out how we are going to go after Excalibur? As a team?"

Mordred nodded. "As a team," he said, dismissing her.

Chapter Eleven

Guinevere let the warm water rush down her face. It made her feel invigorated. She ran her fingers through her hair, washing out the shampoo. The water fell all around her, gently bringing warmth back into her every bone and soothing every sore muscle. She looked up, allowing her face to be covered in its warmth. Sighing deeply, she let the heat into her lungs, rejuvenating every part of her body. She listened to the water as it splashed all around her. Exhaling, she decided that it was time to get out of the shower. She shut off the water and wrapped herself in a towel.

Looking at herself in the mirror, she noticed for the first time how worn-down she appeared. Her long brown hair lay limp around her face. She couldn't make sense of how much time had passed since she had left home. It seemed like a year, but she knew it must have only been a few days. Studying her reflection, she knew she wasn't the same woman who had stolen the map from the library in Avalon. She didn't know who she was anymore. Her old life was gone. That didn't matter at the moment. She slipped her shirt on and then towel-dried her hair.

She aimlessly exited the bathroom, continuing to run the cloth over her head. She saw Arthur sitting on the bed and reading a book.

"Oh, hi," she said, forgetting that she had been in his room, since her room lacked amenities.

"Hello," he said, setting his book down and sitting up from his relaxed position. "How was your shower?"

"Refreshing," she answered, walking into the bathroom to hang up her towel. Her damp hair hung down her back, the ends dancing delicately at her waist. She slipped on her original shorts and cinched the lace of the attached corset. "Surprised you didn't ask to join," she said casually from the bathroom.

Arthur didn't respond. Guinevere peered at him from the bathroom. His face was red with embarrassment, his mouth slightly agape.

"Is it that obvious?" he asked, seeing Guinevere looking at him. She stepped out of the bathroom, slipped her feet into her boots, and stood in the middle of the room.

"You've been fair and even handed with me ever since I boarded your ship; you stood up for me to Mordred. You bought me an expensive bow as a gift; and you fought to protect me from the Rangers at the outpost." She listed the items off, ticking them on her fingers, as was her usual habit. "Need I go on?"

"No," Arthur answered. "It's not what it seems."

"Oh?" Guinevere looked at him, a mischievous smile plastered across her face. "It isn't?"

"Okay," he admitted. "Maybe it is. I don't really know."

Guinevere let out a laugh; it was light and airy, and *real*. Arthur's face remained flush as Guinevere watched him. She couldn't help but smile as she looked at him. Although she had just

122

begun to acknowledge it herself, the guy wasn't so bad. Guinevere hadn't felt this way since her days at the Royal Academy. *I can't let these feelings distract me from why I'm here. After we find Excalibur, things will change forever. I can't take his heart and then rip it out like that. It wouldn't be fair to him. I have to get back to my old life.*

"We should probably head to the lounge," Arthur broke into Guinevere's thoughts. "If we keep Mordred waiting for much longer, he'll start wondering what we are up to. Don't need him to get any ideas."

***

Guinevere sat in the lounge alone after quickly meeting with Mordred and Arthur. She had begun working on solving the code. She stared at the map that sat in front of her on the table. The strange symbols and writings still captivated her. It took her a moment to pull her eyes away. It seemed impossible. *Where do I even begin?*

"Thought you might need these." Arthur interrupted her thoughts, finding his way back to the lounge. In one hand he held a notebook and a miscellaneous collection of pens—an assortment of nib sizes, bodies fabricated from an array of materials, and varying levels of wear. Bottles of random colors of ink accompanied them. He had clearly scrounged the entire airship, finding every pen aboard.

Graciously, Guinevere took the notebook and pens from Arthur. In addition to the writing materials, he had brought her some food: fresh fruit and small basket of bread.

"Figured you might be hungry," Arthur said, setting the food in front of her. Guinevere's stomach growled as she looked at the snack. She realized that she had had little more than alcohol and water the past few days. She was extremely grateful for the meal. She reached for the bread closest to her before he could tell her different. She took a large bite. She closed her eyes and swallowed in delight.

"Mmm…" she said. "So good." She shoved bread into her mouth as fast as she could.

"Woah. Woah. Slow down," Arthur said, laughing nervously. "You don't want to choke."

"Sorry," she said, slowing to a normal pace. "It's just so good," she gushed.

"There is plenty more in the storage room. Feel free to help yourself."

She nodded as she continued eating the food he had brought.

"Any success?" Arthur asked her, changing the subject to the code. He moved over to look at the map.

She looked at him, dumbfounded, trying to figure out if he was serious or not. It appeared so. She shoved the food away and pulled the map back in closer.

"Not yet," she responded shortly, opening the notebook to a blank page. She picked a pen from the collection; it had a solid gold nib and a polished walnut body. She opened a bottle of, what she hoped was, black ink.

"Do you want any help?"

"No." She started writing down the symbols that were on the border of the map.

"Do you want some company?" he asked.

Guinevere sat her pen down. "Look, if you want to help, just leave me alone for now." She knew the stern tone of her voice was harsh, but it was the only way to get rid of Arthur. She was grateful for the food and supplies that he had brought her, but he was a distraction. There were multiple ways really, none of which she wanted to face right now. Not with a map that still needed decoding.

"Sorry," he muttered. Arthur left the room.

Sighing, Guinevere picked up her pen to get back to work. Finding out where Excalibur was located was too important. It wasn't just her future at stake. It was the future of the entire kingdom—the entire Avalon Realm. It was all in her hands. She continued writing the symbols down. Guinevere worked for hours on figuring out the map, in silence and alone, the hum of the ship her only companion.

* * *

Arthur returned to the lounge, having not heard from or seen Guinevere for quite a while. When he stepped into the room, she was nowhere to be seen. The map was sitting in the middle of the table, her notebook open beside it. ink bottles and paper were scattered across the table. Arthur almost panicked until he saw her arm draped off the end of the booth. He walked closer to her. She was lying on her right side with her arm extending straight out. Her left arm was resting beneath her chin. Her legs were bent slightly to fit the length of the seat. She was sound asleep.

He switched his vision to the table. The notebook he had provided was covered in—from what he could tell—a bunch of random writings and scribbles. He picked it up to get a closer look, flipping through the pages. Guinevere had covered them in different symbols and words and diagrams. None of it made sense to Arthur.

"Give me that," Guinevere groggily reached up with her left hand to grab the notebook away from Arthur. She clutched it to her chest remaining laying down. She shooed him away with her free hand.

"If you need to sleep, why didn't you go back to your room? You know, so you could use a bed," Arthur said.

Guinevere shrugged, remaining where she was. "I think this booth is more comfortable than that bed, if you can even call it that."

Arthur chuckled. "I won't argue with you about that. If you want, I'll leave you alone, but, uh, since we are stopped for a while and it's nearing nightfall, I figured you might want to take a break."

"Wait, what?" Guinevere sat up. She rubbed the sleep out of her eyes. "Where are we?"

"Back in Avalon. We couldn't just fly aimlessly forever; we would run out of fuel."

"Avalon?!" She was caught off guard, clearly disturbed by his revelation.

Arthur chuckled. "Don't worry. The ship is locked down. Besides, we aren't at the shipyard; we are parked outside near a smugglers port." He looked at Guinevere. His words didn't seem to lessen the panicked look on her face.

"Actually, this might be a good thing." Her eyes appeared eager as she spoke. She set her notes back down on the table. She paged through the book and shuffled through the loose sheets arrayed on the table in search of a specific entry. Finding it, she copied some text onto a small scrap and handed it over to Arthur. "I'm at a standstill with figuring out the map's code. There is a book—I know Avalon Central Library has it—that should be useful. You'll need help, so ask for Blanche. She'll know where to find the book I'm looking for."

Arthur studied the note that Guinevere had handed him. He looked uncertain and confused.

Guinevere nodded. "I would go get it myself, but..." her voice trailed off. She looked down at the rest of her notes and gathered them up into a pile, avoiding eye contact with Arthur.

"I can go find it."

"You will?" Guinevere head lifted up to face him.

Arthur nodded. "You are going to be the safest if you stay aboard this ship. And Mordred is going to be gone until sunrise at the very least," he said. "Why don't you get some actual rest, in a bed, while I'm gone?" He collected the notebook, map, and scribbles off the table before she could object.

"Alright." Guinevere reluctantly stood up. "There isn't anything else I can do anyway."

Arthur led her down the hall. She was clearly still half asleep, as she didn't protest when he guided her to his room. When he stopped at the door, she finally realized it wasn't the "guest room." She was confused, and her expression showed it. He chuckled to himself.

"I thought you might enjoy sleeping on a real bed, not the cot that we pretend is one," he explained.

"What will Mordred think?" Guinevere asked.

"Let him think whatever he wants," Arthur replied nonchalantly.

Guinevere didn't need any more convincing. She looked at the bed; it seemed to be calling to her, and her tiredness was coming back and overtaking her. She scurried over to the bed, sat down, and removed her boots, dropping them off the end haphazardly. Lying down, she snuggled under the blankets and allowed their weight to rest over her. Guinevere's head nestled comfortably in the pillow. *This beats the holding cell any day,* she thought, *and honestly, it's probably better than the one back in my apartment.*

Arthur was left holding the map and notebook. He set them on his desk and left the room without saying another word, leaving Guinevere alone in darkness. She laid there, quickly succumbing to sleep.

Chapter Twelve

Arthur made his way toward the central district. The outskirts were quiet, nearly devoid of all traffic. He was surprised at the lack of people this early in the night. Everyone seemed shut in their homes, but the lights were off. He had caught a few people looking fearfully at him through their windows. Something seemed amiss. Arthur continued walking with caution, looking out for anything out of place. He passed rows and rows of houses and shops as he neared the heart of the city.

A battalion of Rangers approached, and he stepped into the shadows of an alley. Destruction seemed to follow in their wake as they went from home to home, business to business. The Rangers looted whatever they found and dragged the occupants into the street. Some were shot on the spot and others paraded out of view.

This is the city that Guinevere loves? he questioned. *This is nothing like she described.* He recalled the pride beneath her words when she talked about Avalon. This wasn't that city. This was a military state.

When the battalion had passed, he slipped back into the street and cautiously made his way forward. Arthur couldn't remember the last time he had been this deep in the city. The buildings towered over his head. It was quite different from seeing the skyline from afar, yet his numerous trips flying above Avalon had provided him with a detailed mental map.

There were a few more people scattered about here, but all were wearing formal attire. He stood out from the crowd as they walked in and out of buildings or drove in fancy motorcars. The Rangers, too, seemed more refined, acting more restrained than their pillaging counterparts. He spotted several checkpoints on the roads to the castle, but quick thinking allowed him to stay out of view. He was able to make it to Avalon Central Library without being stopped.

Two young ladies were at the front door of the structure in the distance. Arthur hurried forward to meet them. *It must be closing*, he thought. He dodged a small gathering of people that were milling about on the sidewalk and ran up the stairs. Arriving next to them, Arthur paused for a moment catching his breath; he held a hand up toward them, asking them to wait.

"Sorry," he said, still catching his breath.

"Library's closed," one of the ladies informed him. She looked annoyed.

The other one stared, gaping openly at him as she observed his sharp jaw, chin, and cheekbones. "Maybe we should hear him out." She nudged the first lady, never taking her eyes off Arthur, his dark brow furrowed with worry. She took a small step closer to him and extended her hand. "I'm Raynell," she introduced herself. "But you can call me Ray."

"No one calls you that," her coworker pointed out indignantly.

"I know, but he can."

Arthur laughed uncomfortably. "Arthur," he said, taking Raynell's hand. He planted a soft kiss in an affectionate gesture. She smiled at him, transfixed as Arthur turned to face the other lady.

"I really need a book." He shoved his hands in his pockets feeling around for the piece of paper Guinevere had provided. Finding it, he pulled it out. "*The Compendium of Runic Symbols and Inscriptions?*" he said with a hint of uncertainty. "Here." He handed over the list. She took it from him and stared at it.

Arthur tried to read the name tag pinned to her shirt while he waited.

"Blanche!" he said with excitement.

She looked over at him, bewildered.

"Guinevere told me that I would need help finding this book—" he pointed at the title on the paper she was holding "—and to ask for Blanche. She said you'll know where it is."

Blanche's eyes lit up at the mention of Guinevere. Quickly, she glanced around to make sure that they weren't being overhead.

"Come on in," she said, unlocking the library and motioning Arthur inside. She shut the door behind them, its slam echoing throughout the empty building. Once the three of them were alone, Blanche spoke up again.

"How do you know Guinevere?" she asked him suspiciously and crossed her arms in front of her chest.

"She stowed away on my ship—well, *our* ship," Arthur hurried to explain. As he spoke, he looked from one lady to the other and back and forth. "Long story short, we're helping her find Excalibur."

"Shhh," Blanche hushed him at the mention of the sword. She looked around, paranoid.

"Sorry," Arthur muttered.

"*They* could be listening," Blanche explained.

"Who?"

"Gorlois's Rangers," she whispered.

"What happened to Uther?"

"He's gone," Raynell informed him.

"Gorlois is king now," Blanche continued. "His coronation ceremony is tonight." She walked over to the front door and cracked it open, peeking outside between the slit. She carefully and cautiously pushed it closed, making sure it did not slam this time. She took in a deep breath and leaned against the door.

"What's going on?" Arthur asked.

"There are even more Rangers patrolling the streets," she told him, eyes wide with fear. She turned and made sure the door was locked. "Come on." She motioned to Arthur and Raynell to follow. She led them to a back room, away from potential prying eyes.

The three of them headed up the stairs and toward the offices. Walking up to a door, Blanche fumbled with a key to unlock it. She swung it open, stepping into the room, Blanche flicked the lights on. All three of them took seats around a small conference table.

The far wall of the room was cluttered with wooden crates. They were stacked haphazardly, nearly blocking the only window. Lids were askew on several of them, hay strewn about on the surrounding floor. A couple of small desks rested against the other walls. They were covered in documents, books, pens, papers, and an assortment of other written materials. The room, although typically somewhat cluttered, looked like a windstorm had run through it. Nothing seemed to be in the correct place.

Arthur sat across from the two women. Blanche sat the piece of paper he had handed her in front of her on the table.

"We should be able to talk freely here." She sighed.

"Is this Guinevere's office?" Arthur asked.

"It's *our* office."

"What happened here?" He looked at the chaos.

"Agravain—" Raynell started explaining, loathing in her voice.

"Deputy Ranger?" Arthur interrupted. She nodded, slightly surprised.

"How do you know him?" Her eyes narrowed at him.

"We had a bit of a run-in with at an outpost. Not the friendliest Ranger I've dealt with."

"He and some of his *friends* were trying to find the Excalibur map after Guinevere left. As you know, it's not here, but that didn't stop them from tearing this place apart. They didn't have much respect for the other documents." Blanche sighed. She looked across the table at Arthur. He looked at them intently, taking in their every word. "Enough about us," she continued. "You didn't come here to hear our problems. You came here to help Guinevere."

Arthur nodded. "She sent me here to get a book. She would have come herself, but—" he paused "—I'm sure you've seen her wanted poster." They both nodded understanding. "If you could help me find it, then I'll get out of your way. I don't want to cause you any more problems."

"I'll go grab it. It's in the Special Collection and City Archives room," Raynell said, getting up from her seat. "You can stay here. It'll just be a minute." Before either of them could object, she hurried out of the room. Arthur looked at Blanche.

"Special Collection?" he asked her, wondering what kind of book Guinevere had sent him after.

Blanche nodded. "It's where we house Avalon's rare books, manuscripts, artifacts, archival records, and other historical documents. Much of our work here—" she motioned around the room "—does not go into general circulation. It's why we get annoyed when people confuse us with librarians. Guinevere is after a very special piece of information. She must be close to figuring out the location of Excalibur." Her voice rose with the last sentence, her excitement betraying her.

Arthur nodded. He didn't fully understand, but he knew one thing for certain. He was glad that decoding the map was in Guinevere's hands and not his. He wasn't sure what else he could say. He wanted to ask more about Guinevere, but he didn't know where to begin.

"Just ask the question already," Blanche told him.

"What question?" Arthur was puzzled.

She let out a small laugh. "You want to know if Guinevere was involved with anyone here in Avalon, right?"

"Uh, I—" He was caught off guard. Yes, he wanted to know, but at that moment, that thought hadn't crossed his mind.

"No, she wasn't," Blanche informed him. "But good luck. She isn't going to fall for anyone easily, unlike someone else I know." She glanced over her shoulder. The reference to Raynell was implicit.

"Is it really that obvious?" Arthur blushed.

"Don't be embarrassed."

"Are you two going to be safe here?" Arthur deflected, changing the subject. He couldn't shake the destruction that had fallen over the city.

"Don't worry about us."

A loud thud interrupted their conversation. It was followed by an ear-shattering scream.

"Raynell!" Blanche said sharply, holding back a shout. She jumped up and ran out of the room with Arthur close behind. Blanche pushed open the door to a stairwell and they hurried down the steps. Their footsteps marked their progress in a sequence of staccato beats. Reaching the ground floor of the library, they burst into the back hallway. Raynell lay on the floor near the door to the Special Collections room. An old, worn book was just out of her reach, and a small gathering of Rangers was standing over her.

"What's going on?" Blanche asked as she approached the gathering. Raynell took the opportunity to get back on her feet, scooping up the book.

"Would you look at that. More intruders," the lead Ranger spoke up. The other two flanked him on either side. None of them had their weapons out, but they looked terrifying, nonetheless.

"Intruders?" Blanche scoffed in offense. "We work here." She pulled her work badge out of her pocket and handed it over to the Ranger. He took a moment to look it over before handing it back.

"None of you should be in here," he informed them, studying their every move. He relaxed slightly, his tone softening. "Everyone is required to be at the coronation ceremony or viewing it from an approved location."

Blanche nodded. She bowed her head slightly. Arthur watched her, trying to figure out how he should respond. "Just trying to get in a couple extra hours of work, sir," she responded. "We didn't mean to cause any problems."

Arthur looked over to Raynell, who was clutching the book tightly to her chest. She caught his gaze and gave him a hint of a smile.

"And you two." The Ranger looked at Arthur and Raynell. "Do you work here too?"

Raynell nodded. She handed Arthur the book. Grateful, he took it from her and tucked it under his arm. Raynell reached into her pocket to grab her identification. She handed it over to the Ranger so he could inspect it. Once satisfied, he handed it back.

"And you?" The Ranger raised an eyebrow, looking straight at Arthur.

"I, uh," Arthur mumbled, trying to quickly think up an excuse. He could feel his pair of pistols resting comfortably in their holsters. He was itching to pull them out from under his coat and get this interaction over with, but he didn't, knowing that would only cause future problems for Blanche and Raynell. "I left my badge at home," he lied.

"Hmm." The Ranger eyed him suspiciously, but his answer seemed to appease him. "You should know better than to be in the library after hours," he spoke to all three of them. "Especially since a former employee is wanted for crimes against the crown."

"Yes, sorry, sir," Blanche muttered, hanging her head.

"We should be on our way to the ceremony now," Raynell chimed in. She moved to walk around the Ranger. He held his hand up, stopping her.

"Not yet." His words had turned dark. He turned to his fellow Rangers. "Take them all in. Agravain can sort this out after the coronation." The Rangers advanced at them.

"Get out of here," Blanche ordered him, her words so compelling, that Arthur didn't object. Before the Rangers could approach him, he turned and sprinted to the back of the library.

Clutching the book as tightly as he could, Arthur ran out the back door. He knew the Rangers were behind him, but he couldn't worry about them. He kept running. He ran through the alley, avoiding soiled puddles of water and piles of discarded waste. He rounded the corner and peered out at the street.

Horrified, he watched as Rangers pulled Blanche and Raynell out of the front door and down the large stone stairs. They tried to fight back. Blanche successfully landed a kick on one of the Rangers. He released her from his grasp, startled by the force. Blanche lost her balance, hitting the stairs. When she got up, blood began to drip down her face. A large gash cut through her forehead from where she hit the ground. Arthur caught her eyes.

"Run," she mouthed at him. Arthur didn't listen. With his free hand, he pulled one of his pistols out. Aiming it, he fired at the Ranger who had been holding her. Instantly he fell, the bullet landing squarely between his eyes. Arthur fired off three more rounds, killing the other two Rangers.

"Run!" He screamed at the two of them. The pair took off down the empty street away from carnage. Arthur didn't follow them, knowing he needed to make it back to Hengroen. Avalon wasn't safe—not for him, not for Guinevere, and not for any of its citizens. He darted through the empty streets, ducking down alleys and behind buildings. Arthur feverishly worked to avoid any altercations.

Rangers littered the streets of Avalon, forcefully stopping those who opposed Gorlois's coronation. Arthur watched as men, women, and children were dragged from their homes and marched down the streets. He didn't know where they were going but didn't have time to stay and find out. Their screams followed him long after they had passed.

Chapter Thirteen

Guinevere looked around the dark room, taking in her surroundings and reminding herself where she was. She sat up in the bed, leaving the blankets warming her legs. The light in the bathroom was on, illuminating most of the room she was in as well. She caught a glimpse of Arthur in the mirror. He was standing there shirtless with a hand on either end of the sink, staring into his own reflection. Muscles rippled down his tense arms.

He caught her eyes in the mirror. Embarrassed, she quickly looked away. She heard the door to the bathroom shut, leaving her in darkness. She looked back. Only a slight glow from under the door could be seen.

She looked over to the desk, the map and her notes sitting on top of it. The book that she had asked Arthur to retrieve for her also sat on the desk. It was even more beautiful than she remembered. The dark cover was ornamented with golds, reds, and rich greens embossed into its leather. Along the spine, the title was elegantly written. The pages had begun to yellow, the frayed and bent edges showing their age. Two red ribbons hung out lazily, marking the page of a previous reader.

Excited, Guinevere leaped out of the bed. She rushed over to the desk, flicked on the desk lamp, pulled the chair away, and sat down, hurriedly getting to work. She flipped open the cipher book, searching through it by the glow of the lamp. Fervently, she worked on cracking the code, referencing the cipher book frequently.

Guinevere flipped the page. Out of the book, a folded piece of paper fell. It floated down to the floor next to her seat. Guinevere scooted over and picked it up off the ground. It was a soft white piece of paper scented slightly like perfume. She unfolded it, smoothing it out flat on the desk.

Elegant handwriting covered the page. Guinevere's eyes scanned the writing, realizing quickly what the paper was. It was a love note intended for Arthur, from Raynell. She folded it back up and shoved it to the side, feeling a hint of jealousy. She brushed the feeling aside and went back to cracking the map's code.

Inside the bathroom, Arthur stood, staring at himself in the mirror. He was still angry. After he had returned from Avalon, having found out just how broken the city had become and how corrupt Gorlois truly was, he had stopped by his room to drop off the book. Guinevere was still asleep, and he decided not to wake her.

Arthur had looked at the sleeping Guinevere. After a long day, she had passed out snuggled under the blankets, which had barely covered her body. He had walked closer to her and adjusted her pillow so that it would support her head. He had decided not to risk waking her by trying to adjust the blanket.

Arthur had snuck one last glance at Guinevere. She had been peacefully sleeping, unaware of his presence, her chest slowly rising and falling with every breath. He backed out of the room and quietly shut the door behind him, thinking that he would be able to cool off as he waited for Mordred to return with nervous anticipation.

After drinking had failed him, he decided to take a cold shower in hopes that it would help him regain control of his emotions. He hadn't tried to be quiet, not caring if he woke up Guinevere in his drunken stupor. She slept through the sound of the water running, and only woke up later.

Arthur caught her eyes in the mirror. He didn't need her to see him angry.

He exited the bathroom, leaving the light on, allowing it to continue providing a slight glow to the rest of the room. He walked over to the desk and stood next to Guinevere. She did not notice him walking up next to her, as she continued to focus on solving the code. Arthur watched her work for a moment as she stared at the symbols on the paper and flipped through the book, muttering to herself.

"Guinevere," he said softly. He reached out and rested his hand on her shoulder. She flinched at his touch and recoiled slightly—startled—dropping her pen. Quickly, Guinevere turned to face Arthur, brushing her hair behind her ears. Realizing it was only him, she relaxed.

"I didn't mean to startle you," Arthur apologized, removing his hand.

"No, it's alright," she assured him. "I was just focused on the code. I didn't see you come in." It was impossible for her not to look at his shirtless body that stood before her. Guinevere saw several scars on his chest. Old, almost healed scars, and new fresher

141

scars, littered his ripped chest and abdomen. She bit her bottom lip and looked away.

"How's it going?" he asked her.

"Slow," she admitted honestly.

"Guess it was wishful thinking that you had found something already."

"Well…" She drew the word out as she shuffled things around on the desk, until she found the note. "I did find something." She handed him the note. "It was in the book. I think it's for you."

Arthur took the paper from her hand, slightly confused. He unfolded and read it. As his eyes journeyed down the paper, his face grew red. Guinevere watched him as his expression changed from confused to embarrassed.

"I, uh—this—" He stuttered, trying to form his thoughts into words. He looked at Guinevere, his face now fully beat red. "I, uh, didn't know this was in there."

"So, are you going to take her up on her offer?" She turned away from him, back to her notes for a moment, before turning back as he answered her question.

"Uh, no." He shoved the paper into his pocket.

"Good," Guinevere muttered under her breath. A smile crept its way across Arthur's face. It was clear that he had heard her. "I didn't, uh—I didn't mean that." She hurried to explain herself. Now she was the one who was embarrassed. "Just—I don't think you and Raynell are very compatible with each other. A life of traveling, I don't think is for her. Wouldn't want either of you to get hurt trying something that would be doomed from the start."

"You don't want me to get hurt?" Arthur perked up during her last sentence, ignoring the rest of what she had said.

"Of course not."

"Oh?" he asked her, intrigued. "And there's no other reason you're glad I'm turning her down?"

"Nope," Guinevere responded quickly, too quickly.

"Okay," Arthur relented, still holding onto a sliver of hope, "but, uh, if you think of one just let me know."

"Hmm."

She returned to working on decoding the map, ignoring Arthur's presence. He continued to stand there next to her. He watched her work for a short while before feeling like he was intruding. He looked across his desk, realizing that his belongings were still cluttering the surface.

"Let me get my things out of your way," Arthur told her, breaking her focus once more.

Arthur reached across the desk. His hand collided with Guinevere's as she moved for the same item. She turned and looked up at him; she didn't pull her hand away as she smiled slightly. Arthur closed his hand around hers and squeezed tightly. They stared at each other, frozen where they were. Neither of them moved closer or farther away. Neither of them wanted to make the first move.

"Well, what do we have here?" Mordred said, stumbling into Arthur's room. He stood in the doorway; his arms were crossed in front of his body. He looked at Arthur, who was still shirtless and standing over Guinevere at the desk. The two of them quickly turned around, releasing their hands from each other.

"It's about time you returned," Arthur said. "We really need to be heading away from here—someone may have already recognized our ship."

Mordred sauntered over to them, stumbling slightly as he walked. He dismissed Arthur's comment with the wave of his hand. "How was he? You should feel lucky. So many ladies throw themselves at him, but he never takes any of them up on their offers," he told her with a hint of pity beneath the scorn in his voice. He reached around her to pick up her notes. He fell slightly as he grabbed them, catching himself by resting his hand on Guinevere's shoulder. His fingers dug in.

Before Guinevere had a chance to respond or brush him away, Arthur had joined them. He placed his hand on Mordred's arm, gently removing his grip from Guinevere's shoulder. He stood between them.

"That's not what happened," Arthur said sternly.

Mordred chuckled. He clutched onto some of Guinevere's notes, crumpling them slightly in his hands. Guinevere watched in horror as hours of her work were destroyed.

"But you can't deny that you wish it was." Mordred winked at Arthur. She turned to look at him. His face was flush with embarrassment.

"Are you drunk?" Arthur accused him.

"You're drunk," Mordred slurred.

"Okay." Arthur moved him away from Guinevere. "This isn't like you. You never drink enough to return drunk, or at least not *this* type of drunk. What's going on?"

"Are you jealous?" He stabbed his finger into Arthur's chest. Arthur rolled his eyes.

"Come on," Arthur said to Mordred, shoving him out of his room. Guinevere glared at Mordred as he left, annoyed that he had broken her concentration and ruined some of her notes in his drunken state. Once he had fully left, she returned her gaze back to her notes.

***

"Sorry about Mordred," Arthur apologized, returning to his room where Guinevere was still cracking the map's code. She stopped her work and switched her focus to him as he walked through the door. Before she had a chance to respond to his apology, Arthur continued talking. "I put him to bed, so he shouldn't be a bother to you anymore. We are heading away from Avalon, so we should be safe now."

Guinevere gave him a small smile.

"Perhaps you should get some sleep yourself," she said, seeing how worn-down he looked. His waves of brown hair were disheveled looking, more like a bird's nest than a head of hair. His eyes were bloodshot. He rubbed them, trying to rid them of his sleepiness, but instead he made them worse. "Did you get any sleep at all after coming back from the library?"

Arthur shook his head. "I was a little preoccupied," he admitted.

Guinevere started gathering up her things. "You should get some rest." She stacked her notes on top of the compendium. "Let me head back to the lounge to keep working on this, so you can have your room back." She picked up the stack of papers as Arthur crossed into the room. He sat down on his bed and began removing his shoes.

"Or," Arthur said as he pulled his second shoe off, "you could stay here. And maybe join me?" He turned to Guinevere, a wolfish grin plastered across his face, amusement glittering in his bright eyes.

Guinevere stopped for a moment, considering his offer. She met his gaze. *What am I doing?* she thought to herself. *I need to focus on figuring out where Excalibur is.* She knew that she couldn't allow herself to be distracted at this moment, not after finding out what had happened to her beloved city of Avalon.

She gave Arthur a half-smile. "Maybe a different time," she admitted halfheartedly.

"I'll keep that in mind." He returned her smile.

Guinevere slipped out of the room, notes and documents in tow. She headed back to the lounge where she continued cracking the code. She worked alone in the silence of the airship, the world beyond the windows passing in a blur.

It wasn't for several hours until Guinevere decided that she needed a break from staring at letters and symbols. She regathered her notes and headed to the bridge. She sat her papers down in one of the chairs and seated herself in the other, gazing out over the dash.

Mountains and forests lazily flew beneath her. She let out a small gasp as she watched a herd of apatosaurus running near the edge of the trees. Their bodies were massive but their movements undeniably graceful. They turned their heads upward as the ship flew over them. Guinevere waved; for a moment, she thought she saw one nod at her, acknowledging her wave. Mesmerized by the changing landscape, Guinevere stayed gazing over the dash. The sun rose over the horizon, bathing the land in golden hews.

Sighing, Guinevere decided to get back to work. *Maybe I'll just stay here,* she thought and plopped down on the floor. She grabbed her papers off the chair and flopped them out in front of her. Lying on her stomach, Guinevere got back to cracking the code. For a moment, she felt like she was back at Avalon Central Library, working on processing an ancient document, but a bit of turbulence reminded her where she was.

***

Arthur awoke from his nap. Instantly, he hopped out of bed to go find Guinevere and see how far she had gotten. He pulled a clean shirt over his head. Without tucking his shirt in, putting his shoes back on, or grabbing his holsters, Arthur headed out of the room.

He headed straight to the lounge, thinking he would find Guinevere there. Instead, Mordred was reclined in the booth, relaxing. Arthur contemplated bringing up his behavior from the night before but then decided not to. *Better to just pretend it never happened.* Hearing Arthur approach, Mordred sat up. He smiled at him.

"Have you seen Guinevere?" Arthur asked him.

"I assumed she was with you." Mordred raised an eyebrow at him.

Arthur rolled his eyes.

"You don't think she left the ship, do you?" A hint of panic snuck through.

"Arthur, we are in the middle of the sky."

"Right." Arthur ran his hands through his hair. "I'm going to keep looking for her," he said and left the lounge before Mordred could give anymore sly remarks.

Arthur walked by the holding room. The door was wide open. He peered inside. Unsurprisingly, he found the room empty. He headed on to the cargo bay. Guinevere was nowhere to be seen. Arthur let out a long sigh. There was only one more place to check.

Arthur headed up to the bridge. There he saw Guinevere still working on figuring out the map's code. She was so consumed by her work that she did not notice Arthur approaching. Instead of disturbing her, Arthur watched as Guinevere fervently worked on cracking the map's code. Undisturbed by his presence, she looked from paper to book to the map and back again, all while scribbling down notes. He watched as her long brown hair delicately fell in front of her face when she turned to check something in the book. Annoyed, she pulled her hair back, securing it on the top of her head.

Arthur continued to watch her work, captivated by her. Part of him was jealous knowing that he wouldn't have been able to figure out the code himself. Most of that jealousy was overshadowed by another part of him that found it alluring, though. He couldn't help but find himself more drawn to her.

Satisfied, and thoroughly mentally exhausted, Guinevere let out a long sigh and collapsed back on the floor. She lay on her back, surrounded by the clutter of her notes, clasping the original manuscript in one hand and the final page of her findings in the other. She stared up at the ceiling of the bridge, mind drained of all thoughts.

"Interesting place to work."

Guinevere bolted upright, her hair falling slightly with the sudden movement. There Arthur was, standing in the doorway and leaning slightly against it. He looked well-rested, especially compared to the last time she had seen him. His shirt hung over his body lazily, just tight enough to show off his muscular physique. He smiled at her mischievously, eyes sparkling. He looked directly at her, not wavered by the chaos that surrounded her.

"How long have you been standing there?" she asked him, setting down the documents. She began to hurriedly tidy up the papers around her.

"A while," he admitted, stepping into the room carefully and avoiding the papers strewn across the floor. He sat down across from Guinevere. She stopped gathering up her notes and looked at him. "You were so focused; I didn't want to disturb you."

"You could have gone elsewhere," she pointed out. "I would have come to find you when I finished cracking the code."

"Does this mean that you've figured it out? Do you know where Excalibur is?" he asked, completely ignoring Guinevere's first comment.

"Kind of," she explained, "but I'd rather explain this only once, so we should wait until Mordred is with us."

Arthur nodded, understanding, but he didn't hide his excitement. A large grin spread across his face. "What are we waiting for?"

* * *

Arthur and Guinevere headed to the lounge. Her notes were gathered in her arms haphazardly, nearly falling from her clasp as she walked. Arthur carried the oversized cipher book. Mordred was waiting for them. He was seated in one of the chairs, his back to the arriving pair. On the table was a glass of whiskey.

"Welcome," he said, motioning to the bench across from him. Arthur scooted in with Guinevere behind. Guinevere dropped her notes down on the table and they scattered. She gathered the loose papers into neat stacks, ready to discuss her findings. Mordred passed the bottle of whiskey across to Arthur. He poured himself a generous glass. He offered the liquor to Guinevere who refused.

"I see you were able to solve much of the code while I was otherwise occupied," Mordred said.

Guinevere nodded.

"Why don't you tell me what you were able to find?"

"If you hadn't destroyed some of my notes in your drunken state, I would have figured this out a lot sooner."

"Sorry about that."

Guinevere was taken aback. *Was Mordred actually apologizing?*

"But it's not like Arthur was any help to you either." Mordred continued. "What were you doing while she was working?"

She cracked a smile. There was the typical Mordred response. Arthur was taking a swig from his glass which was already half finished.

"I was drinking your whiskey while she slept," Arthur said.

"That's why my bottle is almost empty."

Arthur shrugged, and they both turned to face Guinevere.

She looked down at her hands and began to speak.

"I was able to figure out the first level of the code."

"The first level?" Arthur asked.

"Yes." She nodded. "It revealed a final cypher that, once cracked, should reveal Excalibur's location. But to reveal the cypher I need dilophosaurus' venomous spit. It appears this technique was common around Constantine's time as the substance was hard to procure. They created an unstable ink that appears for a short time when soaked in the venom." She paused to see if Mordred and Arthur were following. Arthur looked at her contently, but Mordred was characteristically annoyed.

"Where are we supposed to get dilophosaurus spit?" he snapped.

Guinevere took in a deep breath before nervously continuing.

"Well," she said. "I know someone who has a couple dilophosauruses in captivity."

"Who?" Mordred asked, his face lightening up.

"Hueil."

Chapter Fourteen

"What do you mean, Hueil?" Mordred barked. "I thought someone released all the dinosaurs."

"Yes, but when I was there, several technicians extracted the venom into canisters. They were in a lab separate from the dinosaur pens."

"And if it's been moved?"

"Then we could go dinosaur hunting." Guinevere gave them a mischievous smile. Mordred looked at her, about to scold, before realizing that she was joking.

"What can you tell us about the compound?" Arthur asked.

"Hueil's dinosaur complex is made up of at least three different buildings," Guinevere said. She pulled out a blank piece of paper from her pile of notes and drew a rough map of the property.

"The venom canisters are in this one." She tapped the paper with her pen. "About 200 meters from the art gallery."

Guinevere set the pen down next to the map and leaned back in the booth. She ran her hands through her hair unable to sit still. Her nerves were building as she thought about a repeat encounter with Hueil. Once was more than enough for a lifetime, and the prospect of a second was unbearable.

"Do you know where guards will be posted?" Mordred asked after he had taken a long, hard look at the map.

"No," she said. "Did you really expect me to case the joint while dealing with Hueil's advances? I don't want to go back there, but I think this is our only option."

"From what you've described from your last encounter, I don't think we'll have a problem with guards," Arthur said.

"If Hueil shows up, how do you want to play things out?" Mordred asked.

Guinevere paused for a moment before answering. "When I escaped, my guards were being chased by a torvosaurus. One was eaten, and the other barely escaped. I'm fairly sure Hueil either thinks I'm dead or returned home given the chaos."

"A lot has changed since then. You're a wanted criminal now."

"But this time I have two capable bounty hunters with me. You better punch his lights out if he tries to grope me again." She shuddered at the thought of Hueil's unwelcomed touch.

Arthur and Mordred fell silent, and Guinevere turned to look at them. Both men avoided her gaze and looked ashamed, bearing guilt for her trauma.

"I'm going to kill him," Arthur mumbled under his breath. Mordred and Guinevere looked at him. Arthur's eyes were filled with rage and burned with vengeance.

"What?" Arthur returned their stares. "I don't think that's an unreasonable response." He lifted his drink and downed the remaining liquid.

"So long as your vendetta doesn't squander the mission, I have your back," Mordred said. He turned back to Guinevere. "If Hueil does show up, act as if nothing has changed. We might be able to drop his guard and find an opening."

"Easier said than done," Guinevere muttered. She stared up at the ceiling pondering what might go wrong.

* * *

"You ready?" Arthur asked Guinevere.

She nodded, pulling elbow length black leather gloves up her forearms. She led the men out of the Hengroen into the inky darkness of the forest. No celestial light penetrated through the thick hazy sky, just like her last visit to Pictland. The men wore all black and were armed with various weaponry strapped under their trench coats. Arthur even had a small dagger in addition to his twin pistols.

Guinevere tucked her arms inside her capelet to protect them from the crisp, breezy air. It was colder than before and smelled like a mixture of pine trees and decomposing leaves. Apart from the ground crunching beneath their feet, the night was silent. There were no birds calling to each other or aircraft floating above the clouds. The world was uncomfortably still.

She led them out of the woods at the edge of the compound. Arthur and Mordred stopped at the tree line to scope out the buildings. She walked on for several meters before sensing their absence. She turned back to face them.

"Come on," she said, motioning forcefully with her hand. "The lab is this way."

Guinevere continued walking, and the men hurried to catch up.

"What is housed in the large building?" Arthur asked, keeping pace to her right.

"Don't know. Didn't ask."

She kept up a brisk pace, hoping to get their mission over with. The faster they walked, the less chance she had to run into Hueil.

"It might house a brachiosaurus, but I figured it might just store large airships to transport the dinosaurs," she said.

The trio hit the wall of a warehouses and stealthily walked around its perimeter. So far, the area was lightly patrolled, and they had yet to stumble into a guard. When they reached the corner, their target came into focus.

"This is it," Guinevere said to Arthur and Mordred. They shuffled along the side of the building, noting the scorch marks and twisted metal. A giant hole was punched through, large enough for a dinosaur. *This must be how the torvosaurus escaped.*

The trio carefully stepped through the opening and into the oversized stables. There were no dinosaurs here and most of the cell doors were open. Whatever had happened in the aftermath of her escape, Hueil had chosen not to repair this building. *What if the venom canisters have been removed?* She worried. Guinevere led the group to the laboratory section of the building. The double doors were unlocked, and they walked down the corridor. She peered into the lab window. None of the technicians were present, but several jars labeled dilophosaurus' venom were tucked away on a shelf. She let out a sigh of relief.

"What?" Arthur said, checking on Guinevere.

"The venom is here. We just have to get through that door," Guinevere replied.

Mordred walked up to it and pressed Hueil's signet ring into the lock. It clicked, and Mordred pulled open the door.

"After you," he said, motioning with his arm. They walked through the open doorway and into the lab. Mordred let the door swing closed behind them, and it shut with a resounding thud that echoed off the metal walls.

The room was dark, and Guinevere found a recessed light toggle. She pushed the button, and an amber incandescent glow illuminated the space. Various supplies and materials were stacked on shelves that lined the room.

Guinevere walked up to the shelf that she had spotted through the window.

"Here they are," she said and reached up to grab the canister. Something shook the wall and Guinevere nearly dropped the venom onto the floor. She looked around the corner of the room to find the dilophosaurus' stall. She walked up to the edge of the bars and looked into the shadowed space. The two dilophosauruses were still inside, half-starved and abandoned. One lay motionless on the floor, breathing raggedly.

"You'd think with how much money Hueil has, that he could take care of two dinos," Arthur said.

"Get down!" Mordred commanded. Guinevere ducked below a wooden desk and pressed her back to the cabinet. Arthur crouched down beside her, and Mordred hid behind the door. The two men unholstered their weapons and readied them for an encounter.

Outside the room a large metal door slammed shut. *It's just the wind*, Guinevere told herself. *It's just the wind.*

"Guinevere?" A muffled voice said.

She slowly raised her head above the desk and peeked out the window. Hueil was walking past, his shadow silhouetted by the lab's incandescent lights. Two guards followed him, both armed but not brandishing their weapons.

Guinevere dropped to the floor and closed her eyes, taking slow deep breaths. *There is a thick wall between us. I can do this.* She felt a hand touch hers and opened her eyes to see Arthur. He nodded reassuringly and removed his hand. *I'm not alone this time,* she thought, slipping the capelet off her shoulders to reveal the long black dress from the heist. She took one more deep breath before standing up.

"Hueil," she said sweetly, with mock infatuation. "You found me." He was dressed similarly to their first encounter, his expensive suit overshadowed by the radiance of his jeweled fingers. The sight of him made Guinevere want to hurl, and she tried desperately to hide any sign of fear.

"What are you doing here?" Hueil said, his voice muffled by the wall.

"Your dilophosauruses were left behind, and I just couldn't stand the thought of them being alone." She walked over to the cage at the corner of the room and gazed at the muzzled dinosaurs. One creature was hiding in the shadows, the other lay motionless on the floor. She reached between the bars of the door trying to pet the upright dilophosaurus's snout, but it ran from her outstretched arm and cowered in the back of the stall.

"Come here," Guinevere whispered to the creature, fluttering her fingers in the air. It didn't listen. Instead, the dinosaur flared its neck flaps and tilted its head at odd angles. Suddenly, the dilophosaurus charged her hand which she removed with only moments to spare. Its head collided with the metal bars.

Hueil let out a long sinister sounding laugh. She whipped around and looked at him crossly. Two additional guards had appeared bringing their total to four. They remained motionless and arrayed themselves throughout the hallway. Guinevere signaled their number to Arthur and Mordred.

"Careful," Hueil said. "They might not be able to spray their venom, but they are still 400-kilo predators."

Indignantly, Guinevere crossed her arms in front of her.

"Isn't there anything you can do for them? They've been neglected," she said.

"Would you like to feed them?"

"Yes." She smiled.

"Alright, walk over to that shelf and grab the top left container." Hueil said. "Inside you should find several snacks."

Guinevere did as she was instructed and grabbed the canister. It felt empty as she withdrew it from the shelf.

A large metallic click was followed by the squeak of an un-oiled hinge. She froze. Slowly she turned around to find the cage door open. The dilophosaurus stepped across the threshold and looked around. It locked onto her, enraged. The animal moved chaotically rearing its head and banging its snout against the table to free its muzzle. After several attempts, the leather brown bondage dropped to the floor.

Guinevere screamed.

The dinosaur flared its neck flaps and prepared to spit venom. Arthur stood up, shielding Guinevere and covering his face with his trench coat. A stream of venom hit the jacket, which sizzled and smoked from the liquid.

Mordred fired off several rounds, covering their hasty retreat across the room. The men flipped over a lab table for cover and let out volley after volley into the beast.

"I'm out" Arthur called, stopping to reload his pistols. Mordred threw him a pair of magazines which he stuffed into the base of the weapons. Mordred dropped his handgun to the ground and whipped out a dual barrel shotgun. He fired it into the beast, and it screamed in pain.

"Hand me your dagger and cover me," Guinevere shouted, "I know how to take it down."

Arthur tossed her the hilt, and she pulled out the blade. Holding her capelet as a makeshift shield, Guinevere charged the dinosaur. She dove to the ground and slashed at its legs as she passed under the beast. She popped up on a knee behind it and stood up over the creature. She plunged the dagger into its back. It whipped around, smacking Guinevere with its tail and flinging her across the room. She crumpled into a wall as the beast wailed. From her vantage point on the floor, she watched the creature stagger forward.

Mordred walked up to the wounded dinosaur and fired his shotgun point blank into its mouth. Venomous saliva sprayed everywhere from the blast, and Guinevere felt a drop burn her cheek. The animal crumpled to the floor.

Hueil started to clap, slowly at first, before getting faster and louder.

"Bravo. Brava," he said. "I haven't had this much excitement in a long time."

The four guards were pointing their weapons at the group, and they were obliged to disarm. Mordred and Arthur slowly raised their hands.

"Hueil. What is this about?" Guinevere cooed.

"What are you *really* doing here?" Hueil asked. "Last time we met, there was a break in, and all of my prized dinosaurs were stolen. Now I find you with two strangers in my lab, somehow tracking down the last pair."

Guinevere shrugged.

"Oh, hey. I've been meaning to tell you. You're something of a celebrity." He held a projector disk in the palm of his hand and waited for it to unfurl. Guinevere's amber wanted poster appeared, hovering in the air.

"I think I'll collect that bounty. Think of it as your way to repay me for all of my lost capital."

Guinevere noticed Mordred signaling out of the corner of her eyes. He blinked in a rhythmic pattern.

3...

2...

1...

A panel popped open at the base of Mordred's metal palm releasing a round canister. He let it fall directly to the floor, and it released a thick smoke. The trio dropped hastily for cover. The guards let out several volleys from their handguns, totally missing the mark. The glass windows shattered, allowing Mordred to throw a second canister into the hall.

Arthur and Mordred crouched forward through the fog and dropped several guards. Each one thudded onto the concrete floor. Once the last guards were dispatched, Mordred took Hueil by surprise. He wrapped his metal arm around Hueil's throat. He struggled to breathe, and his arms flailed wildly. Hueil's efforts were short lived as Arthur plunged his dagger into Hueil's chest with one clean motion.

Hueil gasped as the life drained from his body. Blood seeped out of his mortal wound, dying his suit crimson. Soon Hueil's body faded away, a mere shell of his monstrous self.

Arthur pulled his dagger from Hueil's chest, and Mordred released his grip. The body fell lifelessly to the floor.

"He's gone," Arthur said, consoling Guinevere who sat trembling on the lab floor. He ran his had gently across her back, and she rested her head on his shoulder.

"We'd better get going," Mordred said. "I'd bet there are more guards coming."

"Don't forget the venom," Guinevere added, pushing herself to her feet.

Arthur walked over and grabbed several new canisters of venom from the shelf and placed them under his arm.

"Come on," Mordred said to Guinevere. She was standing still, somewhat in shock, unable to believe that Hueil was dead. Mordred walked over to her and put a hand on her upper back, guiding her gently out of the room.

Chapter Fifteen

"Are you hurt?" Arthur asked Guinevere. She had sat down in the captain's chair on the bridge. Mordred and Arthur were both standing over her. Arthur had set down the canister the moment the three of them had entered the bridge, none of them considering it a priority at the moment. He had then guided Guinevere to the chair, making sure she was able to sit down safely.

"I'm fine," she told them, feeling embarrassed. "Just some minor scrapes and bruises." She pulled the gloves off her hands and ran her hands through her hair, ridding it of any pieces of debris that had stuck to it.

"Good," Mordred said flatly. He moved away from her. He went and leaned against the wall, still able to watch her and Arthur.

"You sure?" Arthur asked Guinevere. He looked at her, concerned.

She nodded.

"Thank you," she said, looking around Arthur to look at Mordred. "Thank you," she said again, a little softer. "Thank you for saving me."

Arthur took a step away from Guinevere, giving her some space. He turned to look at Mordred, waiting to see how he would react to her words. Mordred's expression did not change.

164

"We are a team, aren't we?" Mordred said with minimal emotion.

Guinevere nodded. She sat forward in the chair, resting her head on her hands and her elbows on her knees. She slipped Arthur's jacket off and laid it on the back on her chair. After she took it off, her bare arms were exposed. They were scratched up, full of mud and dried blood.

"Are you sure you're okay?" Arthur asked again, with even more worry, after seeing a large scratch on her left arm. Guinevere followed his gaze. She hadn't noticed the scratch before. It was caked with dried blood that had been mixed with dirt and small pieces of hay.

"Yes, I'm fine," Guinevere insisted. "Could go for a shower, and maybe a drink, but right now I just need a minute to rest."

Mordred and Arthur nodded. Mordred slipped out of the room and Guinevere sat back in the chair. She turned to look at Arthur. He had sat down in the other chair on the bridge. He had stopped paying attention to Guinevere and had, instead, turned to the dash to get the aircraft into the air. The airship took off into flight, lifting off the ground and traveling nearly vertical. The airship traveled away from Pictland rapidly.

Guinevere sighed. This wasn't how she expected their trip to the stables to happen. Honestly, she wasn't sure how she had expected it to go down, and she knew that it was her fault. Hueil had known who she actually was, but she had been arrogant enough to think that he wouldn't have been able to find out. She had thought that she was smarter than him, but she wasn't. Yet despite all that, they had made it. They had gotten what they were after and had gotten away as a team. And Hueil was gone for good.

Mordred waltzed back into the bridge. In his hands was a large, unopened bottle of whiskey and three glasses. Arthur spun around in his seat to face Mordred.

"Where are we heading?" he asked Arthur, who had turned to look at him.

"Nowhere," Arthur replied. "We are in a holding pattern."

"Good," Mordred replied. He handed Guinevere an empty glass. She took it with both hands. After handing the other glass to Arthur, Mordred returned to Guinevere and poured her a full glass of whiskey. He didn't ask her how much, or if she wanted any, but Guinevere gladly accepted the drink. Mordred filled his and Arthur's glasses as well. Then he lounged against the back wall of the bridge. Guinevere and Arthur remained seated. Guinevere took a long drink from her glass and then looked over to Mordred expectantly, waiting to see what he was thinking.

"What are we doing?" Arthur broke the silence. He looked at Mordred.

"Celebrating our success," Mordred replied, lifting his glass as a toast, before downing it in one, effortless swing.

"It doesn't feel like a success," Guinevere muttered, hiding her words behind her glass. She took another drink.

"We got what we were after," Mordred said. He paused for a moment. "Success."

"I don't care if we call it success or what," Arthur said, interrupting them. He got up from his seat with an already empty glass. "But I am glad to relax for a minute before continuing." He got a refill from Mordred and then returned to his seat. Guinevere couldn't argue with that.

"Fine," she said. She downed her glass of whiskey to keep up with the men. She held the glass up to Mordred to motion for a refill. He poured her another glass.

The three of them drank in silence until Guinevere spoke up.

"So, what's up with the metal arm?" she asked Mordred, leaning forward in the chair, sipping on her second glass of whiskey. She looked up at him as he lazily leaned against the wall still. In one hand he held his glass, and in the other hand—the metal one—he had the nearly empty bottle of whiskey. Mordred reached up and finished his glass. He poured himself another.

"Lost the original," he told her. "Decided to get an upgrade. It's made of titanium, so it is much stronger than human flesh and bones." Mordred paused to take a drink. Guinevere did likewise.

"How'd you lose the original?" Guinevere pried, staring up at Mordred curiously.

"In a battle," Mordred said simply, moving his glass away from his face.

"In a battle?" Guinevere responded with a slight laugh behind her words.

"Yes, a battle," Mordred responded seriously. "It was more than a fight."

"What happened?" Guinevere asked. Instead of responding, Mordred took a long drink of whiskey. "Is that all you're going to say?" Mordred looked at her, cracking half a smile and raising an eyebrow at her. Not satisfied with no answer, Guinevere turned to Arthur. "Do you know what happened?" she asked him.

"Nope," Arthur said. He took a drink then continued talking. "Never asked." Guinevere turned back to face Mordred.

"So, what happened?" she asked again.

"That's for me to know and you to imagine," Mordred told her. He grinned at her. Guinevere sighed and sat back in her chair, knowing that pressing for more information wouldn't work. She finished off her drink and sat it on the floor beside her. Instead of asking Mordred more questions, she turned back to Arthur.

"How about you?" she asked him.

"What about me?" Arthur said, puzzled.

"How did you end up on this ship?"

"It's nothing interesting or special," he said. "I needed a job and Mordred needed a pilot."

"How did you do any bounty hunting or smuggling before you had a pilot?" Guinevere asked, turning to look at Mordred.

"I had a pilot before Arthur," Mordred replied shortly. "Lost her when I lost my arm." Mordred's voice cracked as he spoke the second sentence. She did not press him further. Mordred finished his glass of whiskey, washing down his feelings with the drink. He poured himself another glass and finished that one as well.

Guinevere turned her attention back to Arthur. "How did you learn how to pilot an airship?" She asked him.

Arthur shrugged. "It just came naturally to me. Started going to training camp to be a pilot for the Rangers but dropped out. It wasn't for me. This life, though—this life is for me."

Guinevere nodded. The three of them sat for a while in silence, drinking their whiskey. After a moment, Guinevere spoke again.

"What's the story behind your tattoo?" she asked Arthur, turning to look at him again.

"This?" Arthur asked, pulling up the sleeve on his left arm to show her his black dragon tattoo on the inside of his forearm. Guinevere was able to get a better look at it. It was a silhouette illustration of a heraldic rampant dragon, like those found on a coat of arms. The legs of the dragon were near his wrist and the head of the dragon near his elbow. The dragon itself wasn't colored, but the simple shield shape that surrounded it was inked in black.

"It's the same design as a necklace my mother used to wear. She raised me by herself. My father got her pregnant and then left; I don't know who he is, and honestly, I don't care to know. I got this tattoo when she passed." Arthur paused to look at it himself. "I skipped her funeral to join the Rangers."

Arthur paused, thinking of a way to lighten the mood. "Though, that part of my life is over. This is my life now." He motioned around the bridge. "And maybe you can be my future," he said, speaking with the perfect balance of earnestness and cheeky enthusiasm. He looked over at Guinevere, excited to see her reaction. She was taking a drink as he spoke, abruptly spitting it back into her glass when he finished his sentence.

"What?!" she said, bewildered. She looked over at Mordred. He was smirking.

"You have my blessing," Mordred said, raising his glass to them.

She turned back to Arthur. "You tell me about how your dad abandoned you and how you skipped your mom's funeral to join the Rangers—which you dropped out of—and then, what, you ask me to be 'your future'? How do you expect me to respond?"

"I was meaning professionally. As a part of this team," Arthur said wittily, with a correcting tone, smiling at Guinevere's response. Mordred stifled a laugh but couldn't help smiling.

Guinevere looked from Arthur to Mordred and back again. She rolled her eyes. Arthur let out a laugh.

"It's not funny," Guinevere said, annoyed. She looked down at her glass of whiskey and then downed it, finishing off what she had left.

"Actually, it is," Mordred said, laughing.

"How do I know that you weren't just making up what you said about your parents?" Guinevere asked Arthur. There was a clear annoyance in her voice.

"I don't know," Arthur said slyly. He raised his eyebrows at her.

"Seriously?" She crossed her arms. "What's up with you two?"

"You just started asking us questions. We never said we would answer them," Mordred told her, walking over and refilling her glass.

"Just trying to get to know the other members of this team better." She emphasized the word 'team.' "You know pretty much everything about me. I wanted to know more about you."

"Sorry," Arthur said, stifling his laughter.

Guinevere glared at him. She didn't believe that he was actually sorry.

"Sorry," Arthur said again, raising his free hand in the air in protest. "You just need to loosen up and relax a little bit."

"I am relaxed," she slurred, attempting to sound defiant.

"No. You're drunk."

"Same thing," Guinevere muttered under her breath.

The three of them continued to drink in silence. Guinevere had stopped asking them questions, and they had no questions for her. Instead, the interview ended, and the three of them relaxed, downing drink after drink until the bottle was empty.

"Well, this has been fun," Guinevere said while standing up from her chair. She raised her empty glass up in the air. "But I think I need to shower." She reached forward with her glass to hand it to Mordred; however, she greatly misjudged the distance. She opened her hand and the glass fell to the floor. Instantly, it shattered.

"Oops," she whispered under her breath. "I'll clean it up," she said louder. She looked around the room for something to pick up the glass with, but she saw nothing. Instead, she felt a hand on her back. She turned around. Mordred was standing behind her, his glass and the empty bottle seated by the wall.

"I'll take care of it," he told her. "You should go rest." He guided her toward the exit. "Then you and Arthur can start solving the second code." Guinevere nodded in agreement. She left the bridge and headed down the corridor to Arthur's room to freshen up.

***

Guinevere covered her face with the cowl that she had used when they traveled to Ninniane. Arthur had retrieved both his and her face coverings from the room minutes earlier. Now, the two of them were in the lounge. Mordred had gone off to his own quarters. They both covered their mouths and noses with their cowls to protect themselves from breathing in the dinosaur venom.

Carefully, Guinevere unfolded the Excalibur map and placed it in the bottom of a metal tray. Arthur put on a pair of gloves then carefully opened the canister of venom. As he unscrewed the lid, a soft hiss of air escaped. He poured the yellow-green liquid cautiously into the tray until the map was completely submerged.

"How long is this going to take?" Arthur asked Guinevere as he screwed the lid back on the container.

"I don't know," she told him. "As long as it takes for more information to appear."

"What do we do now?" Arthur asked.

"We wait," she answered him. She took a seat in the lounge so that she could continue to observe the map. Arthur sat down on one of the chairs. He removed his gloves and sat them on the table next to the tray. The two of them had barely sat down for a minute before Guinevere got back up.

"It's changing," she announced.

"Already?!" Arthur stood back up to look over the map.

The two of them watched as it transformed. A new set of symbols was appearing, and the original set was fading away. In the middle of the paper, a drawing appeared. It was Excalibur. They waited, watching, until the symbols had fully appeared. Arthur put his gloves back on and pulled the map out of the venom. He set it down on the table to let it dry. They both stared at the map for a moment, transfixed by it.

"I need my notes and papers," Guinevere said, breaking their trance. She ran from the lounge to get them.

When she returned to the lounge, she quickly got to work on decoding the map. She was certain that this would lead them directly to Excalibur, as indicated by the sword drawing. She, however, was not sure how many other steps would be involved in finding the sword. She wasn't sure how easily they would be able to take Excalibur either.

Arthur sat in the chair next to Guinevere. He watched in silence as Guinevere worked to decode the map. He didn't know how long it would take her, but as she figured more and more out, he got more anxious about their final journey to Excalibur.

Hours passed as Guinevere worked on decoding the map. Eventually, Arthur had gotten up from his seat to go find something to eat and to take a nap. Guinevere continued working, ignoring the hunger that she had started to feel and determined to figure out where they needed to go.

Finally, after nearly giving up several times, Guinevere had an answer. She hurried out of the lounge to tell Arthur and Mordred what she had found. The three of them gathered back in the lounge for her to share her discovery.

"Where are we headed?" Mordred asked her, getting straight to the point. He was grouchy and still a little groggy from being woken from a nap.

"Not sure," she told him. There was no mistaking the excitement in her voice. Seeing the angry and puzzled looks from the two men, she continued. "I'm not sure, because it's a series of coordinates. They will lead us to Excalibur."

She held the piece of paper up, showing it to them. She shook it as she spoke, making it impossible for either of them to read it. Guinevere passed a piece of paper across the table to Arthur. Mordred stood, looking over his shoulder. Arthur looked at the series of numbers that she had written on the page. He grabbed the paper off the table and hurried to the bridge, grabbing an air chart off the shelf near the dash. Mordred and Guinevere stood behind him, anxious to see where they would be headed. None of them could stand still as Arthur paged through the chart finding their destination.

"Looks like we will be heading to Lake Diana," Arthur announced after squinting at the documents.

Guinevere knew very little about Lake Diana. She had heard that it was supposed to be beautiful, nearly untouched by man. It was secluded in the middle of a dense forest in the middle of nowhere, the nearest sign of civilization miles away from its center. It had remained pristine and untouched since the forest surrounding it, Paimpont Forest, was dangerous to travel through. It was filled with every kind of predator. The trees and other vegetation packed together so densely that there was no way to land an airship close to the lake. Very few people were willing to make the potentially dangerous journey through the forest just to view the lake.

"We'll have to land outside of the Paimpont Forest," Arthur said. "Then we can journey on foot to Lake Diana to find Excalibur." He turned around from the dash, now facing Guinevere and Mordred. She nodded in agreement. That matched what she knew of the lake. She was hoping that Arthur might have known more.

"Excalibur better not be a myth after all," Mordred said, turning to face Guinevere.

"It's not," she replied confidently, looking him in the eyes.

Mordred nodded. "I'm sure you wouldn't lie to us," he said, resting his metal hand on her shoulder after walking over to stand behind her.

Guinevere opened her mouth to answer him, but before she could, Mordred continued speaking.

"Arthur," he said, keeping his hand resting on Guinevere's shoulder, "chart a course to Lake Diana. It's time for us to find a mythical sword."

* * *

Guinevere looked out across the dash of the airship. As they traveled closer to the Paimpont Forest, she grew more anxious and nervous about finding Excalibur. At this point, she couldn't let her nerves get the better of her. Excalibur was almost within their grasp.

"When we arrive at Lake Diana, things might get a little messy," Arthur had warned her in all seriousness. She nodded solemnly. "We don't know if we have been followed or who might be guarding the sword."

Guinevere turned her gaze up to look at Arthur. He had not spoken a word since the beginning of their trip to the Paimpont Forest. When he delivered the warning, he seemed rather tense, grasping the yoke with almost white knuckles, even though the airship was on autopilot.

"Are we almost there?" she asked, trying to stay calm herself. A mix of emotions were flooding her; she was excited to find Excalibur. At the same, she was scared and nervous about what was going to happen.

"No," Arthur answered. She breathed a small sigh of relief and relaxed slightly. Arthur remained silent. She wanted to ask him other questions but sensed that Arthur had other things to think about.

"We will arrive in a couple hours," Arthur said, breaking the silence. She noticed that his grip on the yoke had loosened up. She nodded.

They would finally find Excalibur and be able to take it back to Avalon to appoint the true king. She knew nothing would ever be the same, and there was no way out of the mess that she, quite literally, fell into only weeks ago. The future of her safety was questionable, considering that they would be putting themselves in great risk going back to Avalon, especially with Excalibur. Numerous people would be waiting, trying to stop them to destroy

Excalibur or to take the sword for their own gain. Finding it would only be the beginning of further troubles until, hopefully, the rightful person became the bearer of the sword. Then, there would be hope.

Time seemed to crawl by for Guinevere. Every second seemed like a minute and every minute seemed like an hour. Finally, they arrived at the Paimpont Forest. Guinevere gazed out of the airship's front window. Before her loomed an endless forest. A bounty of trees expanded before her and up into the sky, nearly blocking out the sun. Arthur set the airship down near the edge of the forest. The craft knocked over a few seedlings during its descent. Dirt, grass, and pine needles were disturbed, blown up into the air by the ship's drafts and blocking the windows. Once the debris settled back down, mostly on the forest floor, Guinevere looked out the window. The trees looked even taller once they were on the ground. The thick canopy reached up to the sky, birds and flying dinosaurs soaring out of the forest and blocking the sliver of blue sky that she could just barely see.

"Ready to go?" Mordred asked, resting a hand on each of their backs and peering out of the window between the pair. He had joined them on the bridge.

"As ready as I'll ever be," Guinevere said, turning to face him. Arthur nodded in agreement.

Chapter Sixteen

Guinevere, Arthur, and Mordred walked through the forest. The smell of pine was emboldened by the soothing scent of soil after rain. They walked carefully between trees, being sure not to trip over fallen branches or uprooted trunks, and mindful of the numerous creatures that called the forest home. They were the invaders, not the wildlife or vegetation. So, the group kept their heads on a swivel, fixing a watchful eye on their surroundings.

Guinevere blazed the trail with Arthur and Mordred close behind. They all had satchels filled with any supplies they may have needed. Both men had armed themselves prior to leaving the airship, slipping on their holsters and packing them with weapons. The bow and quiver Arthur had purchased were strapped to Guinevere's back. She was also armed with the map to Excalibur, safely tucked away in her satchel. It really wasn't needed, though, as she had memorized where they were going. She had looked at that map so many times that it was burned into her mind.

They continued walking, listening to the sound of the creatures around them. The forest was filled with triceratops, stegosauruses, birds, and other woodland creatures chattering. Some were trying to eat while others tried not to be devoured. The sun's rays creeped in between the trees, providing a dimmed light to their path. The shadows continued to change as they walked forward, the light almost hypnotic. It flashed in and out as the density of the trees changed with every step forward. The sun lowered in the sky as the hours passed, their shadows becoming long and casting sideways as they hiked to the north.

So many thoughts poured through Guinevere's mind. She tried to calm them and focus on the path ahead, but she couldn't. She didn't know what would happen when they found Excalibur. She honestly hadn't thought that they would make it this far. She had only been looking one step ahead. Now they were near the end and she didn't have a plan. This fact wholeheartedly scared her. *Don't think about that*, she told herself. *Focus on getting through the woods. Then focus on finding the sword. Then you will have a chance to make a new plan. There is nothing that can be done now.*

Another thought crossed her mind. *What if we aren't able to find Excalibur? What will happen to me? I can't go back to my old life. Will they let me stay on the crew or turn me in for the bounty? Will they leave me behind in the forest or drop me back off in Avalon for me to fend for myself?* There was no way to know.

It doesn't matter, she reminded herself. *We will find Excalibur and things will only get better from there.*

Arthur's voice broke through her thoughts.

"Do you want to keep going?" he asked, looking at Mordred.

"No," Mordred said, inspecting their surroundings. "It will be dark soon. We should rest tonight and continue our journey in the morning."

***

Guinevere sat by the fire, leaning in close to feel its warmth. They had to keep it small to avoid drawing attention. They didn't know what kinds of creatures could be lurking, and a large fire could draw out the bigger ones—the ones they most definitely did not want to encounter. Guinevere wrapped her arms around herself, leaning forward to warm her face.

"Mind if I join you?" Arthur asked.

"Go ahead," she said, motioning toward an adjacent space.

"Mordred is asleep," he informed her.

"At least one of us is able to," she said, throwing a stick into the meager blaze.

"You've been sitting at the fire all night."

She shrugged. "Someone needs to keep watch. Besides, I'm too anxious to sleep. We are so close!" Her voice raised slightly with the last sentence. Agitated, she picked up another stick off the ground, broke it, and threw the two parts into the fire.

"Why are you doing this anyway?" Arthur asked her earnestly.

"I'm trying to keep the fire going. Isn't that obvious?" She was slightly annoyed.

"No, not the sticks," he said, shaking his head. "I meant: why are you even going after Excalibur?"

"Don't you think it's a little late to be asking that question? We are here after all, in the middle of a forest, hours into our hike. Probably closer to Excalibur than to our ship."

"But why risk everything?" he asked, rubbing his hands over the fire.

"Someone had to. Someone had to stand up for what they believed in—for what was right. If I didn't, someone else hopefully would have. I was just given such a clear chance to try to fix things." She paused for a moment. She turned to look at him.

"Avalon used to be this wonderful place with Camelot as this beacon of hope. It stopped being that. Corruption is everywhere now with Gorlois as king. I mean, even before he took the throne, King Uther had grown so powerless that Gorlois was pretty much ruling anyway. It has likely gotten worse, though, since I left. You know better than I since you were in the streets. I just want Camelot to be a place of hope again. Excalibur is the only way I know how to do that."

As she explained all of this to Arthur, she stared into the fire. She watched the flames change color from yellow to red to blue. She watched the colorful wisps lap over the wood, turning it into coals and ash. She ran her hands through the sand next to her as she stared forward. The two of them sat quietly for a while, listening to the crackling of the flames.

"I know you said something similar to us when we first found you on the ship," Arthur spoke, breaking the silence. "But honestly, I didn't believe you at the time. I thought you were on a self-centered quest for Excalibur that would end with you being the ruler of Avalon."

"Then why did you agree to go on this journey?" she asked.

Arthur shrugged. "Not sure what Mordred's motives were, but I just wanted you to like me either way."

"You don't want to claim Excalibur for yourself?" she asked, skeptical of him.

"Honest," he said, raising his hands up as if to prove his innocence.

"Well, they do say that love makes you do crazy things," she let out a small laugh, throwing another twig on the fire.

"If you were given the chance to claim Excalibur and be the ruler of Avalon, would you?" he asked

"I don't know. I haven't given it much thought." She paused for a moment. "Probably not. I don't think I would be a good ruler. Too many people constantly trying to take advantage of you. I don't even like to talk to people at the library."

"I think you would make a good leader."

She laughed. "Just a minute ago you were saying that you thought I was acting out of selfish intent. Now you think that I would make a good leader?"

"Better than me at least," he said, slightly embarrassed, "but that doesn't take much."

Their conversation paused as they rested around the fire. Arthur fidgeted anxiously, deep in thought, and Guinevere shivered in the cold. She stood up, intending to fetch a blanket, but Arthur hurried to his feet.

"Here," he said, taking his jacket off and holding it out to her. She stepped forward to take it from him, trembling from the cold that had penetrated her body.

He accidentally shifted, lowering the jacket unexpectedly. The moving target caused Guinevere to reach through empty air and she wavered, off-balance, careening toward the fire. His arm went around her, drawing her back up from the flames. His face bent to meet hers as she looked up, startled. Two eyes, bright blue as the daylight sky, glinted in the light of the fire above her. They were only a heartbeat away.

His grip tightened across her shoulders and pulled her into a tender embrace, swinging her away from the danger of the fire. She knew this could never last, but for a moment, she didn't care. His lips reached out to meet hers softly. Her mouth melted into his, the chill of night quickly forgotten. The tip of his tongue brushed her lip. The passion sent a wildfire of flames racing through her body. She clung to him in a universe of longing.

Then she remembered where they were—who they were.

A wave of darkness washed over her; she shuddered and pushed him away, breaking their kiss. *This wasn't a good idea*, she thought. They led two very different lives. They were very different people. How could she explain that to him after this moment? He clearly had fallen for her, and hard too. *Haven't I as well?* she thought to herself, wanting to tell him.

She needed to be realistic. Their relationship would never last.

Embarrassed, she started walking away from Arthur, hiding her face from him. She did not want him to see the tears welling up within her eyes. She wrapped her arms around herself, still feeling the chill of the night.

She heard a twig snap as Arthur walked up behind her. His hands draped the jacket over her shoulder. Still avoiding his gaze, she slipped her arms into the sleeves. She wiped away any potential tears, and then turned to face him.

"We're not meant to be together," she told him, not believing it herself. For the space of a breath, there was silence. Then his voice floated over to her and they locked eyes.

"We could try."

They stood there, both next to one another and far apart, under the stars and steady glow of the moon. The flickering fire cast dancing shadows on their cheek. Both were wrapped up in their own thoughts, their own questions, and their own feelings. The world around them had melted away. The sounds of the forest— the few birds left singing in the night, or the buzz of the insects flying— did not register on their ears. They only felt each other's presence.

"Ok you two love birds." Mordred's voice broke them out of their secluded world. Startled, they both turned to see Mordred emerging from the tent. He yawned as he rubbed the remnants of sleep from his eyes. Before either of them could speak up in protest, he shooed them away with a small wave of his hand. "Go get some sleep. I'll stay up and keep watch."

"You sure?" Arthur asked, looking Mordred in the eye.

Mordred dismissed them. "Yes, now go! Before I change my mind and go back to sleep." He patted Arthur on the back as he walked past him to enter the tent.

Guinevere followed behind. She pulled Arthur's jacket tightly around herself to keep in as much heat as possible. When she was standing next to Mordred, she spoke up.

"Thanks," she muttered.

He gave her a half smile. "No problem kiddo."

Arthur and Guinevere entered the tent. As soon as she lay down beneath the much-needed warmth of the blanket, she realized just how tired she really was. Her eagerness to find Excalibur was equally matched with her desire for rest. She allowed the darkness to swallow her and all her worries, succumbing quickly to the abyss.

* * *

Hours must have passed, but Guinevere wasn't sure. Outside, she heard a noise. Her eyes flew open, suddenly awake. She lay there motionless, making sure she wasn't hearing things. She wasn't mistaken, though, and fear grew inside of her. An animal was sniffing around outside their tent. She could hear the unmistakable sound of a low growl.

Guinevere rolled over. There, on the other side of the tent, Arthur was still fast asleep. He was snuggled under a single blanket, using his satchel as a pillow. Resting on his back, Arthur's right arm lazily hung over his head, his fingers barely touching the edge of the tent. His other arm flopped over his chest. He was so peaceful, Guinevere dared not wake him.

Quietly, Guinevere got up, being careful not to make a sound. She grabbed her bow and swung her quiver over her back. Nocked an arrow to the string, she opened the tent slightly and peered out. She glanced around, but darkness covered everything. The stars struggled to shine through the thick canopy of trees. The moon casted a slight glow, but overpowering shadows fought back. The fire was completely extinguished; there weren't even glowing embers.

There were no animals stirring, no bugs buzzing, and no sign of the creature that had woken her. The silence was eerie and an uneasy feeling overwhelmed Guinevere.

Where is Mordred? she wondered, unable to spot him, and feared the worst might have happened. She shoved the thought out of her head as quickly as it surfaced.

Guinevere took a small step outside of the tent, hoping to spot Mordred and not the creature. She kept an arrow on her bow, holding it down but ready to be released as needed.

Guinevere leaned around the side of the tent, coming face-to-face with the snout of a carnotaurus. She swallowed a scream as it opened its mouth slightly, exposing a toothy smile that dripped with the blood of its previous meal. Slowly, the carnivorous dinosaur blinked, turning its eye directly at her. It breathed heavily, taking in Guinevere's scent. She could feel its hot breath on her face as she gingerly took a step backward. Its head resembled that of a bulldog, and the horns on the top of its head looked like those of a bull. She had to escape before it was too late.

As she stepped back, Guinevere tripped, stumbling over a fallen branch. At the same time, the carnotaurus extended its head all the way toward the sky. It towered over Guinevere and let out a boisterous roar. Its rows of closely packed teeth in its upper and lower jaws, proof that this creature was a champion meat-eater, exposed themselves to Guinevere. They glinted in a stray beam of moonlight.

Letting out a guttural scream, Guinevere let loose the arrow from her bow. It collided with the chest of the carnotaurus, but the pointed tip did not pierce the thick leathery skin of the dinosaur. Instead, it bent and fell to the ground with a disappointing clatter. She hit the ground, arrows scattering out of her quiver and bow knocked out of her grasp. She was defenseless.

Arthur, awoken by the sound of Guinevere's scream, bolted out of the tent in panic. He hadn't taken the time to put his shoes back on but grabbed his holster belt on the way through the door. He stood barefoot, clothed in his simple black pants and a dirtied undershirt, with a gun at his side. He could feel the cool mud seeping in between his toes, but it didn't matter. Frantically, he looked around for Guinevere. She had fallen on the ground. Her dress was covered with mud and leaves, her boots likewise. Her arms were bare, the jacket he'd given her left behind in the tent. Although the night in the forest was cold and damp, Arthur hardly felt it due to the adrenaline coursing through his veins. He turned slightly, hearing a low unmistakable growl. There the carnotaurus was, standing over Guinevere. It prepared to go in for the kill, hungry for its next meal.

"Hey!" Arthur shouted at the dinosaur, waving his arms frantically in the air. "Over here!"

The carnotaurus slowly turned, its red beady eyes staring at him. Intrigued by the movement, it lumbered toward him. Its mouth gaped open, a mixture of saliva and bloody remnants dripping from its lips and sprinkling the ground as it moved.

Guinevere pushed herself up and snatched her bow from the ground. A few arrows remained in her quiver and she nocked one. Without thinking twice, she hurried around the large creature's left flank to stand behind Arthur. She held her bow at the ready, despite its futility. It offered her more comfort than protection.

Once Guinevere was safely behind, Arthur opened fire at the dinosaur. The bullets merely bounced off its skin, angering the creature even more. It lumbered closer to the duo, moving slowly.

"I think it got, Mordred," Guinevere shouted, her voice quivering with fear as she took short and shallow breaths. The carnotaurus marched closer to them, its head barely more than an arm's length away.

"Run!" She screamed, letting loose the arrow and taking off into the darkness. Arthur stopped shooting. He turned and followed, staying close behind Guinevere as she blindly ran through the forest.

The carnotaurus was right on their tail, matching their speed. Its massive feet thundered as they struck the ground. Its large body knocked branches off trees as it crashed through the forest.

As fast as they ran, they couldn't escape it. Guinevere could feel the dinosaur closing the gap. She turned, slowing her sprint, and pulled one of the last arrows out of her quiver. Preparing for what could be her final chance, she nocked the arrow on the string and aimed at its eye.

Arthur stopped running, realizing that Guinevere had stopped. Sweat dripped down his brow, partially from running and partially from fear. He wiped it away and stared at Guinevere as she prepared to shoot the carnotaurus.

Before she could release the arrow, another dinosaur lumbered out of the forest. Guinevere and Arthur watched as an ankylosaurus headed straight at the hungry carnotaurus. It had a wide, low head with two horns pointed backward protruding from the base of its skull; two more horns were below, pointing down. Its leathery-skin was covered in thick, oval-shaped armored plates, and it had a large club on the end of its tail. It bounded in between the trees. In one motion, it swung its tail at the carnivore's head. The club at the end of it collided with the carnotaurus's mouth, knocking loose a few teeth. Blood splattered from their sockets, sprinkling the forest floor with crimson drops.

The carnotaurus turned from Guinevere and Arthur to look at the ankylosaurus. Angry, it let out a primal roar, its bloody saliva spraying from its mouth as its voice echoed in the silence of the night.

Seeing their chance, Arthur grabbed Guinevere's arm, breaking her free from the trance of the fighting dinosaurs.

"Run!" he shouted. She didn't argue.

They continued to run blindly through the forest. There was no use trying to circle back to camp, as they had lost track of it long before. They pushed foliage out of their way as they ran, stomping on fallen leaves, sprouted mushrooms, small twigs, and clover. They could hear the fighting dinosaurs behind them. Neither of them dared look back for fear that they would soon be followed.

Suddenly, and without warning, they broke out of the forest. Their surroundings had completely changed. No longer were they in the dark shadows of the canopy. Past the grassy clearing was a glistening white beach under a multitude of stars. The sky had opened, reflecting off the water that stretched out to the horizon.

They had found it: Lake Diana. Ichthyosaurs were swimming beneath the clear and pristine waters. The clearing, especially the lake, exuded a peaceful calm. It was an extreme juxtaposition from the Paimpont Forest they had just passed through. The melody of the lake was quite different from before. It was filled with a few simple songbirds echoing melodies back and forth. An occasional splash of a jumping sea creature punctuated the chorus.

Guinevere ran from the grassy area near the trees down to the shimmering white sands. Mesmerized by the beauty, she had forgotten for a second that they had just been chased through the forest by a blood-thirsty carnotaurus. She let her knees fall into the soft surface, running her hands through the warm sand. The grains collapsed through her fingers, forming ripples in their wake. Arthur walked over to her, breathless, and barely able to stand. They both remained frozen and stared at the lake, watching the reflection of the stars twinkling and the glow of the moon.

Chapter Seventeen

Guinevere and Arthur looked out at the lake as the sound of rushing waves stole their attention. From across the water, a boat could be seen peacefully sailing. It appeared out of the mist as if rising from the depths of the lake. In the boat was a woman; her long black hair was soaked with water, yet it flowed wispily in the breeze, leaving floating droplets in the wind. She was wearing a simple white dress, saturated with dew, but it did not reveal what was beneath. She clasped her hands across her lap as she lounged against the stern of the boat.

"What is going on?" Arthur asked, breaking the short-lived silence.

"I— I don't know," Guinevere stuttered, unable to peel her eyes off the woman.

The boat slowly approached the shore before running aground on the sandy bottom of the lake. The woman stepped out of the boat gracefully. Her dress flowed behind her as walked toward them, her feet just below the surface of the water. The sounds of the night had stopped—even the waves were silent. The only noise was the water flowing over her feet and the staggered breath of Guinevere and Arthur. The Lady of the Lake continued moving toward the two of them. They could only stand there speechless, staring at her. As she neared the shore, the sounds of the sky and the sea returned. Once she was at the water's edge, she stopped walking. Her ankles were barely submerged in the water.

"Guinevere Cornwall," the woman said, staring at her. Arthur turned his attention from the figure to look at Guinevere, who stood in shock, her gaze straight ahead. The woman's voice was velvet, smooth and silky. She wasn't shouting, yet her voice carried strength. "I am Viviane, the Lady of the Lake. You have traveled a long way." Silence hung in the air. No one knew how to respond.

"Y—you're just a legend. Just a myth," Guinevere was able to mutter while looking at Viviane, mystified. She was still in shock at this mystical figure unable to believe her eyes. The Lady of the Lake was more of a myth than Excalibur. Nobody, Guinevere included, believed that she was real.

"And yet you have come all this way in search of Excalibur," Viviane responded. "Here you will find it." She looked at Guinevere with intent focus, ignoring Arthur's presence. It was as if she was the only one there. Guinevere stood there, looking back at her, afraid that if she looked away it would all be just a dream. Her mind was a blur of confusion and excitement.

Viviane reached down into the shallow waters before her and slowly withdrew the hilt of a sword. Its long blade emerged from edge of the water as she guided it straight out of the deep. Tiny rainbows refracted in the water that dripped from its tip as she raised the sword to her chest. The blade came up to meet her upturned palm, its surface glistening in the moonlight.

"Come closer," Viviane commanded Guinevere. Her voice was clear but still not forceful. It was soft and breathy with an undeniable authority. Guinevere took a step toward the lake, the waves lapping at her feet. The hem of Viviane's dress extended back into the water. It rose and fell with each passing wave as if the lake was an extension.

"Guinevere Cornwall," she said solemnly, "you have made quite the journey to get here, but I am afraid your story has not come to an end. You have found Excalibur, and now the power bestowed upon it is under your command to appoint the true leader of Camelot, the once and future ruler." There was an air of admiration in her voice.

"Take this sword," she said, standing before Guinevere in the water, her arms outstretched, and presenting Excalibur, "and use it anoint the rightful ruler of Avalon. May it serve as a reminder to whomever you choose that they have the power to command. Do not unsheathe Excalibur without reason; do not wield without valor, for the sword can destroy. Even the most steadfast of hearts can be corrupted by its power."

Stunned, Guinevere dropped her bow to the ground and stepped into the water. She grasped the hilt of the sword. Excalibur sparkled with the dew against its hilt, which was adorned with the subtlest jewelry: diamond sparks, myriads of topaz, and reddish-orange jacinth. Arthur scooped up the bow and slung it over his shoulder, still mesmerized by the Lady of the Lake. Viviane released her grasp on the blade, letting the whole weight of the sword fall into Guinevere's hands.

"How should I know the rightful ruler?" Guinevere asked, stunned, while staring at the sword in her hands. She had hundreds of questions streaming through her mind, screaming to be answered, but the one she asked had come out empty.

"You already know," Viviane replied.

"Freeze! You are surrounded!" The command came from the forest behind them. It left Guinevere with no time consider what her words had meant. *We were followed, just like Arthur warned,* Guinevere thought. Viviane slowly stepped backward into the lake, making her way to the boat. When she didn't stop, one of the Rangers fired his weapon, hitting her squarely in the chest. No wounds appeared, and the surface rippled as if like water. A mist rose up from the surface of the lake, shrouding her. When it had dissipated, Viviane was no longer there, and her boat drifted toward the horizon. For a moment, Guinevere didn't move, mystified by the enchanted figure. She slowly turned to face the forest.

There was nowhere for them to escape. Half a dozen Rangers were rapidly exiting the forest. A few had already reached the beach. They were forming a semi-circle around them, pressing the duo's back against the water. Behind them, the expansive lake stretched out for miles. The water lapped against their feet. They were clearly trapped.

The Rangers all had their weapons trained on them. One man stood out in front of the rest; he was clearly in charge and had been the one shouting the orders. The barrel of the gun in his hand was still smoking, and it was evident that he had shot Viviane. Despite that, he had an ease of posture.

"Well, well, well, what do we have here?" the lead Ranger said with a mocking tone to his voice. He kicked sand at them with his steel-toed combat boots. The sand flew up and stuck to their legs, wet from standing in the shallow water. Guinevere looked at the Ranger. *Agravain*, she thought. She was filled with anger and fear.

"Looks like we found ourselves a smuggler and a fugitive." He pointed his weapon at Arthur and Guinevere respectively. He walked up to her, slowly circling and stalking. He stopped in front of her and dragged his gun under her chin. Guinevere stood there paralyzed, clutching onto Excalibur's hilt. She didn't want to move; she couldn't move. Sweat formed on her brow, dripping down to her eyes. Her whole body quivered with fear. She bit her bottom lip trying to stay still. She was terrified.

"The king will surely be happy to see you," Agravain told her. He shoved the gun harder into her throat. He stared into Guinevere's eyes. All she saw reflected back was an empty, black darkness.

She wanted to look toward Arthur. She wanted to gauge his reaction—see if he had a plan—but she knew he wouldn't move, not with the Rangers surrounding them. Not with the gun right at her throat.

Agravain continued glaring at Guinevere. "Huh," he said then holstered his weapon. He took a step back. Guinevere breathed again, but—knowing she was still in danger—did not relax. "What do we have here?" he reached out at Guinevere, attempting to grab the hilt of Excalibur. She took a step back, evading his grasp. Agravain laughed. It was mocking and demeaning.

"Not going to make this easy, I see," he said. His voice was unsettlingly jovial.

"No," Guinevere said. Her voice was starkly flat by comparison.

"I could simply kill you and take Excalibur for myself," he threatened. Arthur moved his hand to his holster but didn't pull out his gun.

"You need me," she said, covering for Arthur before Agravain could reach his weapon. Her voice quivered as she spoke. Agravain froze. He brought his hand back down to his weapon. His fingers danced along the hilt. He stopped short of drawing it out. "You need me," Guinevere continued, "to appoint the true ruler of Avalon. The Lady of the Lake entrusted me with this power."

Agravain stopped reaching for his gun. "Is that so?" he asked, amused.

Guinevere nodded slowly.

"Well, isn't that convenient." He sneered. "And why should I believe you?"

"Because it's true!" she insisted, but her voice wasn't very convincing, trembling as she spoke. She looked over to Arthur, who had pulled his gun out of its holster; he nodded in agreement, but Agravain didn't notice.

"Hmm. Well, that changes things, doesn't it?" He smiled at Guinevere. His voice bounced in a singsong-like rhythm, sending a shiver of fear down her spine. Keeping the lovely expression plastered across his face, he walked back toward Guinevere.

She grasped Excalibur tightly as he approached, protecting it from Agravain. But before he could reach her, she dropped low and rammed into his legs. Arthur kicked up sand at the Rangers who had forgotten he was there. He popped off several shots, causing them to scatter. Guinevere tossed Excalibur to Arthur.

"Run," Guinevere commanded. "They want Excalibur."

He was frozen for a moment, unsure of his next move.

"Come on!" Guinevere grabbed his arm, breaking him free from his petrified state. She pulled him along toward the forest, away from the lake—away from the Rangers.

"Get yourself away from here." She grabbed him by the shoulders and looked him directly in the eyes. There was fear hidden beneath her confidence.

"What about you?" he asked her.

"Don't worry about me," she said, letting him go. "We'll meet up back at the Hengroen. If we split up, at least one of us will make it."

Arthur took off running. He sprinted into the forest, the darkness consuming him. Guinevere turned around to see the Rangers approaching her, weapons trained on her. They weren't shooting. *They need me alive*, she thought. With that in mind, she turned back toward the forest, toward the unknown within its darkness. She started running, trying to disappear before she could be followed.

***

Guinevere had no clue where she was. She had been blindly running through the woods with no plan of what to do next.

197

She ran through the trees and slipped into the darkness. Silence surrounded her. Thinking that she had not been followed, she walked forward slowly. The sound of the leaves crunching beneath her feet broke the hush. She walked for a while, trying to come up with a plan. She knew she didn't have very many options. She would eventually be found; she had no doubt about that.

Guinevere walked deeper into the forest. Every noise made her twitch. She continued to glance around nervously, feeling as if someone was watching her. She tried to brush off the noises as only natural nighttime forest life: dinosaurs eating, birds taking off into flight. She couldn't focus on coming up with a plan; she could barely focus on finding a place to hide.

Guinevere glanced over her shoulder, thinking that she had heard a noise. *Probably an animal,* she reminded herself, continuing forward. Not seeing the roots on the ground before her, she tripped over them, losing her balance and falling to the ground.

She felt a cry of pain building up in the back of her throat. Before it could break the silence, a hand covered her mouth, stifling it.

"Don't make a sound," commanded a deep voice from behind her. She froze as the cold of a gun barrel was pressed against the back of her neck. "Get up slowly," he instructed her as he released his hand from her mouth. Trying to balance herself, she stood up without much ease. Guinevere's mind tried to comprehend what was going on. She started to turn around to see who was holding her hostage.

She felt the barrel of the gun press harder into the back of her neck. "Do not turn around." The man behind her growled. "Walk forward." Quickly, she stepped over a fallen branch and between a couple of trees. "Slowly," he demanded. She decreased her pace as she continued to walk out of the forest toward Lake Diana. The forest was filled with silence. The only sound that could be heard was that of their footsteps and the sounds of woodland creatures echoing around them.

Without warning, a gunshot sounded. It resounded from further in the forest, deeper than where she had sent Arthur. Guinevere figured that he must have been followed. She had put him in danger by giving him Excalibur to watch over. Immediately following her realization was an ear-shattering scream. She now knew that the bullet hadn't lodged itself in a tree or the ground. It had found a home in someone's flesh. Guinevere felt her legs go weak as she slumped to the ground. She felt the soil rising between her fingers.

"Get up now!" the man with the gun yelled at her. She tried, but she couldn't seem to get her legs to obey her. Shock had disconnected her mind from her body.

"Get up." The words were quiet but stern. There was no way to doubt the seriousness in the man's voice as he snarled them. The gun was shoved harder into the back of her neck. Guinevere raised her arms up and placed her hands on her head. She was surrendering. She was preparing to be shot.

Another shot was fired. Guinevere felt the bullet barely skim her arm as it flew over her. It crashed through a tree, breaking off several branches. Guinevere gasped and dropped her arms down to stabilize herself. It was a warning shot. Suddenly an arm was around her and she was pulled up on her feet. The man dragged her swiftly to the clearing that they had been heading toward. It was empty. The lake was empty. No Rangers were in sight.

Guinevere was pushed toward the middle of the clearing and fell onto the ground. As Guinevere looked up from where she lay, the face of the man who captured her met her eyes. She struggled to get up as he advanced toward her, pulling herself onto her feet after a slight struggle.

The man approached her, getting closer and closer, but he never reached her. Before he had the chance, a bullet flew through the air, colliding squarely with the Ranger's forehead. Instantly, he fell to the ground—dead.

Stunned, Guinevere froze. Slowly, she turned to see who had shot the Ranger. Out of the forest, another man was approaching. It was clear by the way he was dressed that it wasn't another Ranger. *Oh great,* Guinevere thought, *who else followed us? Who else is trying to take Excalibur?*

As the man came into view, it became clear who exactly it was.

"Mordred!" Guinevere shouted, a hint of joy in her voice. She ran over to him and collapsed into his arms. She felt a single tear fall. She wiped it away hoping that Mordred didn't notice, but he did. She hated to cry, especially in front of others. She used to never cry. Now, all of a sudden, everything was toying with her emotions. It was too much for her to handle.

"It's okay," he told her. She didn't want to cry, but it was too late. Mordred gingerly placed his hand on her shoulder to comfort her. She leaned against his chest, her tears uncontrollably falling onto his jacket.

"I thought you were dead. I thought the carnotaurus got you. Arthur." Her voice was cracking. "The Rangers. I think—Arthur— I think the Rangers shot Arthur." She blubbered, unable to speak a coherent thought. "I think he's—" She was unable to finish, breaking down once more into tears. Mordred just nodded. He wrapped his arms around her and let her lean on him.

They stood there for a while in the clearing. It was dark and empty. Guinevere sobbed. She had never cried like this before. She let it all out, and Mordred let her. He stood there patiently, trying to comfort her.

"Arthur's resilient," Mordred told her, gently rubbing her back as tears soaked his shirt. "I'm sure he's figured something out."

"You think?" she asked, looking up at him. She wiped the tears away from her face, stopping her crying.

"I'm positive," he assured her. "Come on, let's get you warmed up." He took his jacket off and draped it over her shoulders. He placed his hands on her shoulders and led her away. They walked back into the forest slowly. She bunched up the coat sleeves over her hands and buried her face in them. Together they walked until they reached a smoldering campfire.

Guinevere sat down on a fallen log near the fire. It provided a warm orange glow to its surroundings, but it was impossible to see past the first row of trees deeper into the forest. Guinevere scooted to the edge of the log to get closer to its warmth. She held onto Mordred's jacket, wrapping it around herself like a blanket.

"Wait here," Mordred instructed her, walking further into the woods before she had a chance to question him. Alone, Guinevere sat by the fire. Hearing noises in the woods around her, she continuously fidgeted looking around. She settled down slightly and focused on warming her hands by the fire.

"Glad you're back," Guinevere said, seeing Mordred's silhouette coming back through the trees. She turned back to warming her hands. Slowly, she looked back at Mordred, something not sitting right. He stepped into the light.

Mordred wasn't alone.

Agravain was with him.

Guinevere jumped to her feet. Mordred's jacket fell from her shoulders. She refused to take her eyes off Agravain. He looked across the fire at her, eyes reflected in its light. She stood where she was, feet planted firmly into the ground ready to defend herself.

"What is *he* doing here?" she shouted at Mordred. He did not reply.

"Happy to see you again," Agravain told her with a broad smile plastered across his face.

Guinevere shook her head in disbelief.

"Everyone else is happy to see you also," he informed her. He looked into the forest, past the glow the fire provided. Mordred remained silent.

From the campfire, Guinevere slowly turned around. As she spun around, she saw more Rangers approaching her from behind the trees. In addition to their weapons, many were holding lanterns that lit up the area. It became clear to her that she wasn't at a lonely fire in the middle of Paimpont Forest. She was in the middle of the Rangers' camp. Tents were set up all around, remnants of other campfires were evident. The dark of night and the veil of the forest had provided them the perfect cover. Mordred had led her right to them, and she hadn't suspected a thing.

"No," she muttered to herself. "No, this isn't happening." But it was.

"The Lady of the Lake may have chosen you to appoint the next ruler of Avalon, so we do need you to come with us alive," Agravain informed her, "but that doesn't mean you need to come unharmed."

"What if I told you I already appointed the next king?" Guinevere asked, trying to think fast of a way out. She kept an eye on the Rangers all around her. They hadn't moved, waiting for their next order.

Agravain laughed. "Who?"

Guinevere glared at him.

"You don't even have Excalibur anymore."

He was right.

"Mordred," Guinevere pleaded, "please help me."

He didn't respond. He stood there next to Agravain, expressionless, avoiding Guinevere's eyes.

"Grab her." Agravain nodded toward the Rangers closest to Guinevere. They moved out of the forest. She didn't give them any more time to approach her. Guinevere turned and ran past the Rangers back into the forest.

"Follow her!" she heard Agravain order the men.

She didn't know where she was running, barely able to see more than a couple meters in front of her at a time. She crashed into branches as she sprinted further into the forest. She couldn't think about the multitude of wild animals that were awake in the night like last time. All she could think about was putting as much distance between herself and the Rangers as she possibly could.

Guinevere had no clue where she was, and she had no plan of what to do next. Before she had any more time to consider her options, she was surrounded. Quickly, five Rangers flooded in around her, raising guns as they closed a border in her path. Her eyes shifted from one to the next and down to the forest floor. This wasn't going as she had expected.

"Put your hands above your head," one of the Rangers commanded. Guinevere obeyed. Another one of them stepped out of the group and, before Guinevere had time to react, snapped a pair of handcuffs on her wrists, fastening her arms behind her back.

Guinevere was pushed from behind and forward through the forest. She stumbled, not expecting to move yet. Before she could fall further, two of the Rangers grabbed her arms, causing her to stand upright. Defenseless, she was smacked across the face, and her head pushed sideways with another blow. The cold of metal collided with her cheek. She could taste blood in her mouth. Looking through the tears that welled up in her eyes, Guinevere saw the butt of a gun blocking her vision. Her face stung, swelling as an immediate reaction to the soldier's treatment. Suddenly the barrel of the gun was in her vision instead.

"Move," the Ranger commanded. The other four agents flanked her and escorted her through the forest. They led her back to the Ranger camp.

She continued to stumble as she walked, struggling to maintain her balance without the use of her arms. The Rangers continued to hold her upright forcefully. Her long hair had come undone from the two braids that it was in, no longer held back from her face. With every step, loose hair fell in her eyes, making it harder for her to see.

When they made it back to the Ranger camp, Guinevere could see Agravain and the rest of the Rangers waiting for them. Mordred was gone. The Rangers' faces glowed eerily in the yellow light from their lanterns, their smiles more threatening than before. Long shadows were cast from their glow.

Guinevere was pushed toward them and fell into one of the Ranger's arms. It was all happening so quickly that she hadn't even been given a second to react. She was picked up and heaved in front of Agravain. She braced the fall as best as she could with her cuffed hands. She landed on the ground; the cold earth pressed against her face.

As Guinevere looked up from where she laid, her eyes met Agravain's. She quickly looked away. She struggled to get up, but Agravain kicked her in the ribs, throwing her back to the ground. Her breathing came out as a whimper.

Another one of the Rangers pulled her up off the ground. There she stood, defenseless before Agravain. He walked up to her and gently brushed her hair away from her face, tucking it behind her ears. He took a step back and looked at her. She glared at him. After staring at her for an uncomfortable amount of time, Agravain spoke up.

"Let's go," he commanded the other Rangers. He walked up to Guinevere once more. He placed a cloth over her mouth and nose. She tried to fight him, to look away, but it was of no use. Firmly, he held her face, staring intently into her eyes. Her vision got fuzzy. She blinked rapidly, attempting to get her eyes to refocus but to no avail. Quickly, everything turned to darkness.

Chapter Eighteen

Arthur ran barefoot through the forest. The darkness swallowed him up as he ran. The stars were blocked out by the treetops and the moon was blotted out by their leaves. He didn't look back; he couldn't look back. He ran swiftly but carefully, making sure to keep an eye out not only for Rangers who might have been following him, but also for predatory dinosaurs.

I don't need to see another hungry carnotaurus, Arthur thought, ducking under a branch as he continued deeper in the forest. He clutched onto Excalibur, making sure the sword stayed in his possession. He had Guinevere's bow slung over his back and his guns in his holster. Although heavily armed, he was running low on ammunition: he had no arrows in his possession and wasn't carrying any extra bullets. He wasn't sure how many Rangers or dinosaurs he would be able to fight off.

The cold of the night was beginning to latch onto his skin and seep into his bones. He could feel the crisp breeze piercing through his shirt. He momentarily wished he would have paused to grab his jacket before leaving the tent earlier that night. He pushed the thought out of his mind and carried on. Shivering slightly, he slowed down his run to a brisk walk.

Arthur continued through the forest for what seemed like hours, although it was only a matter of minutes. It was impossible for him to know how far he had traveled in the dark. Everything looked the same. He passed tree after tree, fallen log after fallen log, mossy branch after mossy branch. He kept journeying deeper into the forest, farther away from the lake.

Arthur heard the noise of a gun clicking behind him. Slowly, he turned around. A Ranger was standing there and pointing his gun at him.

"Don't move," he told Arthur.

Arthur understood. The Ranger looked Arthur over as Arthur did the same to him. He noticed that aside from the weapon that the Ranger was pointing at him, he was unarmed. *I'm sure he thinks differently of me,* Arthur noted, thinking of the sword he held, the bow across his back, and the gun in its holster on his waist.

"How about we do this: no weapons, just us two, man to man?" Arthur suggested slowly, setting his weapons down on the ground keeping eye contact with the Ranger the entire time.

The Ranger was hesitant to comply with Arthur's request.

"Or are you too much of a coward to face me without a gun to hide behind?" Arthur mocked him as he stood there without any weapons.

Not wanting to be shown up, the Ranger set his gun down on the ground. "I'm no coward," he said. "Just know that this will not be a fair fight."

"I know." Arthur smiled confidently. "I hope you are up for the challenge."

"Is that so?" the Ranger asked as he walked toward Arthur. They both took up defensive positions.

"Yes," Arthur spoke through gritted teeth as he struck out at the Ranger. Arthur's punch was easily blocked. The Ranger grabbed his wrist and twisted Arthur's arm sideways, attempting to knock him to the ground. It didn't work. Arthur used the momentum to flip himself over backward and land upright on his feet. With a quick twist of his wrist, he was free of the Ranger's grasp.

He took a step backward as he rubbed his wrist, feigning injury.

The Ranger walked toward him, letting his guard completely down. Once he was close enough, Arthur smiled. He twisted his leg around the Ranger's, tripping him and landing him on the ground. He let out a slight laugh at how defenseless the Ranger had been, but he wasn't beat. The Ranger rolled over quickly and jumped back up on his feet.

"Did you think this would be easy?" he asked Arthur as he returned to his defensive position. "I'm one of the king's Rangers. You are just some valueless, dirty vandal." He moved toward him, firing off a series of punches that Arthur strategically blocked.

"Valueless? I have more values than you will ever have," Arthur responded. He took the offensive turn. He ran toward the Ranger and attempted to contact him with a round of sharp kicks.

"How do you suppose?" he asked as he skillfully blocked each of Arthur's strikes.

"I would never blindly follow a tyrannical leader without question." With each word, Arthur delivered an attack against the

Ranger. He separated each word and spoke through gritted teeth. The Ranger caught Arthur's foot in his final blow. He lost his balance and fell to the ground. Angry, he spit out a mouthful of dirt. Arthur wasn't going to let the Ranger beat him that easily. There was too much at stake. With a quick somersault, Arthur was back on his feet. He was now on the defensive, working hard to block each punch and kick.

Arthur and the Ranger stayed caught up in the fight, each taking turns being on the offensive and defensive, neither of them willing to call it quits. They were equally matched.

The Ranger's moves got sloppy. He wasn't focused on Arthur's attack anymore. It was too late to do anything when Arthur's foot came up to hit him on the side of his head. He fell down, stunned. Arthur stood over him, waiting for him to get back up. He never did.

Satisfied that he had knocked the Ranger unconscious, Arthur walked back to the other side of the small clearing and collected his weapons. He strapped them all back to his body and turned around. To his surprise, the Ranger was standing there and staring him down, his eyes a blaze with vengeance.

"Is that all you've got?" asked the Ranger. He pointed his gun at Arthur who didn't have a chance to pull out his weapon. The Ranger raised his gun to fire, but before he could, it was knocked out of his hand. The gun flew across the forest floor. Instantly, Arthur dove after it. Whoever had gotten the gun away had somehow managed to render the Ranger unconscious. With himself pressed against the ground and with the Ranger's gun at the ready, Arthur watched what was happening.

The stranger moved toward Arthur. Preparing to fight, he jumped back up onto his feet and pointed the Ranger's gun at him. He held tight onto Excalibur's hilt with his other hand. Once the stranger was about arm's reach away, he removed his hood and pulled down the bandana that had been partially covering his face. He smiled at Arthur, not intending to fight him.

"I'm Lancelot," he introduced himself mysteriously within the darkness of the trees, extending a hand to Arthur. Arthur looked up at him. Perfectly manicured blonde hair topped his head, and below it, his eyebrows swooped gracefully over two piercing green eyes. A stubble of blonde hairs created a shadow of a beard and mustache, and a smile was plastered on his face. A black hooded coat covered his upper body, with a bandana pulled down around his neck. Draped over his back was a sack of supplies and around his waist a belt strapped with an empty holster. The gun was gripped in one of Lancelot's hands and the other was extended to Arthur to introduce himself to him.

"Arthur," he replied, taking Lancelot's hand, extremely confused.

"I'm here to get you and that sword—" he glanced at Excalibur in Arthur's hand "—out of here. What do you say?"

"Why should I trust you?" Arthur asked, slightly suspicious. "How do I know that you aren't going to take me straight to Gorlois? That seems like a pretty standard issue weapon for a Ranger." He nodded at Lancelot's gun.

Holstering his weapon, Lancelot replied, "I was a Ranger, but I'm not anymore. Not since Gorlois took the throne for himself. We've been looking for Guinevere and Excalibur since her wanted poster was released and, by extension, you."

Arthur wasn't sure he wanted to believe him, but he didn't really have any other choice, not if he wanted to get out of the forest alive. "We?" he asked Lancelot. "Who's we?"

"The knights," Lancelot blatantly answered.

Arthur didn't have time to ask him to clarify when a noise disturbed their conversation. Standing there was another Ranger, armed and ready. Lancelot pushed Arthur to the ground and dodged the Ranger's shot. He pulled out his own gun and shot the man point-blank in the forehead. The Ranger fell to the ground, blood pouring out of the hole in his head. His eyes were still open in shock.

Lancelot pulled Arthur off the forest floor and suddenly they were running for their lives. Presumably another Ranger was back there somewhere, and many more not far behind him.

"Do you trust me now?" Lancelot asked as they tore through the forest.

"I at least believe that you aren't a Ranger," he replied as they continued their pace. He didn't hear any footsteps behind them. Maybe there weren't other Rangers following them. Maybe they had lost them. Either way, they weren't taking any chances.

Without slowing down, Lancelot looked back at him. "Good enough for me."

Arthur nodded, too breathless to reply. Lancelot was still yanking him along. He hoped he knew where they were going. They sprinted through the woods, barely able to see in front of themselves in the dark of night with the stars blocked out by the treetops. Blindly, Arthur followed Lancelot.

Suddenly Lancelot swore and pulled him to a stop. Arthur looked over Lancelot's shoulder. A Ranger was standing before them, having stepped out from behind a tree, with a smug look on his face.

"In a hurry?" he asked sarcastically. He began to pull out his gun, but before he could aim it, Lancelot had tackled him. When the opportunity presented itself, Lancelot grabbed the Ranger's gun and used it to hit him on the head. The Ranger was knocked out in seconds.

Without hesitation, Arthur and Lancelot took off once more, continuing through the woods. They continued in silence, slowing their sprint down to a brisk walk. Arthur looked around, continuously checking for more Rangers to spring out of the forest. Eventually he relaxed slightly, allowing himself to focus on making it safely through the woods in the dark instead of fearing more Rangers. Although he couldn't see very far, he focused on Lancelot, making sure not to lose sight of him.

"Miss me?" a voice behind him asked, both menacing and pleasant at the same time.

Arthur turned around to see the first Ranger he had encountered, the Ranger Lancelot knocked unconscious. Among others from their fight, a bruise was forming on the side of his head from where Lancelot had apparently hit him. Arthur froze in shock, the pounding in his ears making him unable to think.

"Brunor, no! Don't shoot!" Lancelot yelled. The Ranger turned and looked at him. "It's me. It's Lancelot." The Ranger scowled.

"Why would I listen to you, you traitor?" He sneered.

"I'm still the same Lancelot," he tried reasoning with him, walking around Arthur and holding his hands up. "Just listen to me and don't shoot."

Brunor didn't listen.

Arthur felt the bullet graze his leg. He was well aware of it from the moment it contacted his skin, but the searing pain did not come right away. He felt the heat traveling through his leg as it went weak. He unwillingly let out a cry of pain, but he cut it off as soon as he was able. Still keeping his eyes locked on the Ranger who had shot him, Arthur covered the wound with his hand.

Without hesitation, Lancelot shot Brunor.

Then they heard another shot fired. Both Arthur and Lancelot quickly turned their gaze toward where they had come from. Despite everything that had just happened to him, only one thing was on Arthur's mind: Guinevere. He followed the noise as quickly as he could. Blood had already saturated his pant leg and was easily still flowing. Lancelot followed behind.

Arthur pushed his way through the trees, shoving vegetation out of his way. His bare feet pounded against the ground as he ran. He was covered in mud and dirt and blood. Lancelot kept close.

Arthur let out a sudden gasp as the pain in his leg grew worse. He felt it weaken beneath him and collapse. Angry, he tried to pull himself along the forest floor, but there was no use.

"Arthur, stop," Lancelot said, blocking his path. "You are only going to hurt yourself more."

"Don't tell me what to do!" Arthur snapped. "Guinevere is out there by herself. I need to go back and help her!" He threw Excalibur on the ground, filled with anger. Lancelot watched the sword collide with the forest floor. As it hit the ground, fallen leaves were scattered up into the air. They gently floated down to the ground near the sword, which was shimmering in the evening light. The engraving on the blade was even more prominent: 'take me up, cast me away.' The blade shone with soft blue light from the moonbeams barely peeking their way through the trees, and the hilt sparkled as the light danced off the jewels.

"You aren't going to be able to help if you don't look after yourself." Lancelot sat down on the ground next to Arthur, scooping up Excalibur from the dirt and foliage. Arthur stopped fighting and sat up as Lancelot placed Excalibur on his lap; Arthur gently rested his hands on the sword. "Let me at least tend to your wound before we keep going."

Arthur nodded. Lancelot slung his bag off his shoulder and sat it on the ground next to him. Nothing more needed to be said. It was only a matter of minutes before the wound was cleaned and Arthur's leg was wrapped up. With a little help, he stood up again.

They both knew what needed to be done. The two of them journeyed through the forest and back to the lake. Arthur wasn't thinking of Rangers coming after them, or dinosaurs looking for their next meal, or any of the other dangers the forest at night could provide them with. All he could think about was Guinevere.

They broke through the forest to the opening. White sand surrounded them, still glistening in the moonlight, the lake reflecting the multitude of stars.

The clearing was empty.

"Guinevere!" Arthur shouted. He ran across the beach, shouting her name.

He stopped, realizing that she was gone. There he stood in front of the lake, unsure of what to do. Lancelot walked up, joining him by the water's edge.

"She's gone," Arthur muttered. The water lapped at his bare feet. He stared at it, dumbfounded. He looked up at Lancelot. "We need to go after her."

Lancelot agreed. "I'm pretty sure I know where they are going to take her. I think we'll have a better chance of getting her out safely there. Besides, I have some more friends who will be able to help."

"The so-called knights you spoke of earlier?"

Lancelot nodded.

"And where do you think Guinevere is going to be taken?" Arthur asked, turning to look at him.

Lancelot turned and looked him in the eyes. "Camelot."

Chapter Nineteen

Guinevere awoke, feeling extremely groggy. She blinked her eyes multiple times, trying to adjust to the surprisingly bright light. It was overwhelming, and for a time, all she could see was white. An excruciating headache overpowered her, likely from the drug-induced slumber. It left a fog over her mind. She blinked a few more times, registering the faint outlines of her surroundings. She was in a private dirigible with little more than a pilot's cabin and a cargo bay. There were four columns of seats. The middle two, where she was, faced forward. On either side, an aisle ran the length of the ship. The remaining columns faced outward, with clear visibility of the surrounding terrain. Rangers surrounded her. Of those columns nearby, one was sitting beside her, one was in front, and one stood in the aisle. Guinevere felt a small pressure tug at her wrists. They were handcuffed together, attached to a chain that was anchored to the floor. The man in the aisle had his hand resting on his weapon, waiting for her to try to escape.

"Did you sleep well, Miss Cornwall?" the Ranger in front asked as he turned around in his seat. He had one knee on the chair and one leg in the aisle. "I would hope so, given the sedatives. Had to make sure you wouldn't be difficult." He let out a small laugh.

Guinevere was annoyed. She felt irritable from the hangover. Her vision finally cleared, and the Ranger's face came into focus.

"Agravain." She hissed, glaring at her nemesis.

He laughed. "Careful, or you'll end up like Arthur." He had a cheeky grin on his face.

Acting merely out of rage and irritation, Guinevere cried out and lunged at him. Her arms were yanked downward at the expense of the chain.

"Woah there, little one." Agravain stepped back, half-sitting on the seatback of the next row. Her shoulders collided with his seat's metal frames, her head in the now vacant space were Agravain had been. She wasn't thinking clearly about how she was outnumbered and outpowered. She was more than furious, held somewhere between sitting and standing. Like a wild animal, she was affixed to the floor and yanked her arms up in a frantic attempt to win freedom. Agravain watched her from his perch and laughed. He was clearly enjoying her struggle.

"Those handcuffs are made of titanium," his words were mocking, "and so is the chain."

Guinevere glared at him. With one last tug of defiance, she sat back down in her seat. She felt slightly humiliated and even more annoyed. She glowered at Agravain, and he chuckled again.

"Why didn't you kill me?" Guinevere provoked him. "You've had many chances, but here I am alive while your friends are not."

"Turns out you're more useful to us alive." Agravain smiled menacingly.

Guinevere grimaced.

218

"The king seeks an audience with you." Somewhat bored, Agravain turned around and sat back down.

Some time passed and Guinevere watched the scenery outside the craft. She could see the sky mostly but caught occasional glimpses of the terrain below. At some point in their journey, a sack had been stuffed over her head. By that time, she already knew they were headed to Camelot. She felt the craft touch the ground and she felt a presence near her ear. Chills ran down her spine as Agravain whispered.

"The king is very excited to see you," he said.

She heard the chain fall to the floor as two Rangers grabbed either one of her arms. Guinevere was led out the side of the craft and onto the ground. She could hear Agravain's muffled voice barking commands at the other Rangers. She followed behind Agravain for a while before reaching their destination. She could feel grass beneath her feet.

"Stop," she heard him call out.

The Rangers at either side of her paused. She stood motionless, unaware of her surroundings. They released their grip and the sound of footsteps retreated away. The murmuring of voices came to a halt. Seemingly alone in an unknown space, Guinevere felt vulnerable. She knew others must be watching her. Someone approached her. Without warning, Agravain tore the hood off her head. Bright light flooded her vision.

His earlier words echoed in her head. *The king is very excited to see you.* Squinting, she looked around. Guinevere assumed that she was in the atrium resting at the heart of Camelot, otherwise known as the Courtyard Square. She felt the eyes of Rangers surrounding her throughout the complex. There were tens—no, hundreds. It was more than she could count.

Ahead of her, to the north and west, Rangers lined the banisters of the various structures of the castle. To the south was the Great Hall. It was made of granite and stood proudly, a structure worthy of feasts and high celebrations. Gorlois didn't deserve its splendor, especially for his traitorous coronation. To the east was the Royal Palace. The side facing the atrium had two prominent balconies with a stairway leading down into the yard. These, however, were empty as they were reserved for the king and neither Gorlois nor Uther were present.

Hearing a door clang open, Guinevere faced forward. A man appeared through the gap, hidden in the shadows of the castle. The few people still talking stopped instantly in his presence. Guinevere looked him over as he stepped out into the light. He swaggered with authority and a touch of arrogance. Her eyes were drawn to his hands, which were clasped together and displaying his jewels. Numerous rings, many with large stones and others with intricate metalwork, adorned his fingers. They made Hueil's look plain and slight in number. As Gorlois moved, she could tell that his arms were covered in various tattoos. He wore a suit with a jacket fabricated out of red velvet. His eyes were covered with rose-colored glasses. He caught her gaze and smiled, displaying his perfectly white teeth with several gold replacements.

It was Gorlois, she realized, the man who usurped the throne. The Rangers parted before him, making way as he approached. She saw him give a slight nod to Agravain before stopping in front of her.

"I've waited a long time to meet you," he addressed Guinevere with a voice that was sweet and smooth. Gorlois reached down, lifted her shackled hands, and motioned to Agravain coarsely.

"There is no need for these." His voice dripped with venom. There was a murmur that grew from the crowd. Guinevere could hear scatterings of laughter at the man who had displeased the king. Agravain hurried over to her side and roughly grabbed her wrists. He produced a key from his pocket, releasing her hands. She had half the nerve to punch him but was preoccupied with fear. With a curt nod, Agravain was dismissed.

"Guinevere," Gorlois continued. The tone of his voice had changed again. It had an odd, siren-like ring to it. The king began pacing around her, tapping his fingers together. He stopped and looked at her, but she kept a blank expression.

"Thank you for joining us," he said with a grin. While smiling, he looked like a completely different person. Rather than humanize his persona, it made him all the more frightening. "And you *will* join us, if you know what is best."

"Maybe you should reconsider this whole kidnapping routine. It's a great way to build trust," she snapped. Guinevere was unable to keep her cool, her fear replaced with anger.

"Ah, yes, I must apologize for the behavior of the Rangers. It seems they got a little carried away—" he glared at Agravain icily "—but please know that you are valued, and we will make things worth your time." Gorlois smiled.

"I will never join you or give you Excalibur." Guinevere kept her voice steady as she spoke. Underneath, she quivered, her emotions oscillating between panic and fury.

"You haven't even heard what I can offer you: riches, power—nearly anything you could want."

Guinevere simply shook her head.

Gorlois pursed his lips. "Your loss." He paused. "You'll help me whether you cooperate or not."

That's going to be hard without Excalibur, she thought.

"Arthur," Gorlois boomed. His voice echoed off the hard walls of the castle. "I am certain that you are listening right now. Best of luck trying to rescue your lover. Hand over Excalibur and I'll spare her life." Gorlois looked back down at Guinevere. He smiled giddily, and it made her want to scream.

Instead, she looked down at her feet. "Arthur is dead. Your band of idiots killed him," she muttered.

Gorlois laughed. "Yet you refused to join me?" He looked crazed, eyeing his followers to mock her in kind. When the raucousness died down, he settled his voice, inciting Guinevere to meet his gaze. "He's not dead." He pondered a moment. "Well, not yet."

She did not believe him. She couldn't. She refused.

"Huh," he responded with surprise after seeing no change in her expression. "I thought you would be a little more excited. Your lover is not dead." He turned away from her.

"And he still has Excalibur." Gorlois growled at his Rangers. They stepped back slightly, fearful of their leader.

222

Without warning, he turned back and punched Guinevere across the face.

"I hope I have your attention now," Gorlois shouted to the wind like a mad man. He grabbed Guinevere from under her chin and lifted her off the ground. Her airways tightened as she struggled to breathe.

"Come save your plaything, lover boy." He dropped Guinevere. She fell to the ground hard, gasping for air. She coughed for a moment before regaining her composure and pushing herself off the floor.

"You aren't the true king of Avalon," Guinevere sneered under her breath, blood collecting on her bottom lip. She spit into the grass of the courtyard.

Gorlois laughed in reply. She felt her face grow red as anger swelled up inside her.

"You will never wield Excalibur," Guinevere exclaimed, loud enough for all to hear. She tried to keep her voice even, but it wavered with the beat of her adrenaline spiked blood. "You've failed."

"What's that?" the king asked, walking close to her. He was right in her face. His voice dropped with hatred, "Please say it again."

"You failed," Guinevere said slowly but confidently, a fist colliding with her cheek at the moment of her utterance. She could taste the blood in her mouth: old wounds were reopened, and new ones were created. She had expected the punch, but the timing shocked her.

Each punch came before she could brace for the next. Guinevere could feel his rings cutting into her face. She moved her arms up to block, but he swatted them away. She reeled back in pain, knocked to the ground by a final blow. She lay there, gasping for air, eyes closed in agony. She could hear the king circling by the sound of his footsteps. She wiped the blood that was dripping down her face and into her eyes. She pushed herself up to flee, but Gorlois kicked her down in one swift motion, leaving his foot planted solidly on her chest. The sudden pressure caused her to cry out a nearly inaudible gasp. She struggled to get out from under his foot, but he was too strong.

"We have not failed," his voice boomed. Guinevere tried to speak, but her voice came out wheezing.

"What did you say?" Gorlois stepped off of her.

"Where is…is…Excalibur?" She struggled back up onto her feet. Gorlois started laughing maniacally.

"Don't worry yourself about that." He pivoted as the courtyard gate opened. "There is someone here dying to meet you." The king stepped to the side, the door behind him ushering forth a familiar silhouette. Guinevere tried to make out the figure. The man approached Gorlois before stopping in front of her.

"Mordred?" she asked, keeping her voice quiet and even.

"Guinevere," he replied, emotionless and empty. She wanted to shout at the man but chose to remain silent. Mordred stood at her side, facing Gorlois.

"I figured there was no use wasting any more time…" Gorlois announced and began to monologue.

"What are you doing here?" Guinevere whispered to Mordred as Gorlois continued boasting.

"I betrayed you. Isn't that obvious?" He did not turn to face her.

"Why?" she asked, unsatisfied

"My allegiance is with Gorlois." His eyes were unblinking as he responded mechanically.

"What?" she shouted incredulously. She clasped a hand over her mouth, realizing everyone had heard. The king had stopped his speech and turned to look at her. She glanced around nervously and tried to attract Mordred's gaze.

"Surprised?" Gorlois asked her, both angry but curious. "I figured you would be. Don't worry, your 'friend' didn't really have a choice in the matter, but you can still consider him a traitor."

Guinevere looked over at Mordred.

"Noble, isn't it? To save your own skin at the expense of a few friends." Gorlois's words reeked of sarcasm. Guinevere was heartbroken. She didn't want to believe the worst about Mordred. She had seen his loyalty to his missions and even more so to Arthur. He had even started to care about her in his own quirky way. *Was it all just a façade?* she wondered. *Or was he playing Gorlois?* She feared she would never know. Someone she had once trusted betrayed her, and there may not be time to forgive.

The doors clambered open again. Two Rangers were holding a man up by his arms.

"Ah. Now here is the star of the show." Gorlois sneered. "I think you'll be even more excited to see this one."

The figure was not quite lifeless but devoid of all physical strength. As he was moved into the light, he looked up and his eyes met Guinevere's.

It was the former ruler of Avalon. King Uther.

He hung his head in shame as he passed Guinevere. "I have failed you," Uther cried out to her, but the words rang out to all of Avalon. The two Rangers let go of him. His legs violently shook beneath him, but he remained upright. Guinevere ran to his side in support. Agravain reached out to stop her but, with a look from Gorlois, let her go.

"This is your leader, a weak old fool," Gorlois told her. "A man without courage or conviction who begged—begged, I tell you—for his life to be spared. And did I listen?" He beckoned for the crowd to cheer. "For now," he conceded.

"I have failed my people," Uther spoke to Guinevere softly and ignored the hundreds of people around him. She looked into his eyes. They were filled with sadness and regret.

"A confession." Gorlois purred in mock sympathy. "How fitting for the last words of a fallen king." He spat in Uther's face. "You disgust me."

Uther held his head low, no longer having the will to fight.

Gorlois turned around to face Mordred and pulled Guinevere out of the way. "You can shoot him now."

"No!" Guinevere cried and ran back toward Uther. Agravain reached out to stop her, but she slipped away. She placed her life before his to protect him. "Don't shoot," she pleaded to Mordred, who deliberately avoided her gaze.

"It's okay," Uther spoke out to her. "I have accepted my fate. Now go make yours."

Agravain caught up to Guinevere and wrestled her away. She fought back but was shoved to the ground.

"Now," she heard Gorlois command. Looking up, Guinevere saw Uther lifted into the air by Mordred's metal arm. His hand closing around the man's neck. Uther gave a small cry of pain before Mordred released him, crumpling into a lifeless pile.

"You cannot deny my power now." Without saying more, Gorlois pulled out his gun, aimed, and fired. The bullet landed between Mordred's eyes. His face was as expressionless as before.

"No!" She ran to his side. She fell to her knees and flipped Mordred's body over. He was gone. Blood was freely flowing from his head wound. Guinevere collapsed on him, her head lying on his chest, her tears soaking his shirt. She didn't want to move. She couldn't believe that he was dead—that Mordred had so callously betrayed her. He had become her friend. *If he could turn, was there anyone she could trust?*

A hand grabbed Guinevere's shoulder, but she didn't care to look. It was Agravain again. He pulled her off and away from Mordred's body.

"I don't trust someone who's this ambitious," Gorlois started talking again. He walked up to Mordred's corpse and kicked it probingly. He shot him a few more times for good measure. Reaching down, Gorlois yanked off his metal arm. He raised it, holding it out for the crowd. He stood there, content and surveying his subjects, before casting his gaze toward Guinevere.

"This will be nice for parts." He tossed the arm to Agravain, who caught it and placed it under his arm. Gorlois menaced toward Guinevere. "Be grateful we need you alive."

* * *

Guinevere awoke to a cold sweat. She gasped, clutching her chest, and strained to catch her breath. She wiped a lock of hair away from her face as she tried to come to terms with reality. She threw the blanket that had been covering her onto the ground. Her eyes slowly adjusted to the darkness. Sluggishly, she sat up and swung her feet onto the floor. Her whole body felt sore. Bringing a hand up to her face, she noticed the tenderness of her cheek. She felt several places where cuts and scrapes were scabbing. She stood up. Her head throbbed and her muscles screamed in protest. *I'll manage*, she told herself. *I must.*

Guinevere walked around the small room. It was empty save for the bed but even that wasn't much to look at. It was barely more than a metal frame and didn't even have a pillow. She picked up the blanket from the floor, realizing now that it was merely a thick sheet. *Where am I?* she wondered to herself. She tried to recall the events following Mordred's death, but thinking made her head hurt.

She looked down at her clothes. They were the same as the day before, unchanged since the final journey to Lake Diana. Her dress was covered in dried blood. *I will not cry,* she told herself. *I need to stay level-headed if I am going to survive.*

Where am I? She returned to her query. Her memory of previous day did not return and pondering that proved futile. From the construction and furnishings, Guinevere deduced that she must be in a cell at Camelot.

She sat back down on the cot. Her stomach growled, and she noted her hunger. *How long have I been asleep?* Her perception of time was gone. What she thought had been hours or at most a night, could have been much longer. Her thoughts drifted once more.

The door to her cell opened and light flooded the tiny room. Guinevere shielded her eyes. "Come with me," she heard a voice command. *Agravain.* She balked. *I am sure that he is aching to kill me, though his life would be dispatched if he acted out his desire.* Despite the torture and abuse, her life was assured by Gorlois.

Her captor was not alone; five other Rangers were with him. She got up and followed, too tired to protest. Two walked in front, two behind, and one on each side. It was almost as if she were an important dignitary worth protecting, but her experience proved otherwise.

They led her silently back to the atrium, their footsteps echoing throughout the open space. It was empty, unlike the time before. There was no crowd or theatrics—no Rangers leaning over upper deck balusters. Her escort crossed the grass to the center of the courtyard. There, the six Rangers quickly disappeared. She was confused, not quite sure where they had gone or what would happen next.

She looked around nervously, expecting something to appear. Nothing. A few minutes passed: still nothing. She was all alone. Both irritated and empowered by the absence of supervision, Guinevere wandered around the atrium. She tried several doors.

Locked. The main gates and Great Hall—all locked. It was as if the whole courtyard had been transformed into a prison. Bored, she sat on the ground and waited.

Several hours passed and she still waited. The sun rose over the sky and retreated back down. It kept her warm in the crisp autumn air. The birds and wildlife held their breath. *I must be the bait in a sinister trap,* she thought, suddenly self-aware, *but Arthur is already dead. No one is coming for me.* She felt her eyes water and tears drip down her cheek. They stung when they entered her wounds. She lay down in the grass and stared up at the sky, overtaken by melancholy and fear.

"Looks like your time is running out," Gorlois said, startling her. He, Agravain, and several other Rangers made their way into the atrium. Agravain roughly pulled her up and dragged her before the king. Gorlois grabbed her arm and twisted it behind her back, parading her around.

"Arthur," Gorlois sing-songed to the air. "I'm giving you one last chance." Guinevere felt the barrel of a gun shove against the base of her skull. "Show yourself, and save your beloved, or—" She heard the hammer of the gun click. "We kill her."

"Let her go." A demand echoed from the upper levels of the Palace. All eyes turned to look as a brusque silhouette appeared. Guinevere felt the cold point of the gun lower from her head. Slowly, the figure moved into the light.

"Look who decided to show up." Gorlois laughed.

There on the balcony of the palace, Arthur stood, brandishing a pistol. Guinevere's heart skipped a beat, still not believing her eyes. She had been convinced he was dead—that she was all alone—but he stood in the flesh, the proof of his life bearing witness before hers.

Several Rangers made a move to the palatial stairs. "Stay back!" Arthur ordered, and they kept their distance.

Gorlois let go of Guinevere's arm and a Ranger restrained her. He walked toward Arthur, who had stopped halfway down the staircase.

"The hero has arrived," Gorlois announced, spreading his bejeweled hands. "You think threatening my Rangers will aid your cause?" He gestured toward her. "Do I appear to care about their wellbeing?" To emphasize his point, he turned and shot the man restraining Guinevere. She shook as his blood splattered over her person, involuntarily clutching his corpse as he fell. She gently released him, and he lay in a heap. Her heart raced, disturbed by the act.

"Let her go," Arthur demanded once more with a hint of anger in his voice. He pointed his weapon at Gorlois, and his finger hovered over the trigger.

A few seconds passed as Gorlois reflected a cold gaze at the traitor. He opened his mouth to speak, but a deafening screech erupted from the sky. He ducked by reflex as a pterodactyl swooped in. A masked rider, mounted on the majestic beast, released several volleys out of their twin handguns. A few rangers were caught off guard, crumpling as the bullets met their mark. Agravain managed to dive out of the way, but a shot still pierced his shoulder. Startled, Guinevere hesitated at first before bolting for the palace stairs.

Gorlois moved to intervene, but a second pterodactyl swooped in. It collided with his body, knocking him back, and allowed Guinevere to escape. Arthur held out his arms to receive her as she rushed up the steps, his presence forgotten in the midst of the aerial assault. She threw herself into his arms, and he spun her around in a moment of joy.

"Come," Arthur said, setting her back on her feet, and the pair started to run. They passed through the maze-like palace before emerging on the roof. Guinevere looked at Arthur confused, as there was seemingly nowhere for them to go, but he confidently placed his fingers in his mouth and let out a shrill whistle. A lone dinosaur responded to the call. It swooped down from the sky and landed before her. Arthur helped her up into its mount. No sooner than she had climbed the great beast, Rangers appeared from where Arthur and Guinevere had come.

"Go!" Arthur shouted, handing her a weapon.

The pterodactyl took off in flight. Guinevere reached back for him to no avail. She didn't want to leave his side, especially not now. *Did we meet just so I could lose him again?* She watched below as Arthur engaged the Rangers. He shrewdly fended them off and disappeared into the palace. She sighed. *Maybe he'll be all right.*

The pterodactyl shuddered, nearly throwing Guinevere off. A hole had been punched through the wing of the beast. She looked around but did not see who fired the shot. The animal, clearly injured, slowly sunk to the ground where it roughly landed in the palace garden. Guinevere slid down off the back of the creature and brushed herself off. The animal, now free of its rider, took off tenuously into the air. It disappeared from view, leaving her behind.

You're okay, Guinevere thought and looked around. The garden appeared to be fairly remote, and for now there was no one around. Tall vining plants grew up the stone walls, and various flowers bloomed. Not sure where she was or where to run, she decided to stay in place. She found a small bench against the wall and sat down, breathing in the fresh air.

Guinevere examined the weapon that Arthur had given. She balanced it in her palm, feeling its weight. She readied it, aiming at the far garden wall. Satisfied, she dropped it to her side. She took a long, deep breath, feeling her heartrate subside. She was much more comfortable with a bow and arrow, but this would do.

A figure appeared out of the corner of her vision, and she quickly pointed her weapon. They raised their hands and called out her name.

"Guinevere?" a voice asked, soothingly. Feeling somewhat disarmed, she lowered the pistol. She nodded to the stranger. Their head was covered with a loosely draped hood and their face was covered by a tight-fitting cowl. They were wearing a brown leather jacket that was buttoned up to the neck, dark jeans, and calf-high boots. Around their waist was a leather belt, to which a dagger was attached.

"Come with me." The figure motioned for her to follow.

Guinevere strangely found herself trusting them and got up from the bench. At the very least, they weren't a Ranger.

Together, they snuck through the castle grounds, winding their way down the halls. At one point, they were nearly captured. But at the end of their journey, they reached the cliffs just outside the castle wall. A pterodactyl rose quickly from the water below and kicked up a cloud of dust. It perched not more than ten yards away on a rocky ledge protruding from the cliff. Above, she heard the shouts of several Rangers. They had been spotted.

"Get on!" the figure shouted as the pair ran to the creature. Several arrows flew through the air, hitting the ground behind them. The stranger hopped on the dinosaur first before reaching back with a gloved hand. Guinevere grabbed it and was swung onto the back of the beast.

"Hold on," the rider commanded. Guinevere wrapped her hands around the rider's waist as the pterodactyl dove off the cliff.

Chapter Twenty

Guinevere felt the cool mist of the sea as the waves crashed beneath them. She looked out over the landscape as the pterodactyl raced just above the water. Camelot grew smaller in the distance, the rocky edges of its sea wall rising abruptly from the ocean. The dinosaur pulled up away from the water, climbing quickly in the sky. From this new vantage point, she could see much more of Avalon Realms. To her right, the bay shimmered in the daylight, and across it, jagged mountains were littered with vegetation. Once they had crossed the north channel, redwood trees welcomed them to the Avalon wilderness. Here, clusters of triceratops and stegosauruses roamed freely. There were no buildings save for the fading remnants of the Royal Conservatory, its glass dome glistening in the distance. Some time passed as they crossed the forest, landing to its north side in a clearing. The massive redwood trees nearly blocked out the sky, standing mightily over the grasslands.

Guinevere and the rider dismounted the dinosaur. The pterodactyl took off into flight and let out a call. The rider slid their hood back and shook out straight, chin length black hair.

"I'm Merlin," she said, taking off her gloves and extending a hand.

"Guinevere." She shook the mysterious stranger's hand.

"I know," Merlin said. "We've been trying to find you since your wanted poster was published."

"We?" Guinevere asked, surprised.

"You'll meet everyone else when we arrive at camp." With a small motion of her head, Merlin's eyes directed Guinevere's attention to a trail entering the forest. "That's where Arthur is."

"Alright," Guinevere acknowledged. "Lead the way."

They walked for a while in the dense forest with Merlin taking up the lead. Guinevere's gaze kept drifting to the tree canopy above, marveling at the height of the redwoods. Pterodactyls flew far overhead, sometimes landing in the tops of the trees. She walked quietly for a time and took in the scenery along the dirt trail.

"Who are you?" Guinevere asked, breaking the silence.

"I'm a believer in Excalibur," Merlin answered without turning around and continued forward at a rapid pace.

Her response did not satisfy Guinevere. While exhausted both mentally and physically from the day's toll, her curiosity was restless. *Who is this dinosaur whisperer?* she thought, struggling to keep pace with Merlin.

"Why did you rescue me?" Guinevere asked between hurried breaths.

"As I said before, I am a believer in Excalibur. I'll explain more when we get to camp," Merlin said, once again keeping her answer unsatisfyingly vague.

"Why didn't you have the pterodactyl land closer to camp?" Guinevere rushed to keep up with Merlin. She had fallen behind and struggled to catch her breath.

"They don't like to fly through the dense forest and prefer to land in the open field. Since they are gracious enough to provide us with a ride, I like to honor their wishes." Merlin slowed down her pace.

"How do you know that?"

"I used to work at the conservatory before it was shut down," she explained. "Ever since I was young, I've always had a way with animals, particularly the dinosaurs. We have a special connection, them and I."

After a pause, Merlin continued, "It won't be much further to walk, just about a mile or so."

The two women hiked in silence again. Guinevere let herself get lost in the sounds of the forest: the wind broken by the wings of pteranodons, their frequent calls to one another, the crunch of the ground beneath her feet. Before she knew it, they were approaching a cabin. Merlin walked up to the door and opened it.

"Come on in," she said, motioning to Guinevere. She stepped inside and Merlin locked the door.

"Guinevere!" Arthur exclaimed with joy. He jumped up from where he was seated and ran to her. His arms grasped her in a warm hug. She could feel his emotions seeping through his chest.

Arthur leaned back, pulling away slightly to get a better look at Guinevere. He gently pressed a hand against her face and brushed the tip of his finger along one of her many scratches. His eyes processed the wounds that afflicted her. Somewhat startled by his sensitive touch, Guinevere froze until the moment passed. When he let go, he returned to his seat.

She looked around the room for the first time. The air smelled like musty furniture and cigarettes. On the east side, opposite the door, was a ratty tan sofa that Arthur and another guy were sitting on. Excalibur lay between them. Its hilt reflected the lamp light of the two fixtures on either side of the sofa and scattered an abundance of tiny rainbows onto the walls.

In the southeast corner of the room was a large leather chair that was occupied. Its brown surface cracked along the folds of the aged material; it had clearly seen better days. On the floor, a long and shaggy faux fur rug was hiding some of the worn wood floors. It was stained with what Guinevere assumed was wine, although it could have been blood—she could never be so sure these days. On the rug, a short wooden table was placed in front of the sofa. It was missing a leg that had been replaced with a stack of books, their dusty odor mixing with the various other smells of the room.

On the north side was a narrow kitchen with a small dining area, table, and chairs. It was separated from the living space by an open hallway, which connected the front door to a few unseen rooms beyond the east wall. None of the wooden chairs from the table matched. They were scratched and worn but still in one piece. Someone had moved them to the west wall of the space where they sat opposite the couch and continued the circle of seats. Three of the four were occupied.

"Why don't I get you some fresh clothes, and then I'll introduce you to everyone," Merlin said, walking down the hallway. Guinevere was relieved at the thought of wearing something clean. She eagerly followed Merlin through the first door off the hall.

Merlin handed her a khaki-colored dress and an oversized black, knitted cardigan before leaving the room. Guinevere slipped out of her soiled outfit, stained with blood and dirt, and placed them into a neat pile alongside her socks and boots. *Cold,* she thought as she hurriedly changed into the fresh clothes. It wasn't until the sweater was pulled loosely over her arms that she started to feel warm again. Guinevere headed back to the main room, looking for Merlin.

She found her in the kitchen and watched as Merlin pulled various things out of the cupboards. First, she brought down a wooden box and opened it up. Inside were a variety of small amber bottles, one of which she took out and placed on the counter. She returned the box to its shelf. Then, Merlin pulled out a rack of fresh herbs, picking off several different kinds of leaves. Next, she exchanged the rack for a mortar and pestle, made out of white granite. Merlin placed the leaves into the bowl and added several drops of oils from the amber bottle. With the pestle, she ground the ingredients into a fine paste. Finally, she added a little bit of water, stirring the concoction until it was an even consistency.

"Here." She handed Guinevere the mortar full of the green, sludgy liquid.

"What is this?" Guinevere asked her. She looked down at the bowl.

"Drink. It'll help your bruises and wounds heal."

"What is it made of?" Timidly, she held the bowl up to her lips. She started downing the strange substance, choosing to trust the stranger's guidance.

"Roman chamomile, peppermint leaves, and bit of frankincense oil," Merlin explained.

Guinevere finished the elixir, handing the mortar back over to Merlin.

"She's a wizard," the man sharing the sofa with Arthur shouted into the kitchen.

"I'm not a wizard," Merlin said, laughing. "When I worked at the conservatory, I was an apothecarist. I often made elixirs for the dinosaurs." Guinevere smiled slightly, happy to meet someone who talked about their job just as much as her. "Come on, I'll introduce everyone to you."

Merlin exited the kitchen and stood at the edge of the living room. Guinevere followed her, feeling the tuffs of the rug between her toes.

"Gwen, this is Lancelot," Merlin said, motioning to the man on the sofa. His blonde hair was buzzed short. A simple linen button-up shirt was partially undone and hung over his muscular torso. Lancelot held his hand up in a slight wave.

"Arthur," Guinevere said, interrupting the introductions. She turned to face him as he relaxed against the back of the sofa. He looked so comfortable, as if he had lived in the cabin all his life. "Do you know these people?"

"Somewhat." He shrugged. "Merlin read my fortune back in Pictland, Lancelot helped me escape the Rangers at Lake Diana, and everyone else pitched in with your escape." He replied as if it were all old news. She looked around and everyone nodded in agreement.

"Huh," Guinevere muttered, "seems I've missed out on a lot."

After a pause, Merlin continued the introductions. "Gawain." Merlin pointed to the younger man on the leather chair.

"Here," he said, getting up from his chair, "please take this seat, my queen." He gave her a slight bow before breaking his respectful tone and cracking a smile.

"Are you two a thing?" He motioned between Guinevere and Arthur and looked toward him for confirmation. Arthur's face turned red as he averted his eyes. "Well, anyhow, I want to let you know that I'm single and open to anything." He winked at Guinevere.

"I'll keep that in mind," she said, walking across the rug to sit in the leather chair.

"Do you want anything?" Gawain asked, attending her. "Tea? Beer? Whiskey? Anything to eat? Maybe just water? Or some ice for your face? Not that there's anything wrong with your face." The words spilled out of his mouth. "You know what," he said pausing. "I'll just make some tea and grab more beers for everyone." He turned around to head into the kitchen. Arthur shifted in his chair and rested his fist in from of his mouth, hiding a laugh.

"Ice would be nice," Guinevere called. Gawain put a pot of water on the cast iron stove. Then, he reached into the ice box, got some out, wrapped it in a towel, and passed it across to her. She put the bundle against her bruised face. While the rest of the group continued to introduce themselves, he grabbed half a dozen beers and brought them back to the living room.

241

"I'm Percival," the man to her left said. He got up from one of the wooden chairs to grab a beer from Gawain.

"That's Lionel," Mordred continued. Guinevere nodded toward the woman sitting crossed legged. She was wearing a tan-colored tunic with blank leggings. Around her waist was a brown leather corset. Her auburn hair was pulled back with three braids interwoven on each side of her head. Several small curls had freed themselves.

"Call me Lion," she said.

"And Galahad," Merlin finished. She motioned toward the final occupant seated next to the door. His dark black hair was buzzed back in a crew cut.

Merlin took the last open chair between him and Lion. Gawain waited by the stove impatiently, watching the kettle as if to make it boil faster.

"Be another couple minutes on the tea," he announced to the room neurotically.

"Don't mind him," Lion told Guinevere. "He's just a big flirt."

"I heard that," Gawain called back from the kitchen. "You know I'm right here."

"Telling it like it is," she scolded him. Lion leaned back in her chair and took a swig of her beer.

"Who are you guys anyway?" Guinevere asked. She removed the ice from her face. She looked over at Arthur, perplexed. His left hand was resting slightly on the hilt of Excalibur and in his right hand he was casually holding a beer.

"Lancelot, you want to explain to the poor lady?" Gawain asked, bringing Guinevere a hot mug of herbal tea. He took a seat on the floor between Percival and Lion. His feet were flat on the floor, his knees bent.

Lancelot nodded. "We call ourselves the 'Knights'. We met long before all of this started. Most of us, everyone except Merlin really, were Rangers before Gorlois took the throne. At that point, we defected and banded together, vowing to serve the one and future ruler of Avalon—the one appointed to wield Excalibur." He looked at Guinevere with admiration.

"Hold on." She put her hands up. "Do you all think that I am the queen?" She glanced around the room, looking at every knight's face as they nodded one by one.

"No, no, no…" Guinevere shook her head. "Excalibur isn't mine. The Lady of the Lake gave me the sword to appoint the true ruler." The room fell into silence.

Lancelot spoke up, "We would all follow you, should you reconsider."

Arthur turned to face Guinevere. She felt vulnerable sitting in the oversized leather chair. She clutched the mug of tea that Gawain had brought her, hands wrapping around and soaking in its warmth. Her face was battered and bruised: a black impression formed around her left eye and a large cut sliced through her upper lip, caked with dried blood. None of that seemed to register to Arthur. Guinevere sensed him peering into her eyes, looking at her soul behind all the blood and bruises.

He picked up the sword from the couch, walked over to Guinevere, and gently set it in her lap. "I would follow you, my queen," Arthur said before returning to his seat.

Guinevere looked at Excalibur; it was heavy in a way that matched the current mood. She turned her gaze up. Arthur and the knights were all looking at her expectantly, all waiting for her next words.

"I don't know why she entrusted me," Guinevere told them. "I don't know—" She stopped, nervously taking a sip of her tea. She removed one of her hands from the mug to run it through her disheveled hair, brushing loose strands away from her face.

At that moment, she realized what she needed to do. She set her mug of tea down on the coffee table and stood up, grasping Excalibur.

"Arthur—" she turned to look directly at him "—you are meant to be king." The decision felt right the minute she said it, immediately lifting the cloud of indecision she had felt since this journey began.

He opened his mouth to object, but she cut him off before he could speak. "No, you are king. I was entrusted with Excalibur to choose the next ruler. That ruler is not me. It is you—it has to be."

"I'll drink to that," Percival said, raising his drink to the center of the room.

"Here, here," Galahad agreed. The group raised their drinks to Arthur.

"Everyone," Arthur said, stopping the cheers, "I'm no different than any of you. Actually, probably less qualified to be king." He leaned back, resting in the corner of the sofa refusing to rise and take Excalibur.

"That is what makes you the perfect king," Gawain said, looking at Arthur. "You aren't after power and will turn to those around you for support. Plus, she is choosing you, so we know you are meant to be king."

Arthur turned back to Guinevere, who stood before him. "I dropped out of the Rangers because that life wasn't for me. How is ruling a kingdom going to be any different?" he told her.

"That doesn't matter," she assured him. "You are meant to be king." She motioned for him to get off the couch. Reluctantly, he stood. Quickly, the knights got to their feet and cleared the room, moving the coffee table into the kitchen. Arthur stood in its place before Guinevere. The knights formed a line behind him.

"Kneel," she commanded Arthur. Even though the command was clear, her voice was not forceful.

"But Guinevere—" he started.

"Kneel," she interrupted, overriding his objection. He obeyed her this time. He got down on the carpet and looked up at her. She took a step toward Arthur, her bare feet on the rug.

"Arthur Pendragon," she said solemnly, "by the power bestowed upon Excalibur, I appoint you the true ruler of Camelot, the once and future king." She rested the sword first on his left, and then on his right shoulder. After a moment, she brought the sword down in front of her. "Rise, King Arthur," she commanded him. There was an air of admiration in her voice. Arthur rose to his feet.

"Take this sword," she said, kneeling before him, her arms outstretched, the blade balancing in her palms, "as a symbol of your power as king. Let it serve as a reminder that the power you command can also destroy when wielded without care." Looking stunned, Arthur grasped the hilt. Guinevere lowered her arms, letting the whole weight of the sword fall into Arthur's hands.

"Long live the king," she proclaimed.

"Long live the king," the knights echoed.

As they cheered, Arthur assisted Guinevere back up on her feet. She smiled at him and their eyes locked. They inhaled each other's ragged breaths, so close that there was barely space between them.

"Just kiss," Merlin said, breaking their trance. Guinevere let out a small laugh and Arthur's eyes shifted nervously.

A few moments passed that felt like an hour, her king unable to make the first move. Guinevere leaned in when Arthur could not: her arms crossed behind her back, her eyes closed to shut out the world, and her lips planted gently on his cheek. She lingered there, holding in the twinkling. A few knights whooped and cheered. She felt Arthur's face go flush with heat, and she pulled away. She gazed at him, feeling a bit self-conscious herself, then retreated quickly to her seat. She scooped up her tea and hid behind it, her heart in her throat. She watched as the rest of the knights wandered back to their respective chairs. Arthur alone remained standing.

Chapter Twenty-One

"I don't know if I can be king," Arthur admitted, reluctantly wielding Excalibur. He walked over to the sofa and sat down. "There are countless reasons why I shouldn't." His eyes looked at Guinevere anxiously.

"But there are even more reasons why you should be—why you are," she assured him, looking around the room. All the knights nodded in agreement.

"You will have the support of your friends and followers to aid you," Lancelot added.

"What friends?" Arthur asked. "No offense, but I just met you." He motioned around the room. "The one man that I trusted that I would call my friend, betrayed me. The man that I worked alongside for years—that I respected, and I looked up to—was willing to have me killed, and why? For his own reward? How can I be confident it won't happen again? That fate won't repeat?" Arthur spoke fervently, growing visibly more agitated with each passing word.

The room fell quiet. No one spoke or moved. His words hung in the air.

"You have me," Guinevere broke the silence. She spoke quietly, barely more than a whisper. Her mouth was hidden behind her mug, her hands grasping both sides tightly, her nose just visible above its rim. Arthur's eyes met Guinevere's, ignoring everyone else in the room.

"I thought when bad things happened, time slowed down. But to me, it felt fast. Too fast. Everything seemed to happen in a single moment: as I watched Mordred fall to the ground, as I waited for a sign of life, as I realized he would never get up again. Mordred betrayed me. He betrayed us, and now he's gone." Tears were welling up in his eyes. Guinevere did not know what she could say. There were no words that could fix what had happened.

"I'm sorry," she whispered inaudibly. She lowered her mug and looked down into the tea. Bits of leaves clung to the side; the liquid sloshed, revealing the bottom; the dark brown substance reflected her despair. She reached forward and set the mug down on the coffee table. Her eyes drifted to the floor and she pulled her legs up onto her seat. She couldn't face Arthur and no one else spoke.

"This is your fault," Arthur said accusingly. She looked up at him, shocked, and he stared back at her. He wiped his face, tears replaced with rage. There was no mistaking the anger in his voice. Guinevere was taken aback by his tone. She briefly broke her gaze and noticed Lancelot leaning forward. His elbows rested on his knees; he was barely seated on the sofa. He was just as unsettled by Arthur's outburst as she was. Guinevere looked back at Arthur. Daggers shot out of his eyes.

"I'm—I'm sorry?" Guinevere muttered. She didn't know what else she could say without making the situation worse.

"You're sorry?!" Arthur shouted, throwing himself onto his feet. He stood squarely, facing Guinevere. Instinctively, she swung her feet onto the ground, their bare bottoms pressed solidly into the floor. Her hands moved to the armrests ready to spring up and defend herself if it came to that. *This isn't Arthur,* she thought to herself.

He took a step forward toward Guinevere and prepared to speak. She prepared herself to stand. Before either could act, Lancelot rose and took position between the two of them. He looked at Arthur and rested his hands on Arthur's shoulders gently but firmly.

"Get your hands off of me!" Arthur ordered Lancelot violently, brushing his hands aside. Lancelot froze where he was, not expecting this response. Arthur glared at him. He turned around, grabbed Excalibur off the sofa, and stormed out of the cabin. He loosely held the sword in his left hand, dragging the tip on the ground. He unlocked the door and walked out onto the front steps, closing the door behind him with a resounding bang. The knights and Guinevere were left inside the cabin in silence. They all sat or, in Lancelot's case, stood where they were, unsure of what to do. Lancelot eventually sat back down.

More time passed, but Arthur did not return.

"Should someone go check on Arthur?" Lancelot asked, cutting the tension in the room. Everyone shifted in their chairs and seemed to breathe unsteadily.

"I'll go," Merlin said, standing up and heading for the door.

"No," Guinevere responded, her voice commanding. Merlin froze where she was, stopping mid stride. Guinevere pushed herself up. Everyone looked at her. "I will go talk to Arthur. He is right. It is my fault that he's mixed up with Excalibur. If I had not met him, his life would have continued blissfully unencumbered from mine. Mordred might not be dead." She walked past the rest of the knights, past Merlin, and out of the cabin. She closed the door softly behind her.

The sun sat low in the sky. The light danced between the trees, casting the forest in an assortment of reds, oranges, and yellows. The shadows were long, and the air sat still, almost motionless. Guinevere walked down the stairs, their cold, wooden surface pressing against her heels. She stopped when she reached the forest floor, the dried leaves feeling prickly between her toes. She looked out and couldn't see Arthur. Hearing noises to the side of the cabin, Guinevere headed that way. She turned around the corner and nearly collided with the tip of Excalibur, the blade hovering in front of her eyes.

"Who goes there?" Arthur demanded. Both hands grasped the hilt of the sword firmly but trembled slightly.

"It's me. It's Guinevere." She held her hands up in the air, black cardigan hanging off her arms and down past her tunic dress. Her bare legs were exposed to the crisp autumn air.

"What are you doing out here?" he snapped at her. He threw Excalibur to the side. It collided with the forest floor, scattering leaves into the air. They gently floated down to the ground near the sword, which reflected the vibrant reds and yellows of the evening light.

"I came out here to apologize." Guinevere curled her toes into the dirt floor. She did not walk closer to Arthur. Her hands had lowered when he threw the sword. Now she moved them inside the oversized sweater for warmth. Arthur stopped moving to look at her.

"You're right," she said. Her voice was soft as she spoke. "You're right. It is my fault."

Arthur looked surprised by this confession. The anger vacated his expression, but fear replaced it. She could only imagine the anguish he felt at the loss of his friend.

"I'm sorry that you got wrapped up in all of this. I will take up Excalibur so that you don't have to. You can leave now. Leave all of this behind you and go back to your old life."

"No," Arthur said, expressing a brief moment of melancholy. "This is my fight. No matter where I go it will follow me." He reached down to pick Excalibur off the ground. He held it firmly in his hands. "There is no old life for me to go back to. My future, and the future of Avalon, is forward."

Guinevere nodded.

"I'm sorry that I got you hurt," she said, "but you are meant to be king of Avalon. It is one of the only things I've ever been certain of!" Her voice raised slightly, and she looked longingly at Arthur. Ever since Lake Diana, he had seemed like a different man. He was no longer a smuggler and bounty hunter; he was the once and future king. He was the leader to unite Avalon—to bring it to a golden age. Yet despite all this, he had remained the same somewhat aloof but playful boy from their fateful encounter.

"I hope I can be the kind of king you've imagined." Arthur smiled again for the first time; his face still downtrodden but calmed.

Guinevere thought for a minute before answering him. "When I stole the map, I was looking for someone who was: honorable," *you have always looked out for me and others;* "honest," *how many times have you told me the truth no matter how vulnerable it made you?* "and compassionate." *You cared for me from the first day I arrived on your ship—not just because you were falling in love and hoping I would grow to feel the same.*

"You are all of these things and more," she told him truthfully.

Arthur looked at her. He had gazed at her countless times before, but something about this was different. She was beautiful, but not like anyone he had ever seen—not like he had ever seen her before. Something had grown more intense in her demeanor and in his feelings.

Arthur looked into her eyes, eyes that were not honey or golden but dark pools of ink that devoured light in their intensity. They were like billowing clouds of volcanic ash, burying obsidian and jet in their depth—so dark that celestial bodies must have resided in them. Her eyes captured the universe and pulled him in with extraordinary gravity.

Arthur regretted what he had said before. He had been angry: angry with Mordred for betraying them, angry at him for dying, and angry with Excalibur for making him king. To blame any of this on

Guinevere, the only person he could trust and the only friend he had left, would have been foolish. He collected his thoughts and steadied himself, knowing in his heart what must be done.

"As king, I am going to need someone by my side to keep me accountable. Someone who can assist me in leading in a just and noble way."

"Asking Lancelot to be your advisor is a good idea," Guinevere said and smiled.

"I had something else in mind," Arthur said.

"Maybe," Guinevere answered quickly before he had a chance to ask. She started walking away from him back to the cabin door.

"What do you mean 'maybe'?" he asked incredulously. His heart chased after her. "Are you not going to let me ask the question first?" Guinevere had stopped walking and turned back around to face him. She shrugged her shoulders as he caught up to her.

"I'm not sure that I deserve to be your queen."

"Of course you do." Arthur grabbed her hand with his, squeezing it gently. She looked down at their hands. Noticing the shift in her gaze, Arthur let go of her hand. Slowly, Guinevere looked up.

"I just—" she began then stopped. He searched her eyes, trying to discern her thoughts. *It was unfair of me to blame you,* he thought. *Please give us a chance...*

Guinevere restarted and said, "Avalon isn't safe yet. This fight isn't over. How can I think of anything else when we still have a battle that needs to be fought?"

"Guinevere," Arthur spoke her name huskily. "That is exactly why you deserve an equal claim to Excalibur's power. You put the people before yourself, even before me. I look up to you and would have followed you as queen had you chosen Excalibur for yourself." She opened her mouth to reply, but he spoke before she could continue. "You know how I feel about you. I've hardly tried to hide my feelings, and I know that you've felt the same. You think that I am good enough to be king. What more will it take for you to be sure of us?"

"I don't know," she admitted, looking away from him. They stood there for a moment in silence. Neither one of them wanted to be the first one to speak. They avoided making eye contact with each other, both casting their eyes downward. After a while, the silence got uncomfortable.

"Let's go back inside." Arthur looked at Guinevere. He had resigned himself to resolving this later. She shifted her gaze up toward him. "There are some people inside waiting for me to lead."

Guinevere nodded and Arthur headed back toward the cabin. When they had reached the door, he stopped and held it open.

"After you," he said to Guinevere. She walked into the cabin, and all of the knights stared at her. Arthur followed behind, grasping Excalibur firmly. He would give it the respect it deserved this time. The room fell silent when they entered.

Guinevere made her way back to her seat, and Arthur locked the door behind them. Taking a deep breath, he turned around and walked to the end of the living room, standing across from Guinevere at the coffee table. Arthur stood there for a moment, not speaking. He looked from Lancelot to Guinevere to Percival, Lionel, Gawain, Galahad, and to Merlin. All of their eyes were transfixed on him.

"Whether or not I asked to be anointed with Excalibur, I was given the responsibility as the true King of Avalon. It's time I start acting like one," Arthur told them. He stopped talking to look around the room again. Everyone was sitting, watching him and waiting for what he was going to say next. "And yes, I will need your support to rule Avalon. All of you," he said, looking directly at Guinevere. Arthur went and took his seat on the sofa. He rested Excalibur across his lap. He leaned against the back of the sofa, his muscles relaxing as a sense of calm washed over him. The mood in the room visibly lightened.

"The throne is a little occupied at the moment," Guinevere pointed out.

"That is why the knights have gathered, waiting, hiding, and searching until the bearer of Excalibur could be found," Merlin explained. "Now that you're here—" she looked at Guinevere "— and have anointed Arthur, we must prepare to take the throne."

"How?" Guinevere asked.

"Tomorrow night we storm the castle."

Chapter Twenty-Two

Guinevere sat back in the chair after hearing Merlin's plan. *A little suicidal at best*, she thought, *but it just might work.* She pulled up her feet onto the chair then popped her knees inside the sweater.

"Can someone pass me one of the beers?" she asked. "I think I need a drink." Lancelot grabbed one off the table, popped it open, and handed it to Guinevere. She took a large swig.

"Okay," she said after taking a breath. "I'm in. What do I have to lose? Arthur?" she asked and looked over at him expectantly. He was leaning forward, his elbows resting on his knees and his chin resting in his hands. He sat up straight.

"Everyone is willing to sacrifice their lives for me," Arthur said, humbled. "I hope that I can be the kind of king worthy of sacrifice, but we will never know if I don't get a chance to rule, right? So tomorrow we fight!"

The knights cheered.

"But tonight, we celebrate. Because if we don't make it through battle, at least we have tonight," he continued, "and I think we could all go for another round of drinks."

Arthur got up from his seat and walked into the kitchen, opened the ice box, and pulled out some more beers. He brought them back to the living room. He set the beers down on the coffee table and picked up Excalibur. Instead of sitting back down on the sofa, Arthur stood at the end of the coffee table, facing the rest of the room with resolve. He held Excalibur with both hands in front of his chest. The blade pointed down toward the ground.

"I was thinking: if you are going to call yourselves the knights, we might as well make things official." Arthur smiled slightly as he spoke, but his tone conveyed the seriousness of the moment. He looked around the room once more before continuing to speak. "Come here, Lancelot," he said.

Lancelot set his beer down and got up from the sofa. He stood in front of Arthur, between him and the coffee table. He looked at Arthur, who had stopped smiling.

"Kneel," Arthur commanded. Lancelot obeyed. He got down on both knees. "Do you now swear by all that you hold sacred, true, and holy that you will honor and defend the Crown and Kingdom of Avalon?" Arthur asked solemnly. He spoke the words with authority, loud enough for the entire room to hear.

"I will," Lancelot answered after a momentary pause. He looked up at Arthur as he spoke.

"That you will honor, defend, and protect all those weaker than yourself?"

"I will."

"That you will conduct yourself in all matters by drawing your sword only for just cause? That you will enshrine in your heart the noble ideals of chivalry to the benefit of your own good name and the greater glory of Avalon?"

"I will."

Arthur took Excalibur and held it out in front of himself and above Lancelot.

"Then, having sworn these solemn oaths, know now that I—Arthur Pendragon, by right of arms, King of Avalon—do dub you with the sword Excalibur, and by all that you hold sacred, true, and noble…" As Arthur spoke, he raised Excalibur and rested it on Lancelot's right shoulder.

"Once for honor…" Excalibur moved swiftly through the air to Lancelot's left.

"Twice for duty…" The sword arced back to the right.

"Thrice for chivalry…" Arthur grasped it with both hands again and pointed its blade into the ground.

"Arise, Sir Lancelot!"

Lancelot rose from his kneeling position and stood in front of the king. A smile crept across Arthur's face and Lancelot couldn't help but beam.

"Come here," Arthur said with his arms outstretched. He embraced Lancelot, slapping the man on the back. After they stopped, Arthur spoke again, "Go on, take your seat. I've got a few others to knight still." Lancelot returned to the sofa.

"Come here, Percival," Arthur motioned his timbre noticeably more jovial than before. Percival got up from his seat and crossed the room to where Lancelot had stood. Arthur repeated the knighting ceremony one by one.

"Arise, Sir Percival."

"Arise, Sir Lionel."

He greeted each knight with a warm embrace.

"Arise, Sir Galahad."

"Arise, Sir Gawain."

Excalibur moved swiftly and steadily through the air. It's appearance almost magical.

"Arise, Sir Merlin."

With the last of his comrades knighted, Arthur glanced over at Guinevere. She nodded at him knowingly. With her assent, he returned to his seat on the sofa. Excalibur rested across his lap where it continued to shimmer. He sat there silently for a moment, looking once again at all of the knights around the room. They were all looking back at him. He reached over to the coffee table and grabbed one of the beers, popping off the top and taking a long drink.

"Besides promoting anarchy, what do you all do for fun?" Guinevere asked.

"Drink. Smoke. Merlin talks to dinosaurs," Lion said.

"Gawain flirts with anything female," Merlin chimed in, "including the squirrels."

The room erupted in laughter.

"Not true," Gawain interjected. He turned to Guinevere. "Don't listen to them. I'm not a flirt. You are simply beautiful, and I can't help myself."

"Yeah she is," Arthur agreed, shining Guinevere the cheeky smile she had grown to adore. Guinevere looked back at him with a smirk and rolled her eyes.

"What's up with you two anyway? You thought you could avoid telling us?" Lancelot asked, motioning from Arthur to Guinevere.

"Yeah, aren't you going to knight her too?" Lion asked.

"I gave her a standing offer to be the Queen," Arthur explained. He smiled as he spoke and turned his attention toward Guinevere.

"Nothing has changed between us now that you are King. Putting me on the spot won't help your cause," Guinevere said, rebuking him.

"Aye-oh," Gawain hooted. "She got you good."

"I deserve that," Arthur replied, downing the rest of his beer. "I accidentally locked her in our holding cell when she and I first met. I don't think I'll ever live that one down."

"I did stow away on your airship," Guinevere conceded.

"You were the last thing I expected in our smuggler's keep. Much more pleasant than a compsognathus."

"Those little buggers will bite your arm off," Merlin added; she appeared to speak from experience.

"From that point on I had a crush on her. It turns out I care about a random girl who stowed away on my airship."

"Just sleep with him already," Lion blurted out, breaking the silence.

"He clearly loves and cares about you, which is more than can be said for Gawain's relationships," Galahad added.

"Hey," Gawain whined. "Why am I the butt of everyone's jokes?" The knights ignored him

"Yeah," Lion added, "Lancelot is sleeping with Merlin because she can talk to dinosaurs, and she is sleeping with him because, well, look at him."

Merlin shrugged. "What can I say? He's attractive."

"I don't want to sleep with you," Arthur said.

"Pfft. Liar." Lancelot smirked.

"I mean, I do…obviously." Arthur shook his head. "I want to have a real and meaningful relationship and continue learning about you. You're beautiful in every way imaginable and full of surprises," he gushed, "but you already know how I feel."

Guinevere held her drink up to her mouth and drank the remaining contents. "And here I thought that I'd be drinking to our upcoming victory. Not to take part in some sort of relationship intervention." She held up her empty beer bottle. "I think I'm going to need another drink."

"I'll get you one," Gawain said, jumping up from his seat and grabbing her empty bottle. He went into the kitchen, opened a cupboard, and pulled out a bottle of whiskey. He grabbed some shot glasses and brought them, and the whiskey, back to the living room. He poured a series of shots and handed one to Guinevere. She downed it.

"Thanks," she said to Gawain.

"If you and Arthur don't work out, I'm available," he told her, sitting back down.

"Ga-wain!" Lion shouted at him, shoving him slightly. "You're not helping."

"I'm just giving her options," he explained innocently.

261

"What about you, Lion? You seeing anyone?" Guinevere asked.

"Nope, but I don't really go out anymore. There aren't many choices here." She motioned around the room.

"What's wrong with me?" Gawain asked, slightly hurt.

"You know that I'm not into guys," she reminded him.

"What's wrong with Guinevere?" he asked her. "Never mind. Don't flirt with her. I have enough competition with Arthur," he stammered.

"Well I want her and Arthur to be together anyway," Lion replied. "I think she would be a better queen than Avalon deserves." Lion looked around Gawain to talk directly to Guinevere. "No matter your relationship status, you will always be the queen to me." She raised her drink.

"Agreed," Arthur said, raising his glass in agreement. The rest of the group raised their drinks in a makeshift toast.

"Here, here." Galahad exclaimed.

Guinevere blushed from the attention.

"This is not where I expected to be when I stole the map from the archives," she said, "but here we are." She grabbed another shot of whiskey off the table. "I want to thank you all, for believing in Excalibur and for being willing to risk everything for a better future."

"I'd drink to that," Arthur said. He picked up a shot of whiskey and raised it.

The group sat there for a while, talking and drinking the evening away. At some point, Merlin got out some snacks and more drinks for everyone. Gawain brought Guinevere a blanket when she stated that she was cold. Lion got out tobacco and rolled herself and Percival cigarettes. The mood in the room began to simmer down.

Arthur turned on the small radio that was sitting on an end table by the sofa. Upbeat music filled the room. "Come on." He motioned to Guinevere. "Dance with me."

"I don't think so," she said, smiling meekly and shaking her head. She set her feet up on the leather chair and grabbed her knees, hugging them close to her chest under the blanket. "I'm way too comfy to move." She took another drink of her beer.

"These people want you to be their future queen," he said. "Are you going to disappoint them?"

"I might," she answered shortly. "Besides, you're drunk. That's no way for a king to act."

"Drunk on love," Arthur announced to the room, flinging his arms open wide. He walked over to her and grabbed her arm.

"Come on," he pleaded.

She reluctantly allowed him to pull her onto her feet. She draped her arms over his shoulders as he grabbed her waist and they swayed back and forth together. Guinevere rested her head on his shoulder. She let herself get lost in the music and the rhythm of their movement. She breathed deeply, feeling peaceful. Arthur rubbed his hand gently up and down her back.

"You okay?" Arthur asked her in a moment of clarity.

She didn't reply but bounced her chin on his shoulder.

Merlin and Lancelot had joined them dancing. Gawain was trying to get Lionel to dance with him. She was refusing, taking another drag of her cigarette and shaking her head. Guinevere smiled. *This is where I belong,* she thought to herself. She looked up at Arthur. He was staring into the distance, surveying the knights. She rested her head back on his shoulder. He leaned his against hers.

After the next song ended, Guinevere whispered into Arthur's ear.

"You sure?" he asked.

She nodded eagerly.

Arthur grabbed her hand swiftly and led her down to the end of the hall. "Good night!" he called back to the rest of the group, still drinking and dancing. The two of them entered the main bedroom. Arthur closed the door, shutting out the rest of the world.

"You sure?" Arthur asked her, holding himself back.

"We might not make it through tomorrow. I don't want to have regrets—to think about what could have been or what will never be. Let's make the most of tonight," she said. "Are you going to kiss me?"

He did not need to be asked twice.

* * *

"Guinevere," Arthur said, breaking the silence. She was resting her head on his shirtless chest and had nearly drifted off. Arthur was lying there, unable to sleep, staring at the ceiling. Both of them were wrapped in blankets, blocking out the cool and drafty air that had crept its way inside the cabin.

"Yeah?" she muttered groggily. She rolled over onto her side to face him, opening her eyes slightly. She pulled the blankets up under her chin.

264

"I was thinking about what you said—that we might not make it through tomorrow. I want you to take up Excalibur and rule Avalon as the rightful queen. You don't need to agree to be my queen."

Guinevere looked at him confused.

"What I'm trying to say is if I do not make it through the battle, will you lead Avalon in my place? As I said before, you should have been given Excalibur to rule. You would make a better leader than me. Can you promise me this?"

After pausing for a moment to think, Guinevere answered Arthur. "Yes," she said then grinned. Her ran her fingers up his chest, tapping out each word: "Your Royal Highness."

Arthur rolled over so they were face to face, both lying on their sides. He opened his mouth to start talking again, but before he could, Guinevere put her finger to his lips.

"Yes," she said. "Yes, if—when we make it through tomorrow."

She bit her bottom lip while waiting for his response. Arthur looked perplexed at first, and then thoughtful. Finally, a large grin grew across Arthur's face.

"You know that since you are king now, you could be with anyone you want. Raynell totally has a crush on you and you'd sweep her right off her feet. I also heard you turned down Lady Elaine of Garlot and countless other women before my time. Somehow, with all these options, you're still interested in me—the one playing hard to get," Guinevere said, mocking him.

"I want someone to love me for who I am, not my title or my looks. You clearly are not the latter, otherwise we wouldn't have needed a knightly intervention." Arthur grinned playfully.

Guinevere scoffed at him but smiled. "When we make it through tomorrow," she answered him, "I expect a real proposal."

***

Arthur lay on his back, unable to sleep. He looked over to where Guinevere was sound asleep, wrapped in his shirt and the blankets. Her left arm hung lazily over the side of the bed. Arthur's button up shirt had come undone and was falling off her shoulder. With every rise and fall of her breath, it got closer to the ground. He chuckled softly to himself. There was a sense of peace that emanated from her, something that he envied.

Arthur crept out of bed, careful not to wake Guinevere. He removed the blankets from his body, folding them over onto her. He swung his legs over the edge, letting his feet brush the floor. He stood up and crouched forward, turning back to check Guinevere. She was still asleep, unmoved. Arthur slipped on his pants, quieting the belt, and left the room. He gently shut the door behind him.

He snuck down the hallway to the front door. Arthur passed Lion sleeping on the sofa on his way. The living room and kitchen were still a mess from the night's activities. He slipped out the front door and sat down on the steps of the porch. He stared out into the night, gazing at the stars above him. A breeze rustled the leaves of the forest and Arthur felt the chilly blow on his topless chest. He thought about tomorrow's plan. A lot of weight rested on his shoulders. Everyone, including Guinevere, was risking their lives so that he could be king. He hoped against fate that everything would go according to plan, but something could go wrong at any moment. Even now there was a remote chance that the Rangers would find them.

Should I leave the cabin? Arthur contemplated. Anger boiled up inside of him. He wasn't angry at the knights. He wasn't angry with Guinevere. He was angry with himself. He looked behind him at the dark building. *If I leave now, I could turn myself in and turn myself over to the Rangers,* he thought. Maybe his sacrifice would save his friends. No one would need to risk their lives. *Was the danger really worth being king?* Arthur didn't want to rule Avalon. He didn't want the responsibility. He could end it all tonight before the battle had even started. He stood up, having made up his mind to journey through the woods back to Camelot.

Before he could take the first step, Arthur forced himself to stop and cooled the rage that was burning inside his heart. He sat back down on the porch. *Turning myself in won't protect anyone,* he reasoned. The knights and Guinevere would have been hunted down, seen as traitors, and executed as such. Fighting was the only way to secure their futures. *My future is forward.*

"Mind if I join you?"

Arthur was startled as he turned to see Lancelot coming out of the cabin.

"Sure," Arthur said, scooting over on the step. "What are you doing out here in the middle of the night?"

"Having a smoke," Lancelot said. "You?"

"Couldn't sleep," Arthur responded, running his hand through his hair.

"Feeling nervous about tomorrow?" Lancelot asked. He pulled a cigarette out of his pocket and lit it.

Arthur nodded.

"No one is joining this fight out of some obligation. Everyone has chosen freely to support you. We want you to be our king, and no matter what happens, you already are."

"I know that you're trying to reassure me, but the fact that everyone is freely supporting me of their own volition makes the gravity of tomorrow weigh all the more heavily on me. I can't help but feel anxious about our fates."

The men both sat in silence for a while, staring forward into the darkness of the night.

"I don't want anyone dying for me," Arthur said, breaking the silence.

Lancelot took a drag of his cigarette. "Look," he said, "I can't begin to imagine how you feel. Just know that we are all here for you. No matter what happens tomorrow, it won't be in vain."

"Just tell me that you will keep Guinevere safe," Arthur pleaded.

Lancelot nodded reassuringly. "And you should be watching over her tonight." He put out his cigarette and stood up to head back inside. He held out a hand to help Arthur up. They headed into the cabin, Lancelot locking the door behind them. Arthur walked down the dark hallway and rejoined Guinevere in bed. She was still slumbering just as he had left her. He slipped under the covers and closed his eyes, finally drifting to sleep.

Chapter Twenty-Three

Guinevere woke to an empty bedroom. She could hear muffled voices through the door as she rubbed the sleep out of her eyes. Her eyes adjusted to the early light. She wanted to stay in bed, denying what they had planned and casting it to the land of dreams. She sat there for a while upright, alone in the morning glow, and looked at the blank wall opposite the bed. It all seemed surreal to her. She had half-expected to wake in her apartment. The muffled voices weren't unlike her partying neighbors. Guinevere tried to come to grips with reality and force away her wandering thoughts. The fate of Avalon, after all, was in their control.

Guinevere pushed the blankets off and swung her legs around to the floor. Standing up, she stretched her body, feeling the soreness of the past few days. Arthur's shirt had fallen off one of her arms, and she was wearing little else. She pulled its sleeve back on her shoulder for momentary warmth and looked around for something to wear. On the bed next to her, Arthur had neatly folded her outfit from the previous day, tidily stacked on his pillow. Guinevere smiled at the thoughtful gesture. She slipped into the dress and cardigan, brushed her hair, and threw the blankets back on the bed before leaving the room.

She walked into the kitchen, still a little groggy and not quite fully awake. Percival and Galahad were relaxing on the couch while Lionel was in the leather lounge chair. The dining chairs had returned to their home by the table. Merlin, Lancelot, Gawain, and Arthur were seated around it, eating a breakfast of bacon and eggs. Seeing Guinevere enter the room, Arthur put his fork down, grabbed the plate, and got up from his seat.

"Here," he said to her, motioning to the chair. "I'll get you some food."

Guinevere sat down. Arthur deposited his breakfast on the counter and fetched a clean plate out of the cupboard. He started filling it with fried eggs from a cast iron skillet on the stove before finishing with fresh fruit. He walked back over to the table and placed the plate in front of Guinevere.

"There is some fresh coffee," he told her. "Otherwise I can make you some tea."

"Coffee sounds great."

"Milk? Sugar?"

She shook her head as she started eating.

"So," Gawain said, leaning forward across the table and looking intently at her. Arthur was pouring her a mug of coffee and eyed the man skeptically. "How was your night? Did you get any real sleep?"

"Hmm," she said as she took a sip of the coffee. A smile behind the mug betrayed her.

"Missed my chance I guess," he said, disappointedly snapping his fingers. Leaning back in the chair, he interlocked his hands behind his head and puffed out his chest. "I better be invited to the wedding."

"Can't make any promises," she told him. She dug into her breakfast, shoveling the eggs into her mouth.

"How was your night together?" Lionel pressed from the other room.

"It was good," Guinevere sheepishly answered, looking down at her food to avoid eye contact.

"I knew it," Lionel replied. "If this knight thing doesn't work out, I should get a job as a matchmaker."

"If you ever do her wrong," Gawain opined to Arthur, "I will come for you, Excalibur or not."

"Did I just hear someone make threats against the king?" Lancelot asked, smiling deviously at Gawain.

"Woah," Gawain said, raising his hands to his shoulders in a defensive manner. "Not threats. Promises to protect our queen."

"You can start by defending her today," Arthur said. There was no mistaking the serious tone; his voice was flat and solemn.

"Did you get any sleep last night?" Guinevere asked him. She was surprised by his demeanor.

"Enough," he said. He finished his breakfast. "Just have some things on my mind."

Guinevere nodded, not pressing him further. She continued to eat her breakfast, this time scooping up fruit between sips of coffee.

"Want something more to eat?" Arthur asked her.

She shook her head. "Just some coffee." The chair groaned as she got up from the table and crossed toward the kitchen. Guinevere filled her mug.

"Not to rush you," Lancelot said while Guinevere was taking a large sip. Its warmth filled her deep inside her body. "But once you are done, we need to get ready to head out." Lancelot spoke in a flat voice.

"Already?" Guinevere asked, surprised. She lowered the mug away from her face and furrowed her brow. "What happened to the original plan of heading out in the evening?" She looked around the room. No one else was surprised by Lancelot's words. It was clear that a new plan had been hatched while she continued to sleep. She was annoyed to be left out of the loop but grateful for the extra rest.

"Plans have changed," Arthur told her.

* * *

"Here," Merlin handed Guinevere an outfit. They were all preparing for the fight to come. After the announcement, Guinevere had quickly finished her second cup of coffee. She did not want to keep everyone waiting; delay wouldn't gain them anything. Action was the only way to change their future. To stall here, to fall backward, would simply allow everyone's anxiety to grow and second-guess their plan. She had assumed this was why the plan had changed. The time to act was now. Everyone moved around the cabin with purpose, collecting their weapons and changing clothes.

Guinevere took the garments from Merlin. She pulled up black pants, drew down a white shirt, and cinched the brown leather corset. She slipped the black mid-length cloak with an oversized

273

hood and cowl on over the outfit, buttoning its five buttons. She slid her feet into her socks and boots. Merlin handed her a bow with a quiver of arrows that Guinevere secured to her back. She put on a pair of black leather gloves and followed Merlin out of the room.

Back in the living area, everyone else was ready to go. The knights were sitting on the kitchen chairs, arranged like the day before. The coffee table had been removed from the space. Arthur was seated in the large leather lounge chair.

Merlin crossed the room and sat down next to Lancelot on the sofa, but Guinevere continued to stand in the walkway near the door. She looked out over the room. The knights were wearing similar outfits to hers. Everyone had black hooded cloaks to cover their heads and faces, but each cape varied, matching the style of its wearer. Arthur and Lancelot were the noticeable exception, standing out from the rest of the group. Lancelot was clothed in Ranger's attire with Excalibur strapped to his side. Arthur had on his original shirt and pants, his default outfit on the Hengroen.

"Ready?" Arthur asked everyone but looked directly at Guinevere. He got up from his seat. She nodded, as did the rest of the knights. They all stood in unison without speaking, weighed down by the gravity of their quest.

"Before we go," Arthur continued, "there is something I need to do." He turned to Lancelot who nodded, handing Arthur Excalibur.

Arthur looked across the room to Guinevere.

"Come here," he instructed and motioned her to come near. Guinevere was puzzled, not sure of what was going on. She walked forward until she was standing in front of Arthur.

"Kneel," he told her, holding Excalibur in both hands. Guinevere crouched down before him, her bow and arrows still strapped to her back.

"I, Arthur Pendragon, by right of arms, King of Avalon—" He lifted Excalibur above his head for the entire room to see. "— appoint you, Guinevere Cornwall, as the sovereign Queen of Avalon."

He anointed her, moving the sword swiftly and gracefully from one shoulder to the other. He lifted it once more in an arc before flipping the hilt in his hand and bringing it powerfully to the ground. He turned to Lancelot, who retrieved the sword and strapped it back to his back. In exchange, he held out a wreath crown in the palms of his hands. It was made from several green twigs braided together. Different kinds of ferns were tucked in between the various strands. Evergreen needles and cones were attached around it, standing in for jewels. It was the headpiece of a woodland queen.

"It's the best we could do with such short notice," Lancelot conceded.

Arthur nodded. He lifted the makeshift crown up from Lancelot's hands, grasping it tightly. He turned to face Guinevere, slowly lifting the crown and placing it atop her head. It felt surprisingly heavy, she noted.

"Rise," he told her, "Guinevere, Queen of Avalon."

Taking Arthur's outstretched hand, Guinevere rose to her feet. She turned to face the knights, who had erupted into cheers. She gazed upon them. Nothing about the last month felt real. Finding the map, stumbling upon Arthur, discovering Excalibur—even last night when she had agreed to be his and Avalon's queen. The true battle to determine their future was in front of them, and there was much more to come.

Guinevere took Arthur's hand once more. She moved a couple steps backward to stand by his side in front of his knights—their knights.

"Long live the Queen," Galahad cheered. The knights echoed his cry. A smile crept across Guinevere's face.

"Stop," she told them, waving her hands in front of her. She was still smiling. The knights and Arthur stopped their chanting. "We have a battle to go fight and win. There will be time for celebration after our victory." She removed the crown from her head, holding it in one hand. The mood in the room noticeably shifted. It was no longer jovial but instead returned to its prior solemnity. Arthur took the crown from Guinevere's hand.

"This crown will be waiting for you," Arthur said, facing Guinevere. "If I don't make it, if we lose the battle, come back for this crown. It will be up to you to lead. If we win, a different crown will be rested on your head."

Arthur turned to look at Gawain.

"Defend her today," he commanded. Gawain nodded in agreement.

"I don't need protection," Guinevere interrupted. They all turned to look at her. "When I agreed to be the queen—your queen—I did so understanding that I would be an equal."

"You are," Arthur reassured her. "I am not looking to shield you because you are incapable. No, it is because you are invaluable to me. Since we first met, you have been more than able to defend yourself. Simply put, I could not live with myself if you were harmed and there was something within my power that could have saved you."

"No offense, but last night, when we were knighted, we all promised to honor and defend the Crown and Kingdom of Avalon," Lancelot told them both. "You are the Crown. No command need be given, our lives are sworn to your aid. We will be fighting for our kingdom."

Arthur looked around the room at the knights. They were all waiting for him to lead.

"It's time to go fight," Arthur said. "Avalon's future is forward."

Arthur nodded toward Lancelot, who moved toward the door. He opened it and they all filed out. They walked single file, retracing their steps to the clearing.

The forest was the soundtrack of their journey, thick with the distinctive ambience of a late autumnal day. It was unaware of the importance of their quest. The redwood trees filled the sky and air with their sweet scent. Birds sang up in their treetops. Leaves fell from their branches to the forest floor below. The breeze rustled the foliage. Dinosaurs searched for food or a place to rest. Beneath their feet, pine needles and fallen branches crunched rhythmically. The sun shone through the trees, lighting their way.

There is no turning back, Guinevere kept reminding herself. *There is nothing for you to return to. You are a wanted criminal. This is the only path forward. Everyone is here, guided by Excalibur. Everyone is here because they believe in a better Camelot. Avalon can be remade for its people. This is our future.*

The knights, Guinevere, and Arthur made it to the clearing after walking for an hour. From here, the group split up: Arthur and Lancelot traveled further toward the sea, while Guinevere and the rest of the knights gathered around Merlin. She called out to the sky and Guinevere looked up. For a moment, nothing appeared. One by one, four pterodactyls started circling. Their angular path started out large but grew tighter until the four dinosaurs swooped down. They landed next to each other, several meters away from group. Merlin walked up to each of the dinosaurs. She rubbed the soft leathery patch of skin between their eyes. They called out to her as she touched them.

"Come," she said, motioning the knights to join her. They walked over, mounting the pterodactyls in pairs. Lionel and Percival straddled one and Galahad perched on another. He sat near the front of the beast, grasping tightly to its neck. Merlin climbed on the back of the third. She rubbed the back of its head and the dinosaur cooed.

Gawain and Guinevere approached the fourth and final dinosaur. He mounted first and reached back to help Guinevere up behind him. She was nervous, again, about riding such a powerful creature. Merlin had done much to make her feel safe the night before. Guinevere wrapped her arms around Gawain's waist, and they took off into flight. The four pterodactyls soared through the sky, following Merlin and her dinosaur. At first, the wind blew over them and brushed past their faces. But as they picked up speed, the riders leaned forward, shielded in the wake of the beast's neck. Guinevere was beginning to understand why Arthur liked to fly, but she missed the relative comfort of the Hengroen. *I can't look back,* she told herself. *Keep moving forward.*

Chapter Twenty-Four

"King Gorlois!" Lancelot shouted as he waltzed into the Courtyard Square. He pushed Arthur, whose hands were tied, in front of him. Lancelot prodded him forward, leaving Arthur a few feet away in the middle of the castle yard. He felt extremely vulnerable. His face was bruised, and a black eye was forming. His clothes were soiled with dirt and blood. He was nearly unrecognizable. So far, their plan had gone off without a hitch.

Back in the clearing with the other knights, Arthur and Lancelot had separated from the group and headed toward the ocean. Somewhere on its shoreline, Lancelot had hidden a small sailing vessel with branches and leaves. When he had deflected from the Rangers during Gorlois' coronation, he had made off with the craft. In their present situation, they figured this transport would be the least conspicuous. After a short search, Lancelot found the boat, and the two men pulled it out from its hiding place. They worked in silence as they cleaned it off, raised the mast, and pushed it into the water.

Lancelot faced his king with a pained expression. He reeled his fist back and landed a punch on Arthur's right eye. Although he was anticipating it, it still took Arthur by surprise causing him to stumble back. But both men knew this was the only way. Lancelot resumed his attack on Arthur, sullying his eye and torso. With every punch he landed, he grimaced. Once Arthur was thoroughly bruised and battered, Lancelot ended his assault. He helped the beaten man into the boat and tied him up toward the back of the vessel.

Lancelot hoisted the sail, navigating them safely down the coast and through the channel north of Camelot. They barely looked at each other as they made the watery journey. Both men were lost in their own thoughts and concerned about the future.

Reaching the eastern cliff face of Castle Hill, Lancelot moored their ship. The small vessel looked at home amidst the myriad Ranger vessels. They walked the stony path from the water's edge up to the base of Camelot's wall. Arthur could feel the Rangers watching from the castle towers and felt out of place in the palatial grounds. Nevertheless, they had walked up the forecourt without being stopped.

Before they had departed, Lancelot's Ranger attire and Arthur's garb stood out from the knights' dark clothing and hooded apparel. Here, no one saw them as out of place. Lancelot nodded to the Rangers guarding the gate and those stationed in the tower as they passed. A few gave him a cursory once-over since his formal attire was somewhat peculiar. His uniform was typically saved for special events like coronations, high feasts, or ceremonies. Unfortunately, it was the only Ranger outfit that Lancelot could access, having deserted during Gorlois's coronation. The uniform was a simple green jacket that was ordained with many metals and ribbons. They signified Lancelot's numerous accomplishments and honors, which were extensive for a man of his rank. Excalibur completed the look while strapped to Lancelot's hip.

The pair continued walking through Camelot as the knight prodded his bound king forward. Arthur kept his head down, looking at the ground and nowhere else. They stopped when they reached Courtyard Square, the open sky above them and the lush grass beneath their feet. There in the castle yard with the Royal Palace to the east and the Great Hall to the south, Lancelot announced their presence.

"Well, look who dared to show his face," Gorlois proclaimed from the steps of the Great Hall. Several high-profile Rangers followed him, including Agravain, whose left shoulder was bandaged from their previous encounter.

"My king," Lancelot said, kneeling before him.

"Get up," Gorlois commanded. Lancelot obeyed. Gorlois continued to ignore Arthur and pursued Lancelot with questions.

"Do you think you can desert your post and come back without any consequence?" he chastened.

"No—no sir." Lancelot's voice quivered slightly. He rubbed his hands on his pants as they rested by his sides.

"You better have an explanation for your actions. Otherwise, you will end up worse than your friend here," Agravain admonished.

"Friend?" Lancelot scoffed. "This is no friend of mine." He walked behind Arthur, kicked him in the back of his knees, and shoved his shoulders down. Arthur kneeled on the ground before Gorlois forcefully. "This is the reason for my disappearance."

Lancelot shoved Arthur off balance and walked to a place equidistant from him and Gorlois.

"Why don't you tell them, Arthur?" He sneered, motioning between the kings and the Rangers. "About how you thought I was your friend. How I stood by and watched as Guinevere appointed you king with Excalibur. About how you thought I was going to help you take the throne." Lancelot walked over and kicked Arthur in the stomach, causing him to crumple forward and cough up blood.

"Once a Ranger, always a Ranger." He spat at Arthur before moving to the side and standing at attention.

"Well, well, well," Gorlois said, walking around Arthur. "If it isn't the King of Avalon," he jeered. The Rangers laughed. Gorlois yanked Arthur up onto his feet. "What do you have to say for yourself?"

Arthur did not reply. He stared into Gorlois's eyes, unblinking. Although he trusted Lancelot, his words stung, and the punches ached. Arthur attempted to conserve his energy for what was to come. Impatient with his lack of response, Gorlois threw him to the ground before circling Arthur menacingly. He lay there crumpled and unmoving.

"You are nothing without Excalibur," Gorlois derided Arthur and kicked him in the stomach. Arthur gasped, coughing up more blood. He wiped it off onto his sleeve. He tried to get up, rolling onto his knees. Gorlois stopped him, placing his foot on his back and stepping down. Arthurs limbs collapsed under his force, causing him to fall down onto his stomach. There he lay, sprawled out on the grass. His face was pressed into the dirt. He could smell the earth: the combination of soil, worms, and grass that smelt like hay, and warmer weather—like summertime. Its scent was pleasant save for the unfortunate circumstance. Gorlois removed his foot from Arthur and took a step back.

Arthur had been dirty and bloody before, but Lancelot's torment looked like child's play. Now his face was running with blood, dribbling down his chin. His clothes, previously mostly white, were soaked with streaks of reds and browns.

"Kneel," Gorlois ordered Arthur, kicking him again in the side this time. Feeling defeated, Arthur obeyed. Gorlois turned his attention away from his torment and faced Lancelot. He was standing at attention a few feet away from the kneeling Arthur. He was mimicking the position of the other Rangers, who were all standing farther back with weapons at their sides and hands at the ready.

"I have some questions for you," he stated.

Lancelot nodded with understanding. He had been prepared for this—the fury of Gorlois.

"Do you know what we do with deserters?" he asked Lancelot.

"Yes, sir," he muttered.

"What was that, Deputy Ranger Lancelot?" Gorlois barked, stepping up to Lancelot and getting in his face. The former Ranger remained at attention, staring Gorlois straight in the eyes as he answered.

"Yes, sir," he said again, this time speaking with confidence.

"Maybe you would like a chance to exonerate yourself," Gorlois said, taking a step back from Lancelot, "before we resort to those measures."

"Yes, sir," Lancelot retorted. He took a moment to breathe before continuing speaking. "I was going after the traitor, your majesty. I sought his trust to capture him. I was unable to contact command lest I be found out, sir."

"And Guinevere?" Gorlois demanded.

"She's dead, your majesty," he bellowed. Gorlois nodded.

"And Excalibur?"

"On my person, your majesty." Lancelot pulled Excalibur from his hip and held the sword in his upturned palms. The sunlight reflected off the polished blade. He kneeled down, presenting it before the king. Gorlois took a step toward him, inspecting the sword, before confidently grasping it by the hilt. He held it up over his head, marveling, before gently slipping the weapon into his belt.

"Lancelot, I had begun to doubt your loyalty," Gorlois said delicately, as he walked around him and Arthur. Once he was standing behind them, he motioned to Agravain with the flick of his wrist. "Take them both away."

"Wait!" Lancelot turned around, lowering himself onto his hands before the king. His face was nearly at his boot. "Your Majesty, I have nothing but loyalty for you. I implore you to reconsider my fate."

"Loyalty?" Gorlois scoffed. He hoisted Lancelot from the ground. Agravain moved in, flanked by several more Rangers to assist, but Gorlois angrily shooed them away. "Is that what you call running away to the forest to sleep with that grimy wizard girl? Your escapades started long before this conflict." He thumped Lancelot on the chest. He opened his mouth to refute the claim, but Gorlois held a hand up and silenced him. "You think that I am naïve enough to believe your fabricated excuse? You traitor!" Gorlois reached forward and grabbed a handful of the metals and ribbons on Lancelot's jacket. He pulled backward, ripping them free and leaving behind the remnants of metal pins and torn fabric. Gorlois threw the handful to the ground. Making direct eye contact with Lancelot, he stepped on the pile and ground them into the dirt. Lancelot grimaced.

"What gain would I have to bring you Excalibur, or turn in the wanted false king Arthur?" Lancelot turned slightly to look at his true king. There he kneeled on the ground, hands still bound behind his back, facing away from Gorlois. Arthur's form looked listless, dejected, and dead, as if it would fall at a simple touch.

"Prove your loyalty." Gorlois beckoned toward Agravain. He walked up to the two of them. Standing slightly off to the side, he pulled his gun out of its holster and handed it, hilt first, to Lancelot. He took it from Agravain, gripping it firmly in his hand. He turned the weapon sideways while inspecting it; in the magazine was one round.

"Kill Arthur Pendragon."

Wordlessly, Lancelot nodded. He held the weapon at his side and walked to Arthur's right. He raised the gun and slowly pressed it into Arthur's temple. Arthur turned to look at him; he could feel the cold barrel against his forehead. He tried to meet Lancelot's eyes, but his gaze was fixated on Gorlois.

At that moment, Arthur began to regret trusting Lancelot. He was suddenly scared. *What if I was wrong to trust him?* he thought. *What if he is telling the truth and was toying with me all along?* A shiver of fear ran down his spine. *How could I be so stupid and reckless to trust someone I had just met?*

"Lancelot," he pleaded. He tried to read the man's expression, but it was blank. It was impossible to tell where his true loyalties lay. "Don't do this. Please."

Lancelot let out a small laugh. He pulled back the hammer of the gun until it clicked.

"Please, Lancelot," Arthur begged, his voice cracking as he held back tears.

"Shut up," Lancelot commanded.

"Don't do this."

"I told you to be quiet."

"Get on with it already, traitor." Gorlois sneered at Lancelot.

His finger danced on the trigger. "Please," Arthur whimpered, his voice barely more than a whisper. He looked up at Lancelot, begging him not to shoot.

"Is that really what you want your last words to be?" Lancelot asked, dropping his gaze and looking at Arthur for the first time. There was a twinkle of a smile at the side of his mouth.

"No?" Arthur responded, confused by the sudden change in Lancelot's tone.

"Good. I wouldn't either," he confided.

Lancelot pulled the trigger and the hammer slammed.

* * *

Guinevere watched the events unfold from their vantage point in the sky, still riding on the back of a pterodactyl with Gawain. The dinosaur was slowly circling over Camelot. The knights were waiting for Lancelot's signal, but the events below were hard for Guinevere to stomach. She watched, nevertheless. She felt anxious about what they had set in motion. There was no way to run now. If there was, she was sure to take it. She could feel the anxiety growing in the pit of her stomach, creeping up into the back of her throat. Her chest felt tight. *Breathe*, she told herself. *Breathe*.

"You alright?" Gawain asked, turning ever so slightly to look at her. He pulled down his cowl as he talked.

"Yeah," she said, trying to shake off her feelings. She pulled down her cowl as well. "Just some pre-fight jitters. I've never done this before."

"Honestly," Gawain replied with a smile, "neither have I."

"That isn't very comforting," Guinevere said, but the jovial tone of his words actually settled her stomach. She was reminded that she was not alone. There were other people present that were looking out for her.

A shot rang out as Lancelot fired into the sky.

"That was the signal," Gawain announced. Both of them drew up their cowls. Only their eyes could be seen. Guinevere pulled an arrow out of the quiver and nocked it. She held the bow at the ready, drawing the string back and waiting for a good shot. Gawain steered the pterodactyl closer to the fight. The dinosaur swooped down toward the ground.

Guinevere released the arrow, aiming at Agravain. It soared past his head and made contact with the grass behind. Frustrated with herself, she quickly nocked another arrow. This time she took a moment to breathe, steadying her aim before letting it fly. The arrow cut through the air and found its home, gliding straight into Agravain's chest. He looked down at the arrow for a moment, pausing. Guinevere felt time slow down. No one reacted as blood soaked out in a ring around the arrow. Agravain crumpled to the ground. One of the Rangers let out a cry. Their cover was blown, but it didn't matter anymore.

Guinevere held her bow at her side, shocked that she had actually hit Agravain. She had never killed anyone before and wasn't sure how to react. On the one hand, she was happy that Agravain was gone, no longer able to torment her. But on the other hand, she had just taken someone's life. There had been no trial to weigh his crimes. What gave her the authority? Her mind stuck in a loop between these conflicting emotions, unable to process the urgency of her surroundings.

"You did it," Gawain said sometime later. There was admiration in his words. He had guided the pterodactyl higher into the sky after Guinevere's shot met its mark. They sat there, hovering in relative safety, ready to swoop down and rejoin the fight.

"I did," Guinevere barely whispered, still shocked but snapped out of her spiral. She pulled down her cowl and shook off her hood.

"Arthur wasn't lying when he said you were a pro," Gawain stated.

"Yeah…" she said, trailing off. "Maybe at hitting targets. But people? That is a completely different thing."

"Come on," Gawain reassured, removing his hand from the pterodactyl's neck and resting it gently on Guinevere's hand. "You are a knight now. You are a warrior."

Guinevere nodded. Something about his words was comforting. They didn't excuse killing people. They didn't say it was right. They meant she, like the rest of the knights, had come to Camelot to fight—and she was not alone.

"I thought you said I was your queen," Guinevere replied, a small smile creeping across her face.

"My warrior Queen," Gawain said, motioning his hand with a flurry and slightly lowering his head to mimic bowing. Guinevere laughed.

"Come on," she told him this time. "We came here to fight, so let's get back to it."

Gawain nodded and faced forward again. Guinevere pulled her cowl back up and covered her head once more with the hood. He steered the pterodactyl back down toward the Rangers. As the dinosaur dove toward the action, Guinevere nocked another arrow from her quiver, readying herself for the next attack.

* * *

When Lancelot had fired his gun into the sky, he ran forward to free Arthur. Moments later, two pterodactyls swooped down to the ground. The first carried Lionel and Percival with Galahad close behind them. Around this time, Guinevere's shot made contact with Agravain's chest, throwing the Rangers into chaos. Merlin swooped in, dropping Arthur a sword, and circled back up into the sky.

Lionel, Percival, and Galahad dismounted from their moving dinosaurs as they reached the ground, using the momentum to run full speed at the Rangers surrounding Lancelot and the dueling kings. All three knights had swords strapped to their backs, but they weren't using them. They un-holstered their guns and shot at the Rangers as they ran toward them, adding to the disorder. Their aim was wild, barely hitting anyone or anything as they charged. Still, they were running with purpose and dodging the bullets that were fired back. All of them were in the open field with nowhere to hide. As they got closer, their shots started landing and they were able to hit several Rangers, knocking them to the ground.

After dropping the sword earlier, Merlin guided her pterodactyl over to the rest of the knights. She did not dismount the dinosaur but instead used the creature to fight. It swooped down, nearly landing, and picked up an unfortunate Ranger. They were lifted into the sky before being dropped from quite the distance. An unsettling crunch emanated from where the Ranger's body contacted the ground.

Somewhere in the commotion of the fight, Gawain and Guinevere rejoined the battle. She loosed multiple arrows upon the Rangers, her steady aim and watchful eye protecting her fellow knights. Gawain skillfully guided the pterodactyl, avoiding incoming fire.

"Hold on!" he shouted to Guinevere sometime later. She slung her bow over her shoulder and grabbed onto his waist. Gawain guided the dinosaur down. They dove, just missing a flurry of arrows that passed over their heads. Startled by how close they had been, Guinevere ducked down, pressing her head against Gawain's back.

"We're okay," he reassured her, guiding the pterodactyl back up into the sky, but he had spoken too soon. The dinosaur let out a terrible screech. An arrow had plunged into its chest. The gravely injured creature, along with its two riders, started falling from the sky.

"Be ready to jump!" Gawain shouted as the ground rushed up to meet them. Another arrow tore through one of the pterodactyl's wing. They were no longer gliding but were thrown into a spin. Guinevere let out a scream as the dinosaur flipped over onto its back and she slid down its spine. She clutched onto its lifeless body as she hung upside down. She wanted to close her eyes and give up as she felt them racing for the ground, but she knew she couldn't.

"Guinevere!" Gawain broke through her thoughts. She lifted her head to look at him. Tears blurred her vision. "I'm going to need you to trust me," he shouted over the wind.

Guinevere nodded, knowing that he couldn't see her. She wanted to speak, but all that came out was a gasp for air.

"When I say, jump," Gawain told her. He continued to watch the ground, waiting for an opportunity for them to land safely.

"Now!" he shouted.

Guinevere let go and allowed herself to fall. The two of them dropped a couple meters before colliding with the ground. Guinevere rolled a couple times before steadying herself. She kneeled on the grass and looked up. Gawain had landed not more than a few meters from her, but the pterodactyls mass kept it moving. It had collided with a couple Rangers, leaving a trail of blood and broken foliage in its path.

Seeing that Gawain was alright, Guinevere paused for a moment. She readjusted her hood and cowl since they had come free during her plummet. Although the quiver was still secured to her back, all the arrows were scattered across the battlefield. Her bow had come free when she had landed and lay just out of arm's reach. She got up off her knees to go retrieve it. Before she could move, though, a voice spoke up behind her.

"Well, what do we have here? Another knight," he scoffed at the word, "coming to join the fight?"

Guinevere turned around slowly to see who had spoken.

It was Gorlois.

With a flurry of Excalibur, he struck down a distracted Arthur and ended the kings' duel. He crossed the distance to her at a slow pace, drawing out the moment of his victory. His figure ominously blocked the sun as he drew nearer, and he motioned for the Rangers to approach. They closed in like the walls of a fortress, shutting out the knights and any hope of escape.

Guinevere's body was frozen in place, unable to react—unable to breathe. She was horrified at the sight of her king's defeat. She looked over to where Arthur's lifeless body lay in a heap. A sense of dread welled up within the pit of her stomach. She nearly let out a scream.

Arthur meekly lifted his head to face her and Guinevere eagerly met his gaze. Nothing could be done to change their fate, but for the moment she didn't care. The pair willed time to stop, frozen before the instant of their demise. Their eyes were transfixed on each other and reality fell away. There, in the iridescent depths of their souls, the past month replayed.

The awkward meeting, as if these star-crossed lovers had been orchestrated by the fates.

The time on Hengroen, soaring boundlessly throughout the skies of Avalon and the realms afar.

The knights, a family found and not asked for, tied by loyalty and valor.

Their first kiss in an enchanted forest under an endlessly twinkling starlight.

The final moments passed together in a mystical embrace.

Chapter Twenty-Five

A hand grabbed Guinevere, breaking the incantation. She felt the cool blade of Excalibur press against her skin. Her hood was pulled off, exposing her identity to the world. Her face was stoic but fearful. Laughing at his good fortune, Gorlois shook heartily. Her flesh stung as the sword brushed her neck and a warm liquid trickled down to her chest.

"Choose your next move carefully, my queen." Gorlois lingered longer than necessary on the word. It dripped off his tongue like poison. She stood motionless before him, but her fear was replaced with rage.

Gorlois lowered the sword and guided Guinevere toward the Great Hall. She strained against him but lost her footing. Rather than confront his belligerent captive, Gorlois let his hand slip down her arm. It caught her wrist and pulled. The joints in Guinevere's arm and shoulder protested the force and ached under the pressure. When they reached the steps of the Great Hall, Gorlois slung her around before him. The momentum carried her into the stairs, where her knee collided with its stone surface. It throbbed in pain as she tried to stand, unable to support her full weight. She stumbled to her feet despite, trying to distance herself from the insidious king. Nevertheless, he overcame her. Gorlois shoved his fingers under the back of her corset and hoisted Guinevere to her feet. He thrust his other arm across Guinevere's chest, crushing her against his body. She staggered forward as he pushed her across the threshold of the stone structure.

The large doors of the Great Hall slammed closed behind them, leaving Guinevere alone with Gorlois. Apart from a few pieces of furniture littering the tile floor, the room was empty. Sunlight streamed in through windows that covered the upper walls. The sharp rays formed crisp beams in the otherwise dark space. Dust danced in the light, moving in chaotic patterns. Still clutching Guinevere, Gorlois propelled them toward the front of the hall. There, on a slightly raised platform, two thrones were illuminated by a perfect ray of sunshine.

Gorlois threw Guinevere before the seat of power. She fell to her knees, bracing herself, and stared down at the floor. He sheathed Excalibur and climbed onto the throne, situating himself in its cushions. He leaned back, relaxed, as if nothing else mattered in the world and as if there wasn't a battle waging just outside the doors. Guinevere prepared to get up, but he lowered his feet onto her back as a makeshift footstool. She strained under the force of his weight before collapsing.

"If I were you, I would consider joining forces with me before this petty fight is all over. That is," he paused, "if you have any desire to survive this mess." Gorlois presented the familiar offer to Guinevere once more. She continued looking at the ground, not moving and not ready to admit defeat.

"Look at me!" Gorlois commanded, indignation and dominance seeping from his words. Slowly, Guinevere turned her head. She held back the tears of her fury to stare straight at him.

"What do you say?" His tone had changed again. It was sickeningly cordial and carefree. "Will you join me? You could have this throne." He motioned to the adjacent seat. "That is what Arthur promised you, no?" He looked down at Guinevere, resting his chin on his hands and smiling sweetly. The rings that ordained his fingers sparkled in the ray of light, their multicolored gems casting off a variety of hues. His countenance made her stomach churn.

Guinevere did not grace the king with a response. She pushed herself up, sloughed off his feet, and stood before the throne. She held herself regally and stared at her adversary.

Sighing, Gorlois leaned back. "I'm disappointed," he said flatly.

Gorlois remained expressionless as he snapped his fingers. Several men, dressed in all black, appeared out of the darkness of the room. They flanked Guinevere, and she allowed herself to be captured. They grabbed her arms, gripping so tight that it caused her nerves to tingle. She kept her face smooth through it all and stared sourly at Gorlois. He rose off the throne and stood in front of her.

"You're making a big mistake," he taunted as he grabbed her face in his hand. He pulled her closer to him, his hot breath smacking her face. She wanted to turn away, but he was too strong.

"If you are going to kill me, do it already," she spoke through gritted teeth, voice trembling. Gorlois laughed as he released his grasp.

"No. I have plans for you. When all your troublesome knights have died, you will anoint me king." He gently tucked one of her loose hairs behind her ear. The gesture made her skin crawl. "Tie her to the throne," he commanded, "and bring word when the traitors are dead."

Gorlois watched as his men threw Guinevere onto the throne. He smiled as she struggled against them. Her wrists were bound to the armrests, the ropes tied tighter than necessary. Gorlois took a step closer.

"Anything you would like to say?" Gorlois jested.

She spit in his face.

"Gag her," he commanded, clearly agitated. A cloth was tied through her mouth and the men disappeared back into the darkness

"Somehow your ragtag band of deserters thought that you could beat me and the entire force of the Rangers. You actually thought that Arthur would be king? And why? Because he found this sword?" He pulled out Excalibur, holding it up in front of himself. The blade glistened in the sunlight, casting pockets of light around the room. "And what? You would be the queen?" He laughed mockingly. He put Excalibur back away as he lamented, "If you want to be a queen, you really need a crown."

Gorlois walked away, leaving Guinevere alone for a moment in the large room. She struggled, trying to free herself from the bonds, but they were securely fastened. She had only caused herself more pain. Guinevere tried to scream out for help, but the gag muffled her words, making her call barely more than an inaudible whimper.

"I thought you didn't have anything to say," Gorlois laughed, reentering the room. In his hands he held a crown as if it were a discarded piece of clothing—something soiled or to be burned, not respected. Yet, the headpiece wasn't ordinary or plain; it was the late King Uther's. The crown was gold and came up into four separate points: one in the front, one in the back, and one on each side. It was not ordained with jewels but was ornately carved, impressed with geometric swirls and laurels.

"A queen needs a crown, doesn't she?" Gorlois belittled Guinevere. He placed the crown upon her head. The crown felt heavy, but in a different way than the woodsy ornament fashioned by the knights. This one was too large and sat ajar, sliding down to slightly cover her eyes. Gorlois laughed again, pleased with himself. As he sat back on the throne, he placed Excalibur across his lap and waited for word from the ongoing battle.

* * *

The doors to the Great Hall banged open and Arthur burst forth. Several Rangers rushed in after him, but he deftly kept them at bay, brandishing his sword and lunging at them as necessary. The fight to the Great Hall had already taken a toll on Arthur. He wiped the sweat off his brow on the sleeve of his shirt, smearing blood and dirt on his forehead. His arm had been cut, dried blood covering the tear in his shirt and trailing down his arm, but he was of one mind; no one—not a Ranger nor a King—would stand between him and the throne room. Arthur turned away from the parrying Rangers at the sound of clapping behind him.

"The king has returned," Gorlois mocked, standing and applauding his entrance. Arthur stared at him. He did not appear to be touched by their duel. There were no scratches on him, his clothes had barely been dirtied, and his hands were washed. Not a drop of blood was visible on his person. Excalibur rested in his palm wantonly as if at any moment he might drop it to the ground.

Arthur turned away from him, noticing Guinevere. He was startled to see her bound to the throne, struggling and in pain. She was battered and bruised; the ill-fitted crown precariously balanced on her head. Despite the ropes, and despite Gorlois mockery, she looked like she belonged on this throne. She was the ruler Avalon deserved—who he was fighting for. Guinevere stopped wrestling against her bonds and nodded reassuringly toward Arthur. In that moment, he knew what he needed to do. He raised his sword and charged down the hall toward the thrones.

"Stop!" Gorlois commanded. Instinctively, Arthur obeyed. He stood halfway down the room. Gorlois crossed the thrones and stood next to Guinevere. He dangled Excalibur in front of himself, his fingers dancing on the hilt.

"Take heart, your king is alive. Maybe I should have saved him the crown." He laughed at her helplessness. Leaning in, he adjusted the crown to sit properly upon her head and whispered in her ear, "What do you think, Guinevere?"

"Let her go!" Arthur shouted. Gorlois turned back to look at him. "It's me you want—not her." He motioned to Guinevere. Gorlois didn't move but cocked his head slightly in a sardonic expression.

"Let. Her. Go," Arthur threatened, readying his sword and resuming his march toward them at a slow pace.

"Where's the fun in that?" Gorlois laughed. He stepped off the platform and walked to meet Arthur. "Why don't we continue our duel? This time just the two of us—man to man." He gestured between them dispassionately as the two of them approached. "We fight to the death, though. You are an annoying brat and I have no need of you in a cell. Your demise will bring me a modicum of entertainment when compared to the pathetic battle your knights have waged." He readied Excalibur.

"Agreed," Arthur responded as the two kings began circling, studying one another's balance and form, "but be prepared to die. That haughty look does not serve you well."

Arthur suddenly lunged forward and charged at Gorlois through gritted teeth. He struck at him, trying to release all of his anger: at Gorlois, at the corruption—at all of it. Gorlois blocked his strike easily with Excalibur, deflecting the other man's sword. The motion twisted Arthur sideways, nearly throwing him off balance. Instead, he used the momentum to flip over backward and land upright on his feet. The maneuver placed him in a strong defensive position, ready for the next attack.

Gorlois sauntered toward him, firing off a series of sword strikes that Arthur strategically blocked. He switched to the offensive and flanked Gorlois, attempting to make contact with his unguarded side. Gorlois deftly pivoted, and their swords collided with each assault. The percussive clamor of metal echoed throughout the Great Hall, punctuated by moments of emptiness.

Arthur remained on the offensive while dodging his adversary's counter strikes. Gorlois skillfully blocked any attack, stepping back and raising Excalibur to meet his sword. Sweat dripped down Arthur's forehead and into his eyes, stinging and blurring his vision. Gorlois took advantage of the momentary weakness, sidestepping Arthur's final thrust and knocking the younger man to the floor with the hilt of Excalibur.

With a quick somersault, Arthur was back on his feet. He wasn't going to be beaten so easily. Now it was his turn to defend as Gorlois lunged forward with a vengeance. Several minutes passed as the men traded blows, each alternating attack and defense—victory and near defeats. Neither was willing to concede and pushed themselves beyond their limits. Arthur worked hard to parry each attempted strike, but as the duel wore on, his moves became sloppy. He grew fatigued from the arduous day from the ceaseless fighting, their previous duel, and Lancelot's beating. His mind slipped from the ongoing fight. As Excalibur came down, he couldn't evade. Arthur's sword barely managed to deflect the blade; its flat body impacted his wrist. His sword clattered to the ground. He was stunned, unmoving for a moment. Gorlois raised Excalibur, ready to plunge it into Arthur's chest.

Have I just lost this fight? Arthur thought. He quickly glanced behind him at the Rangers who were blocking the exit, then toward Guinevere at the front of the room. *This isn't over.* He rolled over, just in time to escape Excalibur's blade, which buried itself through the floor. He picked up his sword with his other hand, springing to his feet. He lunged at Gorlois, who was still off balance from what should have been a finishing strike. His thrust made purchase, piercing Gorlois' side. Gorlois staggered backward, and Arthur plucked Excalibur from the floorboards, its surface reflecting the scattered sunlight. He brandished both weapons as he approached his unarmed nemesis. Gorlois tried to take a step away from Arthur, but he stumbled, tripping over the raised platform holding the thrones. He fell backward, catching himself with his arms. He held himself in a reclined position, eyes locked on Arthur.

"Kneel," Arthur commanded, but Gorlois refused. There was no mistaking the authority in his voice. Gorlois shimmied backward to the edge of his throne as Arthur followed, the tip of Excalibur placed gently under his chin. "Surrender now, and I may spare your life." Arthur lowered his sword, waiting for the man's response.

"I will never surrender to you, scum," Gorlois said with contempt. "An outcast like you will never be my king." Gorlois covertly reached into the leg of the throne and produced a knife, throwing himself to his feet and lunging for Arthur.

But he was ready. Arthur held out his sword and plunged it into Gorlois' chest. The outstretched dagger scratched Arthur's cheek before dropping to the floor. Arthur pulled Excalibur out of Gorlois, the blade dripping with blood. Shock was plastered across his face as his limp body dropped first to his knees and then teetered sideways onto the floor. His lifeless body spilled off the platform, and blood pooled on the tile.

Arthur did not see any of this as he ran up to Guinevere. Quickly but gently, he removed her gag after setting his swords on the adjacent throne. She coughed a couple times before going to speak.

"You don't need to say anything," he told her. "You will be fine. We are fine now," he assured her. Arthur reached back and picked up Excalibur. Using the sword, he cut Guinevere free from her bonds. She rubbed her wrists as Arthur stepped aside, allowing her the room to stand. Guinevere got onto her feet and removed the crown. She placed it atop Arthur's head. The two of them looked at each other in numbness and disbelief, amazed that they had survived. For a moment, the pair forgot the ongoing battle hadn't fully been won.

Commotion ensued at the entrance of the Great Hall, catching Arthur and Guinevere's attention. The knights had broken through the door. Lancelot led the forward group attacking, a knife in one hand and a pistol in the other. Merlin appeared from behind him, her fists at the ready and her knuckles bloodied. Gawain came out from the other side. His left arm, banged up from his impact with the ground, hung by his side limply. In his right hand he held a pistol, pointing it down. The three of them quickly dispatched several Rangers. Behind them, Galahad, Lionel, and Percival covered their rear flank. More Rangers poured through, encircling the knights.

Lancelot looked through the chaos of the fight to see his king and queen standing in front of their respective thrones. Gorlois' lifeless body was heaped on the floor in front of their feet. Excalibur hung down in Arthur's right hand, blood still dripping off its blade.

Uther's crown rested upon his head prominently. Guinevere stood before the crowd majestically.

"Long live the queen. Long live the king," Lancelot shouted, breaking through the chaos of the Great Hall. He placed his weapons down and kneeled on one knee, the violence around him slowing to a halt. The Rangers' heads slowly turned away from their prey as the remaining knights unmasked and kneeled in unison before their royalty. They bowed their heads slightly in reverence and closed a fist against their chests.

"Long live the King and Queen of Avalon," they chanted. The Rangers were frozen. They looked out over the Great Hall before one of them, a female Ranger, deigned to speak.

"The true rulers of Avalon stand before us. The sword of legend is in his grasp. With its blade, Gorlois has been struck down." She motioned to her fellow Rangers to kneel and took up a humbled form, resembling the knights. Persuaded by their comrade's appeal, one by one the Rangers kneeled.

"Forever may you rule before us," she shouted, and the Rangers joined in. The Great Hall rang out with their fealty toward Guinevere and Arthur. They were the true rulers of Avalon.

Arthur and Guinevere stood, speechless, in front of the crowd. They looked at each other with pride and giddy excitement. The knights before them—Lancelot, Merlin, and Gawain; Lionel, Percival, and Galahad—held themselves with admiration and respect.

Arthur turned back to look at Guinevere as she gazed out over the crowd. Her demeanor had relaxed, and she looked as beautiful as ever. Without saying anything, he kneeled before her. He wiped the bloodied sword on his pants to make the blade sparkle once more. She slowly rotated to face him. Her expression was empty and maybe a bit unsure. Arthur took the polished Excalibur by the hilt with both hands and stabbed it into the floor in front of him. The blade sliced cleanly through the wood of the platform, its hilt at his chest.

"Guinevere Cornwall," he spoke out, nearly shouting for the room to hear, "will you make me the luckiest king in Avalon and all the realms? Will you be my bride?" He looked up at her, eyes as enchanting as the moment he first saw them. They sparkled as she replied.

"Yes," she whispered just loud enough for Arthur to hear. She dropped to his level, caressing his face with her hands. She did not see the blood and dirt that covered him, or the fresh wound upon his cheek. All she saw before her was the one true King of Avalon. She looked him in the eyes and kissed him.

"To the bride and groom!" Lancelot shouted. The rest of everyone whooped and hollered. Slightly embarrassed, Guinevere leaned back on her legs. She covered her mouth with her hand, blushing. She looked around at the knights and the Rangers. They all continued cheering. She looked back to Arthur; they were both reflecting admiration and love toward the other. Arthur stood up from the ground and pulled Excalibur out of the floor. He held out his hand to Guinevere helping her up.

The two of them turned to face the crowd, and Arthur raised Excalibur over his head. The sword shone, catching the light streaming in through the windows. Excalibur shone across the Great Hall as if it were the sun itself.

Guinevere gazed upon the people—her citizens, her subjects—and reflected on her journey. Nothing on that first day of discovering the map with friends and colleagues would have hinted at this moment. But here in the midst of battle, amongst new friends and family, she ruled. Still holding Arthur's hand, Guinevere took a step back with him in unison, sitting together on the thrones as King and Queen of Avalon.

Thank you for reading *Rise of Knight & Sword*.

Please consider posting a rating or review to sites like Goodreads and Amazon.

Reviews are the lifeblood of authors and help more readers like you find their new favorite books!

About the Author

Miriam Wade is a Minnesotan transplant to Kansas City. She writes young adult fantasy, adventure, and urban fantasy driven by resilient young women, filled with twisty plots, and garnished with a hint of romance. She loves coffee, renovating her home, and riding her motorcycle. When she is not writing, she enjoys spending time with her husband, Ryan, and their two cats, Freya Virgo and Modi Taurus. *Rise of Knight and Sword* is Miriam's debut novel.

Twitter: @wade_author
Instagram: @miriam.wade.author
Website: oneswordsaga.com